THE ANGEL IN THE GLASS

Alys Clare

Severn House

This first world edition published 2018
in Great Britain and the USA by
SEVERN HOUSE PUBLISHERS LTD of
Eardley House, 4 Uxbridge Street, London W8 7SY
Trade paperback edition first published
in Great Britain and the USA 2018 by
SEVERN HOUSE PUBLISHERS LTD

British Library Cataloguing in Publication Data
A CIP catalogue record for this title is available from the British Library.

ISBN-13: 978-0-7278-8804-4 (cased)
ISBN-13: 978-1-84751-930-6 (trade paper)
ISBN-13: 978-1-78010-984-8 (e-book)

All Severn House titles are printed on acid-free paper.

Severn House Publishers support the Forest Stewardship Council™ [FSC™],
the leading international forest certification organisation. All our titles that
are printed on FSC certified paper carry the FSC logo.

MIX
Paper from
responsible sources
FSC
www.fsc.org   FSC® C013056

Typeset by Palimpsest Book Production Ltd.,
Falkirk, Stirlingshire, Scotland.
Printed and bound in Great Britain by
TJ International, Padstow, Cornwall.

for Sue and David White,
bibliophiles,
in celebration of a quarter of a century of friendship.

ONE

Summer 1604

On a warm June evening of long, quiet daylight, I left my house and, with my big black ginger-eyebrowed dog Flynn beside me, walked down the path to wait for my sister. Celia had gone visiting, as she often did, and would be coming home soon. She knew I worried about her being out alone after dark – an elder brother's right – and, although my anxiety clearly irked her, she endured it with no more comment than an occasional irritated sigh.

Few people could put as many unspoken words into an irritated sigh as my sister.

It was only a little over a year since she had been widowed, under the most terrible circumstances, and I found it hard to persuade myself that her apparently miraculous recovery was as wholehearted as she made it appear. But that, as Celia would have robustly reminded me, was her business.

I had reached the place where the path up to the house met the track that wound its way along beside the Tavy river. I went over to the grassy bank and sat down, my back against one of the big old oak trees that stand either side of the path. Flynn was off on pursuits of his own – sniffing out cony trails, probably – and the soft silence fell around me like a silky sheet.

It was good to have these moments to myself. The day – bright sunshine after a misty start – had been busy, not to say hectic, and now was the first chance I'd had to think. And I wanted to think, for in the space of the past fortnight two disturbing events had occurred. My instinct told me they were connected, although I couldn't for the life of me see how.

The first event had been pretty unpleasant.

Two young lads from the village – Tavy St Luke's – had trespassed on a farmer's land, creeping down into a tree-shaded hollow, known locally as Foxy Dell, on the boundary of the property. If they'd had the sense to do it discreetly, refrain from causing damage and not steal anything, the farmer would probably have been none the wiser and no harm would have been done. But the lads – they were brothers, and aged about nine and seven – hadn't had that sort of sense. They'd come flying home from their adventure, yelling about having found buried treasure – 'Jewels of every colour, some big as your fist, all shiny and gleaming in the sunshine!' – and bragging about how they'd enlarged the hole in the bank to get a better look and picked up a couple of the jewels to bring home to show their mates.

The farmer caught up with them just as they reached the village and the safety of their own front door. He'd heard their excited jabbering and he had a good idea of where they'd been and what they'd been up to. He caught hold of them by the worn fabric of their collars, tried to grab back what they'd stolen from the cavity in the dell's side and then set about them, trying to lam into both of them at once and yelling that if he caught them on his land again he'd paddle their arses for them so hard that they wouldn't sit down for a week, and that he'd had more than enough of folks sneaking into his dell and he'd set his dogs on the next ones to try it.

In the midst of the uproar the boys' father had shot out of the house, shoved the furious farmer off his sons and gone for him. Abandoning the small fry, the farmer had turned his attention to the father, and the resulting fight had escalated swiftly and dramatically. A sensible neighbour had thrown a bucket of cold water over them – 'It's what I do for randy dogs,' she'd been heard to remark, 'and these two are little better' – and brought the fight to an abrupt end, although not before both participants were bruised, battered and bleeding profusely. Someone had come to fetch me and I'd done what I could, setting a broken bone in the lads' father's right hand and, after patching up a long cut on the farmer's palm, informing him that the best thing to do for his splattered nose was to keep applying cold compresses and hope that when the swelling went down, he'd be able to breathe through it again.

It wasn't that unusual for fights to break out, but this had been a savage one. And what troubled me was that it had been, really, over nothing. I wasn't sure what the lads had excavated from the bank – the farmer had grabbed back whatever it was and hidden it before anyone else could see – but I was quite sure it wasn't valuable and most certainly not precious jewels.

And now we were suffering the aftermath, with deep, angry resentment between the farmer and the village – almost all the villagers sided with the lads and their father – and no opportunity missed for one side to have a snipe at the other. Other than a few servants and farm hands whose loyalty probably owed more to fear than any appreciation of their master's finer qualities, the farmer lived alone but, big, loud, red-faced and choleric man that he was, he could shout and bluster enough for half a dozen. Moreover, he had made good his threat of letting loose his dogs and now the boundaries of his land were guarded by two huge, mastiff-like animals who were terrorizing everyone going about their business on the track that ran alongside the farmer's land.

The villagers had asked me to have a word with the farmer and I'd tried. His nose was still spread across the lower half of his face, however, and just now he wasn't listening to reason. I'd been going to ask Jonathan Carew, vicar of St Luke's, Tavy St Luke's, to try, but there was something the matter with Jonathan.

That was the second event: only the previous Sunday, the one after the fight, the vicar had had some sort of attack, for want of a better word, in the midst of his sermon. Come to think of it, *attack* isn't the right word, for it implies violence and there was nothing violent, or even dramatic, about what happened, and it's possible that those placed further back in the church observed nothing. Celia and I, however, were near the front, and both of us saw Jonathan go pale suddenly and clutch at the sides of the lectern, hands white-knuckled, appearing to forget what he was saying and simply stand there, staring out blankly over the heads of his congregation. It was as if he had suddenly seen a horrible vision; as if something had reminded him of some awful memory he was trying not to think about. Or, as my sister said with a touch of the macabre, and not entirely in jest, as if he'd seen a phantom.

He was quick to recover himself, however, and, after a couple of false starts, resumed his sermon. Afterwards I heard one or two remarks – 'Vicar had the hiccups, I reckon!' and 'Lost his train of thought, he did, and I thought we were going to get away with a short one this week!' – but overall it seemed that my sister and I were the only ones to realize that something out of the ordinary – something quite disturbing – had happened.

The superstitious say that if two events of a certain type occur, then it's only a matter of time before the third one. Well, I'd been more shaken than I should have been by these first two troubling occurrences, and I feared what might be about to come.

Which was why I was at the end of the track up to Rosewyke, waiting for my sister, in the twilight of a late June evening.

She came trotting up on her pretty grey mare, a smile on her face, her cheeks slightly flushed, and I knew without asking that she'd had a good time. The women she'd been visiting were wives of her late husband's business associates, and they had rallied round her after Jeromy's death. They didn't know the whole story – hardly anyone still living did – and they had taken Celia to their collective bosom out of the kindness of their hearts, wishing, I think, only to help, comfort and support her in her loss. Some of them irritated my sister to distraction – Celia is quite easily irritated – but two or three had found their way under her protective shell and become valued, even beloved, friends.

'You don't need to act like my bodyguard,' my sister greeted me. 'I'm perfectly capable of riding home safely and finding my way up the path to the stables, you know.'

'I know,' I agreed. I also knew better than to defend or even explain my actions.

But she wasn't really cross. She slipped off the mare's back, handing me the reins as if I was indeed the bodyguard she had just spurned and tucking her arm in mine. We set off towards the house, and just for a moment she leaned in towards me in a rare demonstration of affection. I called to Flynn, and obediently he abandoned whatever fascinating scent he'd found and came trotting after us.

'So, what's the talk of the wives of Plymouth this evening?' I asked.

She sighed. 'I have no idea since, as you very well know, I haven't been further than Dorothie's house at Foliot, and I've only been talking to two wives anyway.'

I smiled. 'Very well, then. What did the three of you speak of?'

'Oh, you wouldn't be interested,' she said airily. 'It was—' She stopped suddenly. 'Actually, there was one matter that you might wish to hear about.'

'And what was that?'

She hesitated, and I had the impression she was slightly abashed. 'Well, it's going to sound as if we were being sour-tongued old gossips, but I promise you, Gabe, it wasn't like that – we were really concerned because we like him.'

I had an idea what was coming. 'Go on.'

'Well, we were all in church on Sunday, and the others also noticed Jonathan's strange moment of . . . inattention? Absent-mindedness? Fear? Anyway, whatever it was, we agree it was out of character and we were wondering if someone ought to go and see him and make sure he's all right. That he's not ill, or something.'

'I see,' I said. 'So, me being a physician and you being a physician's sister, you suggested it should be I who goes to visit Jonathan and—'

'Don't flatter yourself!' she interrupted. 'Your name wasn't mentioned. In fact I offered to go, since we live nearest, and I'm going to do so tomorrow morning, with a pot of Sallie's strawberry preserve and a posy of roses. I shall rise early in the morning,' she added, 'because roses are at their best picked with the dew still on them.'

'It's a kind thought,' I said cautiously.

'He'll probably invite me in and offer refreshment,' she went on, 'and I'll find the right moment to say I'd noticed he looked rather pale on Sunday and is there anything I can do to help?'

I wasn't sure how to reply. On the one hand, Celia's impulse was a good one, for Jonathan Carew is a regular visitor at Rosewyke and my sister and I enjoy his company. Besides, he had been extremely kind to her when she was widowed, and I know she had been very grateful. But on the other hand he was our parish priest, a person of standing in our community, and, above all, a reserved and private man. While he might recognize Celia's enquiry as having a generous inspiration, how would he feel at this evidence that his brief lapse in the pulpit on Sunday hadn't gone unnoticed?

In the end I just said, 'Be careful.'

She turned to me, and I saw from her expression that she understood. 'I *know*, Gabe,' she said softly. 'I know what he's like. Of course I'll be careful.'

We reached the courtyard, where darkness and deep silence, other than tenor snores with an accompaniment of reverberating bass ones, told us Samuel and Tock were already asleep. My outdoor servants have their quarters off the yard, and they don't keep late hours. I helped Celia stable the mare, rubbing her down while Celia filled the water bucket and put the saddle on its tree and the bridle on the hook. Then, still moving quietly out of consideration for Samuel and Tock, we went into the house. Sallie must also have retired for the night, for no light showed around the door to her room off the kitchen. As usual, she had left her domain in an immaculate state and the stone flags of the floor were still slightly damp from the final mopping of the day. Her snores, too, were audible, although in a higher register than those emanating from Tock or Samuel. My servants all work long hours, and they earn their rest.

But I wasn't ready for sleep, and I didn't think Celia was either. I led the way through the kitchen, across the hall, then through the parlour to the library, where I took a bottle of brandy from behind a row of books and poured a measure for each of us. My sister took her glass with a nod of thanks, then went to stand by the open window, where the sweet, clove-heavy scent of gillyflowers rose up from below.

After a brief pause she said quietly, 'You feel it too, don't you? This sense that something's about to happen?'

'I do,' I agreed.

She turned to stare out through the window. 'Is there a storm brewing?' she asked. 'Is that what's oppressing us?'

I shrugged. 'Possibly, although there's no wind tonight and the weather seems set fair.' I too looked out over the peaceful land. A mist was rising, emanating out of the earth like thin smoke.

She nodded slowly. 'I believe you are right. Besides, if this apprehension were due to an approaching storm, then others too would feel it, yet neither Dorothie nor Phyllis mentioned an awareness of anything amiss.'

I went over to her and put my arm round her, drawing her to me. 'It's only to be expected that you are fearful,' I said. 'It is not very long since the events of last year, after all.'

'I know.' She put up her hand to take hold of mine. Then, with a sound that was a mixture of a sigh and a sob, she added, 'I wonder at times if I am even the same person.'

'You are,' I said firmly. 'You are my little sister, and much as you have always been, save that you are older, wiser and have a better understanding of what you can endure, and do, and still survive.'

She nodded, but didn't speak.

After a while she finished her brandy, bade me goodnight and went to bed. I sat a while longer, then followed her upstairs and into my own chamber.

Eventually I slept.

I wasn't there to see her rise early to pick her roses and I didn't even know if she did, for something happened just before dawn that took me away from the house.

I was awakened by what sounded like hailstones hitting the diamond-shaped panes of my window. Roused from deep sleep, my first thought was that the storm had come after all. But then the pattering sound came again and a voice called my name.

I got out of bed and went across to look down.

There, foreshortened so that he looked even bigger and broader than he is, staring up anxiously and in the act of picking up some more little stones to throw up at my window, stood Theophilus Davey the coroner.

'Gabe? Gabriel Taverner?' he hissed again. 'Is that you?'

I refrained from asking who else he expected to be in my bedchamber as dawn broke. 'Yes. What is it?'

'I need you,' Theo replied. 'Will you come down?'

'Shall I dress?'

'*Yes*,' he said impatiently, as if I should have known. 'And be swift, for we have some miles to go.'

I hastily put on the garments I had taken off the night before and, picking up my boots, went soft-footed down to join him.

'I'm sorry about the stones on the window glass,' Theo said as we rode off. Samuel had woken and come stumbling out into the yard, still half-asleep, to help me, and we had saddled and bridled my black horse as swiftly as we could. I was still trying to kick the resentful Hal into some semblance of eagerness, or even willingness, for this early outing. 'I hope there was no harm done.'

'No, there wasn't.'

'I didn't want to go banging and pounding on your door and waking the household,' Theo went on. He turned to me, grinning. 'Bad enough that you and I are roused so untimely from our beds.'

I grunted my agreement. I hoped he would take the hint and not try to engage me in conversation. It really was too early for chatter.

He did.

For several miles we rode in silence. The previous evening's mist still hung in the hollows. Ahead, to the east, the faint glow of light above the high moors strengthened, and presently the first brilliant edge of the sun's great curve appeared. The birds were singing all around us. I identified blackbird, chaffinch, wren, robin and thrush. We were heading steadily uphill, into the wide, desolate, unpopulated places.

Presently I spotted a small cluster of buildings on the track ahead. It hardly warranted the term hamlet; it looked more like a run-down, abandoned farm. As we approached, I saw a man standing by the head of a stout mare in the shafts of a two-wheeled, flat-bedded cart, and two others leaning against the front wall of the largest of the buildings. Not that that was saying much, for it appeared to be little more than the sort of one-roomed dwelling with a second roofed space attached for the animals. The door of rotting wood was half off its hinges and had been propped in place.

One of the men stepped forward, giving Theo a curt bow; a mere nod of the head.

'Anything to report, Arthur?' Theo asked as we dismounted. The man – Arthur – reached out to take our horses' reins. Along the track the mare shifted and gave a nervous whinny, her ears twitching back. I guessed she'd caught a whiff of what we were smelling.

'Nah,' Arthur said. 'Quiet as the grave.' He inclined his head towards me. 'That the doctor?'

'Yes,' Theo said shortly.

Arthur was eyeing me, a faintly supercilious expression on his thin face. 'Hope you didn't pause to break your fast,' he said. 'Or, if you did, that you've a stronger stomach than young Gidley there.' He nodded towards the other man standing by the dwelling, who I now saw was little more than a boy. Pale, shivering, he had wrapped his arms round his lean body and was hugging himself. A few paces away I spotted a pool of vomit.

Poor lad.

Theo had pushed aside the door and was entering the dwelling. I went in after him.

The body lay huddled on its right side facing the back wall of the room, beneath the portion of ruined roof that remained most intact. Animals had found it before humans, and there was evidence of predation. I noticed in my first swift glance swellings or lumps on the face, and the ghastly thought occurred to me that the predation must have begun ante-mortem, for the body so to have reacted . . . In addition, the garments were torn and ragged; perhaps from where the rats had tried to get at the dead flesh, perhaps because the deceased had been a vagrant and the clothing had consisted of ancient cast-offs.

Despite the plentiful fresh air afforded by the holes in roof and walls and the ill-fitting door, the room was heavy with the stench of decaying flesh and urine.

For a few moments Theo and I simply stood there, and I think he, like me, was silently regretting a world in which someone could die like this, alone and in deepest poverty, starving and in all likelihood wretched and sick.

'Who found the body?' I asked.

'A pair of merchants on their way up from the coast to Tavistock,' Theo replied. 'Apparently they thought to shorten their journey by cutting across the moor, and got lost in the mist. They stumbled on this place and were all for sheltering until conditions improved, only then they smelt it. They came down into the river valley seeking someone to report it to, and thus I was alerted.'

I nodded. I said a prayer inside my head for the departed soul. Then I stepped forward, pushed up my sleeves and muttered, 'I suppose I'd better have a look, then.'

The body was that of a slender person, not tall. The skull was neat, the brow ridges not very prominent. The bones were gracile, the limbs slender.

Theo said softly, 'Man or woman?'

'Good question,' I replied.

I leaned over the corpse and unfastened the fraying ties that held the outer garment – tunic, coat, I wasn't sure – together, and pushed aside the flimsy chemise. The chest, bared, showed very faint swellings that might have been the small breasts of a woman or the fatty deposits of a man. With a sigh, for I had a strong sense that I was violating what remained of this poor, lonely soul, I thrust my hands inside the hose and pushed them down over the upper thighs.

The penis was tiny, shrunken and curled against the top of the right thigh like a little finger. 'A man, then,' breathed Theo, right in my ear.

'Wait,' I said softly.

I pushed my hand deeper into the crotch, behind the small testicles. It was too dark to see, so my fingertips had to be my eyes. I advanced them, step by step, and then came to the anus. Withdrawing my hand – I felt an urgent need to clean it – I said, 'Yes. A man.'

Theo was looking at me curiously. 'Did the penis and balls not tell you what you needed to know?'

'Yes, with hindsight,' I agreed. 'But very occasionally it

happens that a body displays the sexual characteristics of both male and female. A person will have the appearance of an effeminate man, or a masculine woman. These people are called hermaphrodites and the condition is found elsewhere in nature. In snails, for example, and if you have ever seen a pair of garden snails in the act of regeneration, you'd have observed that both creatures are equipped with male and female genitalia, and the—'

'Yes, thanks, Gabe, I'll remember to look out for it,' Theo said hastily.

'Human hermaphrodites are, I believe, very rare,' I went on. 'I have never seen one, only read of the condition.'

Theo was still looking faintly horrified. 'The sexual characteristics of male and female,' he repeated, 'in the one body. So, when you thrust your hand down between the legs, you thought to find a—' He stopped abruptly.

I smiled to myself. I guessed he'd been about to use one of the vernacular terms, of which there are so many, but stopped out of respect for a physician's presence. 'A vagina,' I said calmly.

'Er – yes, quite,' he agreed. I'll swear he blushed.

'Yes. I thought it best to check.'

'But this is definitely the body of a man?'

'Yes, Theo, it is.'

He gave a deep sigh. 'We'll get him on the cart and back to my house, then, and together we'll begin the challenging task of finding out who he is and how he died.'

TWO

We were back at Theo's house by early to mid-morning. He lives on the edge of the village of Withybere, towards Warleigh Point, which is on the river. He and his family inhabit the upper storeys of the house, and his three young children are under the strictest orders *never* to sneak through the door that divides the residence from their father's official quarters. The work of the coroner frequently involves sights, sounds and smells – particularly smells – that are not suitable for the young, and the children, in particular the bright lad Carolus, Theo and his wife Elaine's firstborn, showed far too much curiosity and had been known to open the forbidden door unless carefully watched.

This morning there were no signs of the family's presence. Perhaps the children were at their lessons, or maybe Elaine had taken them out. The corpse was lifted from the cart by two of the three men who had come out with Theo to fetch it – the weight was so slight that two could easily bear it – and, once it had been deposited on the trestle table in the cellar down beneath the house, Theo thanked them and accompanied them back upstairs to dismiss them. I was vaguely aware of their muttered conversation – somebody laughed briefly – but most of my attention was already on the pathetic remains lying on the boards before me.

Sunlight was streaming in through the series of narrow windows set in the south-facing wall up near the ceiling, so now I had plenty of light to work by. The men had laid the dead man on his back, and, before I did anything else, I spent some moments looking down into his face. I wanted to gain an idea of what he had looked like, before poverty, sickness, starvation and desperation had brought him to his solitary death.

I picked up a strand of the filthy, matted hair. He had lice. There was a bucket of water set beside one of the trestles, in it a wash cloth. I picked up the cloth and ran it several times along the hair. With the dirt removed, the hair revealed itself to be fair, stranded lightly with silver. It was the first clue to the dead man's age: although people sometimes begin to go grey in their thirties, or even their twenties, normally the loss of hair colour doesn't begin until the fourth decade.

I rinsed out the cloth and gently began to bathe the face. The skin was pale and fine; surprisingly smooth. I raised the right eyelid and saw that the iris of the eye had been light, clear blue. The other eye had gone, and I turned my thoughts firmly away from what had happened to it.

I stared into the dead face. Cleaned, I had a better view of those swellings, that I had originally taken for infected animal bites.

They were not.

They were firm, fleshy lumps, one on the end of the nose, a larger one obscuring much of the cheek beneath the left eye and some smaller ones distorting the lines of the face.

Several possible causes crossed my mind.

For now – until I could return home and consult my reams of notes and my small library of medical reference books – I would just have to go on with the examination.

I heard Theo's tread on the steps down into the cellar. Theo is a big man, tall and broad, and although he can be light on his feet when need arises, people usually hear him approaching. He came to stand beside me, observing but not speaking. With an inward sigh – the next action is one that I always find a distasteful sort of intrusion when working on the dead – I began to strip off the tattered garments.

Coat, shirt, hose, a worn leather belt from which hung a purse, and a pair of soft shoes with holes in the thin soles and worn-down heels that had surely been inadequate for someone who lived on the roads. *If* he'd lived on the roads. I removed the garments and made a small pile of them on the second trestle table, beside the bottom of the steps. Theo went over and began turning them this way and that, looking, I imagined, for clues to the man's identity.

I rinsed out the washcloth once more and began to clean away several weeks, or perhaps months, of accumulated filth from the naked body.

Presently Theo said, 'The purse is empty of coins, much as you'd expect, but I found this inside his coat.'

I turned to see him unfolding and then holding up a small piece of heavy, artist's paper on which there were dark lines. 'What is it?'

'I have no idea.' He set it aside and returned to his task.

As I did to mine. We worked in silence. As always, Theo was the perfect companion, for, even though he didn't speak, I was aware of his strong presence and it helped me; I felt almost that the power of his personality was supporting me.

He is a good man; there's no better adjective to describe him. He is, as Jonathan Carew might have put it, on the side of the angels.

Jonathan. I wondered, in a swift thought that momentarily took me away from the reeking cellar and the sad corpse before me, if Celia was even now knocking on the door of the Priest's House, presenting her roses and the pot of Sallie's strawberry preserve . . .

When the body was as clean as I could make it and I had examined it minutely, I said quietly, 'I cannot be sure, Theo, but my initial thought is that this man died of natural causes.'

I sensed movement as Theo came to stand beside me. 'Yes?'

'He might have starved to death.' I indicated the concave stomach and, just above it, the arch of the ribs, sticking out so starkly and stretching the skin. 'But he was diseased' – I pointed to the lumps on the face and to other swellings on his limbs and torso; to a distortion in the joints of his legs – 'and whatever he was suffering from may have finally killed him.'

Theo suppressed a gasp. 'Is it leprosy?' he whispered. Brave man that he was, he had managed not to obey the instinct that must have been yelling at him to take a step back. Take two steps, five, ten, get out of the cellar and away from the corpse.

'Possibly,' I said. 'If so, there is no danger to you, or even to me, and I've just been handling him.' I heard the question Theo hadn't asked. 'Leprosy is infectious, or in fact I should say contagious' – I decided to answer it anyway, to set my friend the family man's mind at rest – 'but contact has to be over a long period of time. People habitually living in close quarters with victims catch the sickness, which is why lepers are removed and kept apart. But a swift, casual encounter offers no danger.' *Or at least*, I thought but didn't add, *I'm fairly sure it doesn't* . . .

'Should we arrange for a quick burial?' Theo suggested.

I was on the point of agreeing, but something stopped me.

'Have you still access to that crypt you found for me last year?' I asked him. We'd had need to store a particularly malodorous corpse, and, exhausted by the perfectly understandable complaints of his agents and his wife, Theo had found somewhere other than his own cellar in which to keep it: the crypt of an empty house close by.

'Yes, indeed,' Theo said. 'I had been using the crypt from time to time, and a while ago I thought it was time to see about obtaining formal permission.' He made a faint grimace. 'Which, at a price, I have done. I contacted the owners, and they've let the crypt to me in exchange for a monthly rent.'

Men will always make a few coins where they can, I reflected. 'Then I will wrap our dead man up tightly in a clean binding, if such a thing can be found?' Theo nodded. 'And we'll take him there, straight away.'

Theo hurried off, returning with a bundled-up sheet. 'This was put out in the rag bag,' he said. I could see that it was worn very thin in places. 'It's a bit stained, but it's all right for our purpose.'

I wrapped the body, rolling the cloth a couple of times round. I refused Theo's help: even though I knew that any risk was minuscule, I'd touched the naked body already and he hadn't. Then, when every piece of flesh was safely covered, I picked up the dead man – he was even lighter than I'd imagined – and followed Theo up the steps, out of the house and along to the empty dwelling and its crypt.

We left him there, our unknown dead stranger.

But I didn't believe for a moment that I'd seen the last of him.

I went home.

I was so eager to get to my books, my shelves of notebooks and my papers that I barely answered Sallie's cheerful greeting. I was intent upon laving my hands out in the yard, over and over, the stench of the corpse still in my nostrils even after all trace of it had left my skin, and it took a couple of repetitions of her remark before I took in what she was saying.

'Mistress Celia has eaten an early dinner and gone out again,' my housekeeper said once more with the painstaking slowness and clarity of one speaking to the deaf or the slow-witted, 'and I'm wondering, Doctor, if you wish me to prepare something for you?'

I finished my washing and turned to her. 'Thank you, Sallie,

I'll have bread, cheese, ham and pickles up in my study. And a mug of ale,' I added as she hurried off.

'Big or small?' she asked without turning round.

'Big.'

My study is probably my favourite room out of all of them in this house, Rosewyke, that I love and that has come to feel so thoroughly like home. I found the place when I was at my lowest ebb. I'd been a ship's surgeon, a sawbones serving in the magnificent vessels of the late queen's navy, but an accidental blow to the side of the head had left me with acute, permanent, debilitating and agonizing seasickness. Being forced to give up the life I'd loved broke something inside me that I had despaired of ever mending. But then one day I came across Rosewyke, empty, unloved, beautiful, and, it seemed, waiting for me to find it. From the moment I first set eyes on the place, I began to heal.

My study is up on the first floor, adjoining my bedchamber, and faces out to the front of the house, roughly south-westwards over the thicket of soft fruit bushes and small trees that stand on the top of the higher ground above the Tavy river. The big oak table that serves as my desk is placed in the window, either side of which are the shelves where I keep my books, notebooks and papers. My doctor's bag is always stored in the same spot: on a small table beside the fireplace.

I barely noticed Sallie coming in and depositing the tray with my food and my mug of ale – she'd take me at my word regarding the ale, I saw when she'd gone, and filled a vast pewter tankard that probably held almost a couple of pints and might actually have been a jug – because I was already engrossed in the reference work I'd been thinking about all the way home.

The one that included a treatise on leprosy.

Since I'd stared down at those swellings and distortions on the dead man's thin, malnourished body, I'd been unable to escape from the awful thought that Theo and I had between us unleashed that dreaded horror from biblical times not only on ourselves and the three men who had brought back the corpse but also on Theo's unsuspecting wife and children.

Before I began on any other branch of investigation – and I had several in mind – I had to reassure myself.

The words I was reading were bringing me such comfort that I paused to say a swift prayer of gratitude. It was as I'd remembered: for some reason, wrote the learned authority who had produced the text I was studying, the incidence of leprosy appeared to be declining. Hospitals dedicated solely to the care of lepers had been closing, or else changed into places where all and every sort of sickness and injury was treated. The learned authority speculated tentatively as to the reasons: perhaps, he suggested, people were dying from the many other more swift-acting diseases that were so common, such as the plague, before the slow development of leprosy had a chance to deform or kill them? Perhaps, even, the policy of isolation had been successful, so that new cases just weren't occurring?

His arguments were plausible, but I spent no more time on them. I had verified my original thought – that the incidence of leprosy had declined – and the next thing to do was to remind myself of the symptoms and, the relative rarity of the disease notwithstanding, determine if they fitted the dead man.

After quite a long time, I closed my books with a sigh of relief and a long, luxurious stretch of my cramped muscles.

Whatever had killed that slender, graceful and, perhaps, once beautiful man, it wasn't leprosy.

I almost set off straight away to tell Theo the good news and to reassure him that our isolation of the corpse had been unnecessary, but just in time I stopped. Perhaps it hadn't been leprosy, but the possibility remained that *something* had infected him. Until I could work out what it was, celebration was premature.

I sat down again and once more began trawling through my books.

Celia had woken early – not quite as early as she'd planned – and wasted no time in going outside to pick the roses. They were as dewy-fresh as she had anticipated, and she took care in her selection, choosing colours that blended and, for fragrance, one or two more open blooms. She took them into the kitchen and, incorporating the foliage she'd also picked,

made up a pleasing posy and put it in a jug of water to keep
fresh.

There was no sign of Gabriel. Observing that his black horse
was also absent, she guessed he'd been called out. It happened
with such frequency that she barely noted it. She flew back
up the stairs – the bright morning had filled her with happiness
– and set about selecting a gown that was suitable for visiting
a man of the cloth.

She knelt before the big clothes chest set against the wall
of her bedchamber, picking up folds of different-coloured
silk garments. She had so many: the one good memento of
her marriage was the amount of fine silk in her possession,
in the form both of garments and of bolts of cloth, for her
late husband had been employed in the import of the
gorgeous fabric. The very best of its kind, too, that came
from Venice.

Celia made her selection. Straightening up, she tightened
her corset and stepped into the wide skirts of the gown, then
pushed her arms into the tight-fitting bodice and laced it up.
She had chosen for modesty rather than flamboyance, and the
neck of the bodice came up to her collar bones. The silk was
a soft lavender shade which she knew full well became her
fair hair and sea-coloured eyes.

She reproved herself silently for her vanity.

*Look where vanity and the love of fine raiment took me
before*, she told herself.

There was a tap on the door and, after a brief pause, Sallie
came in with fresh bread rolls, butter and preserve. 'Off out,
Miss Celia?' she asked, smiling broadly. 'That's right, on such
a fine morning!'

'Yes, I am,' Celia agreed. 'Oh, is that your strawberry
preserve? Delicious!' She bent over the tray and, scooping up
some butter and preserve onto the warm roll, stuffed in a large
mouthful and began chewing. 'Mmmm!'

Sallie's beaming smile intensified. 'You eat up, my lass,'
she said approvingly, although it must have been evident Celia
need no encouragement. 'Build yourself up, my lovely,' she
added softly, watching Celia out of slightly misty eyes.

Celia swallowed, then said, 'I'm going visiting, Sallie, which is why I've put the posy of roses ready in your kitchen. May I also take a jar of this delicious preserve?'

'Of course you may!' Sallie exclaimed. 'As much as you like – we've soft fruits aplenty and I can always make more.'

She moved around the chamber for a few moments, straightening objects, tidying, picking up a discarded stocking, then nodded, bobbed a sketchy curtsy and left.

Celia smiled. Sallie was one of the joys of living with Gabriel in his lovely house. Sallie had been Celia's staunch supporter ever since her trouble the previous year, and sometimes Celia was all but certain that Sallie knew far more about the terrible events than she let on. She was kind, generous and loyal, and Celia knew that she and Gabriel were lucky to have her.

Celia glanced back at the chest through which she'd lately been searching. Stowed away at the bottom, well out of sight of the casual glance, was the widely gathered, deeply frilled russet silk underskirt that she was making as a gift for Sallie. It was going to be a surprise – hence the hiding-away at the bottom of the chest – and Celia couldn't wait to see the housekeeper's expression when she was presented with it. It was a costly gift, and perhaps unsuitable, but Celia had made up her mind. If anybody deserved a luxurious gift, it was Sallie.

Some time later, mounted on her grey mare, the roses and the preserve carefully tucked inside a soft cloth bag slung across her body, Celia was on her way to the village, and the small house beside the church where Jonathan Carew lived. She rode astride: her father and her late husband had both disapproved, and Celia had been forced to subterfuge. Gabriel, however, didn't seem to mind. If he thought it was unstable for a lady to abandon the side saddle, he had the tact not to say so. Nor, Celia thought with a grin, had he objected when he discovered she'd appropriated the riding boots he'd loved so much when he was a boy. Well, they hadn't fitted him for years, she reasoned, so why should he?

She was aware that her mind was throwing up these thoughts to keep at bay her anxiety for, in truth, now that she was on her way, she was having doubts about the wisdom of her mission. Yes, it had been inspired by concern for a friend who might be suffering in some way, but now it occurred to her that if Jonathan had wanted to seek out someone to talk to, he'd have done so. Might have done so, in fact, and the person he'd selected someone other than Celia or her brother . . .

Oh, dear, should she turn back?

But she was already entering the little village of Tavy St Luke. There, right before her, was the church, and there the vicar's house.

With its inhabitant – oh, wouldn't he just be? – standing in the doorway, calling out a greeting.

Celia forced her stiff face into a smile and, kicking the mare to a trot, rode up to the gate.

'Have you come to see me?' Jonathan Carew asked, shading his eyes from the morning sun with a long-fingered hand as he looked up at her. 'How very pleasant!'

He came through the gate in the low fence, held out his arms to her as she slipped off the mare's back, then took the reins and secured them to the post set beside the gate. There was a water trough next to the post and the mare, despite the fact that it was only a short ride from Rosewyke to the village, took the sort of advantage of it that suggested she'd been ridden hard for hours.

Jonathan led the way up the brick path to his door. 'I was about to take refreshment,' he said over his shoulder, 'so I hope you will join me, then you can tell me what I can do for you.'

The Priest's House was tiny. He indicated the pair of chairs set either side of the hearth, and she went to sit in the one that she guessed wasn't his; the other had a small table beside it on which was a small leather-bound book, some sheets of vellum, a pen and an ink horn. Jonathan had gone across to what appeared to be the kitchen area, although, being little more than a series of shelves with a few mugs, platters and knives on them, it scarcely warranted the term. He reached down for a jug of ale, stored on the cool stone flags of the floor, and poured some into a pair of pewter mugs.

'I'm interrupting you,' Celia said as he handed her a mug

and sat down. She nodded towards the vellum and the pen. 'You were writing. A sermon, perhaps.'

'I was attempting to, yes,' he agreed. 'Inspiration, however, is not forthcoming.' He met her eyes, and she knew he was about to ask why she had come.

He was pale. His green eyes were circled with darkness, as if he wasn't sleeping, and there were shadows under his cheekbones that suggested he wasn't eating either.

She decided to speak first. She took a breath then spoke. 'You said I was to tell you what you could do for me,' she began, the words tumbling out too fast, 'but actually it's what I can do for you.' His expression changed and for a moment he looked alarmed; hostile, even. She plunged on. 'We – Gabe and I – wondered if something was troubling you on Sunday, and we – I – thought I'd call on you and bring you these.' She reached inside the cloth bag and thrust the roses and the jar of preserves at him.

There was a silence.

She wished she was anywhere but in Jonathan Carew's little house, facing his immobile face and his astonished disapproval.

But then suddenly he smiled. He took the roses, raising them to his face and inhaling deeply. Then he took the strawberry preserve, instantly removing the piece of cloth that Sallie had carefully tied over the top and sticking in a finger, licking off the deep red jam with evident pleasure.

'What a kind thought,' he said warmly. 'The roses are beautiful, and will brighten up this room. The preserve is delicious.'

'I didn't make it,' Celia blurted out. 'It's Sallie's special recipe – she's our housekeeper. Oh, you probably know that.'

'I do,' he agreed gravely. 'Please compliment her from me.' His eyes were on hers again, and she couldn't read the expression. She had the fleeting sense that there was something there, lurking just beneath the affability and the warmth; something disturbing. Something dark. As if he felt her sensing it, probing, assessing, he smiled again and said, 'It might be somebody else's work, but it was you who had the generous thought to bring it, and the roses, to me.'

'As I said, Gabe and I thought you might be troubled. Unwell, even.' He didn't speak. 'It was just that there was a moment when you seemed to freeze,' she hurried on, not knowing how, having begun, to stop. 'You stood there, and I saw your hands gripping the lectern as if it was the only thing holding you up.'

The frightening silence fell again.

Then, after what seemed to her a very long time, Jonathan sighed and said, 'I hoped nobody had noticed.'

'Gabe and I were close by, and Gabe's a doctor,' she replied. He nodded.

'Are you ill?' she whispered. 'Is there anything we can do?'

He came back from wherever his thoughts had taken him and now she sensed that his smile was true. 'No,' he said softly. Then – and she had the feeling he was finding it hard to say the words – 'It is good of you to have come. To have braved the renowned reserve of your vicar and dared to ask such a personal question.'

She felt the hot blood flush her face. 'I'm sorry, sorry, I had no right to—'

'Yes you did,' he interrupted. 'You had the right of a friend. Of someone who, observing what they believed to be another's distress, was prompted to do what they could to assuage it.' Before she could comment, he added, 'Is that not what the scriptures tell us to do? What Our Lord would command to any of us who see a fellow human being suffering?'

'Then you—'

'Dear Mistress Celia, it was but a thing of a moment,' he said very firmly. 'I am most grateful for your solicitude, and for your gifts, but I must assure you that all is well.'

I have to leave, she thought. *He wants me to go, despite the kindly words.*

She rose to her feet. 'I will pass on your compliments to Sallie,' she said, stepping across to the door. 'And now I must be on my way.'

He walked up the path with her and gave her a leg-up onto the mare's back. 'My regards to your brother,' he said pleasantly. Then, with a farewell wave, he turned and went inside his house.

*   *   *

Gabriel was still not back when Celia returned to Rosewyke. She went inside, ate a bite or two of dinner, told Sallie how much the Reverend Carew had appreciated her preserve – 'Aha, so *that's* where you were off to!' the gleam in Sallie's eye seemed to say – and then, far too restless to spend the afternoon indoors, she rode out again.

She let the mare amble aimlessly for a while, for she couldn't think where to go. Her friends the wives of Jeromy's colleagues were welcoming and she knew they wouldn't turn her away, but there was something about their solicitude that was beginning to disturb her. It was as if they were saying, those generous-hearted women, *You've been through sad times and, young, grieving widow that you are, we will do all we can to look after you.*

But Celia wasn't grieving. She'd been through an experience that had almost finished her; it hadn't. She had recovered, and sometimes – quite often, if she was honest – it was uncomfortable to be perceived as in need of care and comfort when she wasn't.

No. It wasn't Phyllis, or Dorothie, or Jennet, or gossipy old Catryn – *particularly* not gossipy old Catryn – whose company she need now, when she was still feeling so raw from her morning's experience; she'd felt both anxious and embarrassed at the same time, two emotions that, she had discovered, sat ill together.

Then all at once she knew exactly who she *did* want to see.

Turning the mare's head and kicking her out of her lazy shuffle, Celia set off for the village of Blaxton, where the ferry crossed the Tavy, because nearby was the house of Judyth Penwarden. And, apart from being a midwife and a healer, Judyth was Celia's friend and the holder of her closest secrets.

THREE

Theo was in the big room that served as his office and his agent Jarman Hodge stood before him, chewing away on a heel of bread.

'Any idea who it is?' Jarman asked.

There was no need to ask what he was referring to. 'Not the least one.'

'Description?'

'Male, fair-haired, filthy, diseased. Might have starved.'

Jarman nodded. 'Vagrant.'

'Probably,' Theo agreed. *But even vagrants have a name*, he wanted to add. *This man had a name, once.*

Jarman was still in his office. Theo guessed he had something pertinent to say, otherwise he wouldn't be.

'Found where?' he asked.

'Up on the edge of the moor, quite some way from any dwelling currently inhabited.'

'Elfordtown direction?'

'Not far from there. Why?'

Jarman shrugged. 'It might be nothing, but I heard they'd had a spot of bother out at Wrenbeare. The big house, set up above Elfordtown, and no more than four, five miles from it, if you take the tracks over the moor.'

'What happened, and when?'

'I can't swear to this, mind,' Jarman warned. 'I overheard it in the tavern on the road out to the moor, and it was quite late in the evening, but the man who was letting his tongue run away with him was saying how he'd joined in the chase after a skinny, ragged vagrant caught lurking around Wrenbeare. Word was the vagrant had tried to break in, or maybe he *had* broken in. Like I say, it was late, plenty of mugs of ale had been drunk, and it could just as well have been wild talk to impress the lassies serving the ale.' He paused, his expression thoughtful. 'As to when, I heard the talk about two weeks ago, maybe less, and the loudmouth seemed to be saying it had happened a few days before.'

'And it wasn't clear if this vagrant had actually broken in, or, if he had, whether anything was stolen?'

Jarman Hodge shook his head.

Theo thought for a few moments. The time probably fitted, if the assumption was made that, having failed to break in and steal food – probably what he'd been after – the vagrant slunk away to starve in that lonely hovel. How long did it take a man to starve? You needed water to go on living, Theo recalled being told – probably by Gabriel Taverner – but the body could go on for a surprisingly long time without food. As much as two and a half weeks? But then the vagrant might have had the remains of some paltry food supply, and only run out after—

Jarman Hodge appeared to have tired of waiting. 'Want me to see what I can find out, chief?'

Theo came out of his reverie. 'Why not?'

He returned Jarman's nod of farewell and, once the man had gone, went back to his thoughts. Vagrants were all too common, and there was nothing to say the one he and Gabe had just brought in was the same man who had been lurking about at Wrenbeare. If anyone had in fact been lurking. But he thought it was worth having his agent check.

He knew better than to ask Jarman Hodge how he proposed to go about his task. The man was a highly efficient investigator, and Theo had had many an occasion to be grateful for his tact and his tenacity. But he had decided some time ago that it was better not to ask too many questions.

I heard the sibilant hiss of silk, and Celia was beside me, perching on the edge of my desk and picking up one of my reference works.

'*Eugh!*' she said, her expression horrified. 'Whatever was wrong with that poor soul?' She was pointing at a drawing of a man with a hole in his face where the nose had once been. It was in one of the books I'd consulted earlier when I'd been so fearful that the corpse had suffered from leprosy.

'The illustration shows one of the effects of leprosy,' I

admitted reluctantly. Before my sister could react, I hastily added, 'It's not pertinent to anyone I'm treating.'

She whispered a swift prayer, then added, 'Thank God for that.' She slid off my desk and sat down in one of the pair of chairs beside the hearth. It was as if even the mention of the terrible word *leprosy* made her want to keep her distance.

I closed up my books, tidied my papers and, standing up, began the long task of putting them away. The light outside told me it was evening. As I'd done so many times, I'd allowed the day to pass by without noticing.

'So, what have you been doing?' I asked, looking round at Celia with a smile. I turned my mind back to earlier in the day. 'Sallie said you'd been in for dinner and then gone out again.'

'Oh, I've just been visiting,' she said, although I didn't miss the swift glance she shot me under her long eyelashes. 'The day has been far too lovely to waste it indoors. Unless, that is, you're a stuffy old physician who's more interested in his books and his studies than in *living*.'

'I had something I needed to check,' I muttered.

'Whether someone is suffering from leprosy?' she replied swiftly.

'Well, yes,' I confessed. I didn't really want to tell her, but then I thought, why not? 'A body was found up on the edge of the moor. Theo came to fetch me and I had a look at it once it had been brought back to his house.'

'But that – leprosy – wasn't what killed him.' She made it a statement, not a question.

'I'm almost certain it wasn't.'

'*Almost?*' She had paled. 'But Gabe, you—'

'Enough, Celia,' I said very firmly. I got up and went to crouch before her, taking her hands. 'I have more work to do on the body, for, apart from anything else, Theo needs to know whether this was a natural death. Whether he died of disease or starvation.'

'Or whether someone killed him.'

I didn't recall that either Theo or I had actually voiced that possibility, but, of course, it existed. 'Yes,' I agreed. Then, for I had spent far too much of this beautiful day preoccupied by the dead body, I forced a smile and said, 'I was forgetting, you went to see Jonathan Carew this morning. How did you find him?'

She took her hands from mine and covered her face. 'Oh, Gabe, it was so embarrassing!' She dropped her hands. 'He spoke very politely, and said it was a kindly thought, and that the roses were beautiful and the strawberry preserve delicious, but he left me in no doubt whatsoever that he thought I was intruding and had no right to ask if he was all right.'

'Really?' I was surprised. 'He was curt with you?'

'No, *no*! He was polite, I just said so. But he sort of—' She struggled to explain. 'It was as if I'd been peering in through a window, and he noticed and very gently closed it.'

'Ah.' That I could understand. 'And you still think he's unwell? Disturbed?'

'I think it all the more now,' she said. 'He was ashen-faced, and I'd swear he doesn't sleep. Something ails him, of that I'm sure.'

I stood up, stretching. Appetising smells were snaking up from the kitchen and I realized how hungry I was. Well, food would have to wait.

'I'll go and see him,' I said. 'Now, before supper.'

She looked horrified. 'But he'll know I've told you he's ill!'

'If he is, then I'm the right one to call on him,' I pointed out.

'But—'

I didn't listen to Celia any more. 'I won't be long,' I said, and then I hurried away.

I found Jonathan Carew in his church. He was standing in the low doorway that leads from the main body of the building through to a small chapel, little used for services but convenient, I've always supposed, for private prayer.

Hearing my footsteps, he turned. He smiled faintly.

'Ah,' he said.

'My sister feels she may have intruded upon you the morning,' I began, 'but—'

'It was an act prompted by concern,' he interrupted. 'As is your own appearance here now.'

'You don't look very well,' I said. 'And on Sunday, Celia and I both observed your brief moment of inattention.' I was watching him carefully. 'Was it a spasm of pain?'

His expression registered surprise. 'Pain? No.' He paused. 'Well, of a sort, I suppose, although not physical pain. I do not fear, Doctor, that I am suffering from some deep-seated malaise.'

'I see, and I am glad of it. Something on your mind, then?'

For some moments he didn't reply, and I thought he was going to shut the window, in my sister's expressive phrase. But then he sighed, and I heard him mutter, 'What is the harm?'

I waited.

'I thought I saw the ghost of a man I once knew,' he said eventually. *Celia was right*, I thought. 'Or, to be more exact, who I once met, for our acquaintance was too brief for it to be said that we knew one another.'

'I am not entirely sure that I believe in ghosts,' I said.

'Nor I,' he agreed. 'This was, I think, rather a manifestation of a matter that presses on my mind.'

Again I waited. I didn't want to prompt or hurry him. I was sure it would serve no purpose.

'He has always stayed with me,' Jonathan said softly. 'Ever since – ever since the very short time we spent together. Of late, he has occupied my thoughts, both in the waking hours and when I sleep. My dreams, Gabriel, have been shaking me into wakefulness, so that I fear the night and try to stay awake.'

No wonder he looked so thin and white-faced. 'I can prepare a mild draught,' I said.

He smiled swiftly, the expression there and gone in an instant. 'A kind thought, but no.'

He feared, I guessed, that the deep sleep induced by the sedative herbs might intensify his nightmares, as well as prolonging them. 'Then will you not speak to me of why this man haunts you?' I asked gently. 'Words spoken to me are treated with the same discretion as to you, Jonathan.'

'I realize that,' he agreed. 'Thank you,' he added. 'If I—' But abruptly he cut the sentence off. 'I'll bear it in mind. Do you know what this chapel is called?' he went on, the change of subject so sudden and so ruthless that I found I couldn't challenge it.

'Er – no, I don't believe I do.' You can't make a potential patient confide in you, and I understood there was nothing more I could do for Jonathan Carew until or unless he asked for my help. 'Why not enlighten me?'

He waved an arm behind him, indicating the mysterious darkness of the tiny chapel. It was separated from the main body of the church by an interior wall with five small apertures at the top, about a foot and a half high by a foot across, topped by pointed arches.

'Those are called clerestory windows,' Jonathan said, noticing the direction of my gaze. 'The chapel – it's called St Luke's Little Chapel – has no other source of light, save that coming through the apertures from the church itself.'

In its outer walls our church has windows of thick, slightly greenish glass, set in lattices of lead. There are six of them, and the dim light inside is augmented by candles.

'St Luke was a physician,' Jonathan was saying, 'as of course you'll know, and it's believed that when the church and this little chapel were constructed – both are very old – the chapel was used as a healing shrine.'

I nodded. 'Perhaps we should resurrect the tradition,' I remarked. Instantly I wondered if I ought to have done. What was the Church's view on healing shrines? Might it not smack of miracles, and popish ways, and the vast store of ancient superstitions we were meant to have put firmly behind us?

But, whatever the Church's position, Jonathan's seemed to be one of tolerance. 'Yes,' he said mildly, 'I've often thought the same. People have long memories, I find, and the old traditions can still give comfort.'

He had unobtrusively been edging me back into the aisle of the main church, and now, side by side, we walked slowly to the door.

As I took my leave, I turned back to him. 'If you change your mind about having a mild remedy to help you sleep, come and see me.' I hesitated, then added, 'Come and see me – us – anyway. Company can be of help when we have something on our minds.'

He didn't answer, save by a nod and a smile. He went back inside his church and closed the door.

I was kept busy the next morning with a series of calls on patients in varying degrees of distress. I set a child's broken leg, stitched a long cut on a man's head (he'd taken too much beer the previous evening and forgotten all about the low branch that overhung the entrance to his yard), and reassured an anxious and exhausted young mother that her little girl was on the mend and the fever definitely abating.

My final call before I went home to dinner was to a farm where an angry old woman was making life hell for her son and daughter-in-law. They were by no means young themselves – it was their sons, the old woman's grandsons, who now did the bulk of the labour – and would, I was sure, have preferred a bit of peace and quiet and a well-earned rest to being at the mercy of the old woman.

As I always did, I took a deep breath as I went into the frowsy, overstuffed, airless recess that she had shared with her late husband since the day she had married him some sixty years ago. It appeared, to the visitor's eye, that she could not have thrown one single thing away in all that time. Given that she refused to open the tiny window set high in the wall for fear of a wicked draught sneaking in and taking her off, as she phrased it, the stench was all but unendurable, even to one in my profession well used to bodily smells. I sat with her for a while and listened to her complaints, accepted her furious criticism that the tonic I habitually prepared for her was less than useless except for making her costive – 'It turns my bowels to stone,' was what she actually said – and she might as well drink her own piss, then, when she drastically changed tack and demanded to know why I hadn't brought more, promised to do so in the next day or two. I felt her pulse, made her breathe deeply while I put my ear to her chest, examined her eyes and throat, then tucked her up and backed out of the room, closing the concealing curtain behind me.

The farmer had joined his wife in the kitchen. He was helping himself to a bucket-sized mug of small beer from the barrel in the cold pantry, and as I watched he raised it to his lips and drank a good half of it in a few gulping mouthfuls. He had a prodigious swallow. Seeing me staring, he raised the huge mug with an enquiring look and I nodded. The mug he gave me was fortunately more modest. I wouldn't have minded a draught as generous as his, for his wife's brew was excellent, but I knew I'd sleep the afternoon away if I copied him.

'How is she?' the wife, Jane, asked wearily.

'Much the same.'

The farmer, Gregory, gave a great gusty sigh. 'She doesn't get any easier,' he muttered.

The pair of them had my sympathy. 'The old man's death last year shook her more than she'll admit, I dare say,' I said.

Gregory nodded. 'Aye, aye, you're right there, Doctor.'

There was a brief silence. I was trying to find a tactful way of asking if they had any other family and friends to share the care of the old woman when, almost as if she'd anticipated the question, Jane said, 'We're lucky in that both the Reverend and that lovely midwife call in to give comfort, so, what with you and all, Doctor Taverner, we're not short of help.'

I was pleased to hear that Jonathan came; and the news of Judyth Penwarden's visits – for I guessed that was who Jane was referring to – gave me a secret lift of the spirits. 'What has his reverence to say to comfort your mother-in-law?' I asked Jane.

She grinned. 'Oh, he told her she'll see her Humphrey again one day, when she gets to heaven, and she said, "I bloody well hope not, Vicar, I'm trusting the old bugger's gone the other way." Sorry, Doctor,' she added, blushing.

I waved the apology aside. It wasn't really the moment to tell her I'd been in the navy for years and acquired the sailor's imperviousness to bad language. 'And how did the Reverend Carew reply?'

Jane chuckled. 'Well, he said something about God's understanding and forgiveness, and a bit more in the same vein, but I could see he was trying not to smile.'

I finished my ale, refused a refill – reluctantly – and, promising to bring or send round a fresh supply of tonic very soon, left them.

*   *   *

My route back to Rosewyke took me quite close to Theophilus
Davey's house. Turning Hal's head away from the road home,
I went to see if he had any news.

I found him in his office, his desk even more loaded than
usual. 'If you've come to see if I've an identity for that vagrant,
the answer's no,' he greeted me grumpily.

It was just past noon, I reminded myself, and Theo was still
at his desk. He's always tetchy when he's hungry.

'I'm as certain as I can be that he wasn't suffering from
leprosy,' I said. 'I've checked every reference I can find to the
disease among my papers, and the symptoms don't match.'

'Thank God for that, at least,' Theo muttered. Then,
mellowing, he looked at me with a faint smile and said,
'Something to interest you, Doctor. My agent Jarman Hodge
heard there'd been a suspicious figure loitering around the big
house at Wrenbeare and we wondered if it might have been
our vagrant, so he went to see what he could find out.' He
strode across to the door, flinging it wide open. 'Wait there,
I'll see if he's around.'

He went through to the big room at the rear of the house
where his administrative staff, his agents and his officers
congregate, and I heard a brief conversation. Then Theo was
back.

'Jarman's on his way,' he said, and, after a moment, the slim,
unobtrusively clad, nondescript and totally unmemorable figure
of Theo's most efficient officer followed him into the room.

'So, Jarman, what did you discover over at Wrenbeare?'
Theo demanded. 'Does it sound as if it was our dead skinny
vagrant who was hanging around?'

'Who lives there?' I interposed before Jarman Hodge could
reply. 'I know the name, I think, but not the occupants.'

Jarman turned to me. 'It's a grand old house, the long-time
home of the Fairlights,' he answered. 'Sir Thomas was a man
of substance and position, a justice of the peace, I believe,
and wealthy. He died, a decade or more back, and now the
house is run by his widow, name of Clemence, who is supported
by her two daughters. The elder one, Agnes, is wed to a man
called Avery Lond – seems the two of them are resident at
Wrenbeare – and there's a younger daughter, Denyse.'

He gave me a significant sort of a glance when he said the name of the second daughter. 'Yes?' I asked. 'What of this Denyse?'

Jarman Hodge looked discomfited; an expression I'd not thought to see on that carefully bland face. 'She's – er, well, this is only talk, mind you, and probably an exaggeration, but they say locally she's – er – she's not right in the head.'

'Ah.'

But Jarman went on staring at me, and I realized he had more to say. 'That, then, is the gossip,' I said mildly. 'What did you make of her?'

He smiled. 'You don't miss much, do you, Doctor?' he murmured. 'You're right, I did have the chance to see the young lady with my own eyes. I went and knocked on the door,' he went on, turning to Theo, 'and managed to get myself admitted to the lady Clemence's presence – she had the daughters with her but not the elder one's husband – whereupon I told her who I was and that I was from the coroner's office, and I said we'd had word that they'd complained of an intruder, or a burglar, or someone suspicious hanging around, and could I be of assistance?'

'And they didn't ask what a coroner's agent was doing asking about a burglary?' Theo demanded.

Jarman Hodge shook his head. 'I doubt if any of them has the least idea of the different interests of coroners and constables,' he said. 'Anyway, they seemed to accept my question as legitimate, and straight away they denied it had ever happened.'

'What, the burglary? The vagrant peering in the windows?' Theo asked.

'None of it,' Jarman agreed. 'Lady Clemence sat up very straight and pushed her shoulders back, then said in a haughty sort of voice that she couldn't imagine where I'd heard that unpleasant little tale but there was not an iota of truth in it.'

'So then what did you do?' I said.

'I apologized for disturbing them, agreed that I must have been mistaken – her ladyship made some remark about it being unwise to listen to tavern gossip – and took my leave.'

'And then?' Theo persisted. He knew his man well,

I reflected, for he didn't assume for a moment that Jarman had simply walked away.

'I set off down the path back towards the road, and as soon as I was out of their sight – I guessed they'd be looking out of the window – ducked back and went to speak to the groom and the stable lad. As I'd expected, since it was their conversation I overheard, they told a different story. At least, they'd just begun to – the lad said there'd been a bit of an upset some two, three weeks ago, which was what he and the groom had been talking about in the tavern, and he insisted there most certainly had been an intruder, who fled when they gave chase – but then there was an almighty scream from within the house and the groom shoved me out of the yard double-quick. "That's Mistress Denyse," he said, his eyes wide with alarm, "and it sounds like she's having another of her attacks, so you'd better make yourself scarce." The screaming was still going on, and it was sending chills up my spine, so I didn't stay to be told again.'

Silence fell. I was intrigued by Jarman's story and I was sure Theo was too. Presently, looking first at Jarman then at me, Theo said musingly, 'Why should Lady Clemence and her daughters pretend that this burglary, or whatever it was, didn't happen?'

'Maybe something was stolen that they don't want known about,' Jarman suggested. 'Something they shouldn't have had in the first place.'

Theo nodded. 'It's an idea,' he said.

'Maybe the vagrant saw something he shouldn't have,' I said.

Theo spun round to stare at me. 'And, if it was the same man who currently lies in the crypt of the house up the road, perhaps somebody had to make quite sure he didn't speak of what he'd seen,' he said softly.

'So we're saying now that our skeletal vagrant was *murdered*?' I was taken aback. 'But I saw no marks of violence, no signs of death by another's hand!'

'Did you look for them?' Theo asked swiftly. 'Or did you simply assume he'd died from sickness or starvation? Not that it would have been unreasonable,' he added charitably, 'since we had no cause to believe otherwise.'

I sighed. I'd planned my visit to Theo to be brief, and I wanted my dinner. It looked, however, as if the pleasures of Sallie's cooking were to be postponed.

I said resignedly, 'I'd better take another look.'

FOUR

The crypt beneath the empty house has little natural light, so Theo and I each took with us three lanterns. By their flames, down there below ground level, I unwrapped the corpse and began my second, more careful examination.

And I found quite a lot that I had missed in my first cursory inspection. I found the hard skin on the heels and the deformities on the toes that indicated this man had walked for endless miles in inadequate, poorly fitting footwear. There'd been little left of his thin little shoes when he was found. I found the swollen, distorted knee joints that backed up the impression of a man who had wandered far. I found more of the lumpy growths I'd noticed before. And, on his back, buttocks and elsewhere on that poor, thin body, I saw the marks of ill usage. At some time in his life, this man had been beaten hard enough to leave deep scars.

I looked carefully over every inch of him and eventually I concluded that he hadn't died by violence.

'You're sure?' Theo said when I told him.

'Yes,' I confirmed. 'He wasn't stabbed or strangled, he wasn't hit on the head, he wasn't beaten to death.'

'Could he have been poisoned?'

'It's possible, but poison usually involves a voiding of the body as it tries to rid itself of the toxins, and I'd have expected to see vomit or evidence he'd been passing loose stools, or perhaps both, on the body and in the place where he died, and I didn't.'

'Not on the body, perhaps, but you're sure about that ruin where we found him? It stank, right enough.'

'Yes, of urine and decaying flesh, neither of which suggests a body responding to having been poisoned.'

But still Theo wasn't satisfied. 'Could he have done all the throwing up and stool-passing before he got to the ruin? Crawled in there to die?'

'It's possible,' I conceded.

He nodded, as if I'd given the answer he wanted. 'So, let's say he was the man apprehended at Wrenbeare by this Lady Clemence and her daughters, and he saw something he shouldn't have done, and her ladyship decides to make absolutely sure he doesn't tell anyone by slipping him some food – in the guise of a charitable gift to encourage him on his way, perhaps – and it's poisoned.' He looked at me, eyebrows raised. 'What d'you reckon?'

It didn't sound very likely to me. 'If she'd caught him trying to break into her home, would she really offer him food?' I said. 'And, if she did, wouldn't he be suspicious? He could hardly believe she wished him well.'

Theo frowned. 'I suppose you're right. All the same, I think I'll head out to Wrenbeare and have a word with Lady Clemence Fairlight.' He met my eye, and he was smiling. 'Since I'm quite sure you're keen to have a look at this mad daughter – oh, I saw the spark of interest there when Jarman Hodge spoke of her – I reckon you'd better come with me.'

We had our midday meal with Theo's comely wife, Elaine, and the three children. Carolus entertained us with a lively recounting of the story of Noah, which apparently he'd been studying with his tutor, although the child's lively imagination had added a few colourful touches such as Noah being considerably more censorious than in the original version and trying to ban the pigs because they were too smelly and the hens because they were stupid. The two younger children, Isabella and Benjamin, sang us a song that Elaine had taught them, although they had to be discouraged firmly by their mother from the substitution of rude words – I distinctly heard Benjamin say *bum* – for the rather more staid original version. The meal was delicious, as was the ale. All in all, it was with reluctance that Theo and I finally tore ourselves away.

It was a ride of some half a dozen miles to Wrenbeare. We were trusting to post-prandial somnolence to have kept the family at home, and so it proved. We were admitted by a musty-smelling servant – few, it appears, are willing to turn away a coroner in pursuit of his duty, and Theo can be very imposing – and, after a short wait in a lofty wood-panelled hall with dark, unfaded rectangles on the floor to indicate where items of furniture once stood, shown into a long, dimly lit but very evidently dirty room where the Fairlight women awaited us. There was no sign of the son-in-law and no explanation was given for his absence.

Lady Clemence sat straight-backed on an elaborately carved chair by the fireplace. She was large, fair, exceedingly plain and aged, I guessed, in the fifties. She wore a brocade gown that must once have been gorgeous, but now its deep blue shade had faded in places and there were stains and worn patches down the bodice and on the front of the skirts. Her posture and the severity of her gaze, however, gave authority to her bearing, and as she spoke a greeting that superficially welcomed us while at the same time seemed to demand what we thought we were doing disturbing her in this way, she eyed the pair of us with sparse-lashed, bulging, light hazel eyes.

'I am here to enquire about an intruder reported to have been hanging around your house some two or three weeks ago and—' Theo began.

Lady Clemence raised a plump, imperious hand. 'No, no, *no*,' she said. From somewhere in the room I heard someone echo the words, and a slightly hysterical giggle. But Lady Clemence was still speaking, and I made myself listen. 'Your man came before,' her ladyship said, 'and I told him he was mistaken.'

'Mistaken!' came the mischievous little echo.

Other than a disapproving frown, which might well have been for Theo and me, Lady Clemence ignored it.

'The reason for the enquiry,' Theo went on, almost as if he hadn't heard her protest, 'is because a body has been found that appears to match the description of the man seen lurking here.'

Lady Clemence sighed. 'But nobody *was* lurking here.'

'We hear differently,' Theo said baldly.

The woman sitting in the matching chair on the other side of the fireplace now chose to speak. 'You should not listen to gossip,' she said reprovingly. 'If my mother says there was no intruder, there was no intruder.' She gave a nod as if to emphasize her utterance.

I studied her. She was obviously Lady Clemence's daughter, with the same big-boned, chubby body and the same fair hair and skin. Her nose was like a lump of clay that had been pulled into a point, so that the nostrils were distorted into long, narrow slits. She wore a wedding ring on her left hand, and I assumed she must be Agnes, the elder daughter.

'Mistress Lond,' Theo said, turning to her with a brief bow. He had obviously reached the same conclusion.

'Indeed,' the woman said. 'We know nothing of dead bodies, Master—?'

'Davey,' Theo said.

'Master Davey. Thank you.' Agnes Lond's tone was icily polite. 'As I was saying, no dead bodies have—'

'*Dead bodies!*'

This time the echo was too loud for any of us to pretend we hadn't heard it. And now the source of the mimicry came out of her hiding place behind one of the long, drooping curtains half-drawn against the bright day and skipped forward to stand beside her mother.

For this woman, too, was clearly Lady Clemence's daughter, although her resemblance to her mother and her sister was twisted and strange, like a reflection in a distorting mirror. She was squat, and her arms – and probably her legs too, although they were covered by the skirts of her gown – were short and malformed. She had somehow arranged her tight bodice so that the flesh of her breasts was pushed up and spilled out. If the intention had been to attract, to seduce, then the failure was total. Her almost colourless eyes were set at an odd angle in her face, and her widely smiling mouth – although in truth the expression was closer to a grimace or a rictus than a smile – revealed gaps between her teeth, which were jagged. There was something wrong with her nose, too, for it appeared truncated and turned up at the tip in an exaggerated way, so that one was all but staring up her nostrils.

She went up to her mother and sat on the arm of her chair, wriggling herself close and leaning her head on her mother's shoulder. I saw Lady Clemence edge away slightly, and her face wore a mask of distaste. 'Run away now, Denyse,' she said, her tone chilly. 'These men have come to speak to me, not you.' She looked around anxiously, and I heard her hiss to her elder daughter, 'Where is Mary? Why is she not here?'

Without a word, Agnes got up and left the room.

'*I* saw a dead body,' Denyse said. She was watching Theo and me slyly, and the intensity of her pale gaze made me uneasy.

'Did you?' I heard the spark of sudden interest in Theo's short reply.

'Yes, yes, *yes!*' Denyse sang. Then abruptly she leapt off her mother's chair, dashed at Theo and, flinging her stubby arms round his waist, pushed her face up towards his, her wet lips pursed as if for a lover's kiss.

'*Denyse!*' thundered her mother.

Denyse spun round. 'I did! *I DID!*' Her voice rose to a deafening screech. 'This nice, big man says there was a dead body, and I want to help him! And *you can't stop me!*' Now she flung herself at Lady Clemence, all the time screaming, 'Dead, dead, *dead!*'

Although short, Denyse was sturdy, and I feared for Lady Clemence. Hurrying forward, I took hold of Denyse's shoulders and, trying gently but firmly to pull her off, said, 'That's enough, now, come away and sit down quietly.'

Denyse spun round and, quick as a cornered cat, raised her hands and tried to scratch my face. I caught her wrists just in time, holding the hands with their sharp nails inches away from my eyes.

Behind me I heard footsteps running across the floor, and then a calm, maternal voice said kindly, 'Mistress Denyse, so this is where you've got to!' Arms were wrapped round Denyse, pinning her own arms to her sides, and, turning, I saw a tall, well-built woman of around forty clutching the young woman to her. Denyse was whimpering. This, I guessed, was Mary; a supposition borne out by the way Lady Clemence was glaring at her.

'You were supposed to be looking after her!' she said in an all too audible whisper.

Mary turned calm eyes to her employer. 'She escaped,' she said.

Lady Clemence looked as if she'd like to say more – probably a great deal more – but Theo's and my presence, it seemed, prevented her.

We watched in silence as Mary took her charge away.

Then Lady Clemence gave a deep sigh. 'My younger daughter refers not to recently having seen a dead body, Master Davey,' she said, staring up at Theo, 'but to an occasion when she had the misfortune to observe, many years ago, the corpse of my late husband.'

Theo, it seemed, was at a loss as to how to reply.

'That must have been a very disturbing experience.' I stepped into the breach. 'She was a small child?'

Lady Clemence turned to me. 'She was ten years old.'

'Ah.' Not an infant, then. I wondered briefly whether the late husband had died by violence, that the sight of his body should so have distressed his daughter, possibly to the extent of turning her mind. Then it occurred to me that it was far more likely that the insanity had predated the unfortunate viewing of her father's corpse, and that this had been the reason for the distress.

Something, definitely, was not right with Denyse Fairlight.

Theo was staring at Lady Clemence, a faint frown on his face. 'It is my job to identify the body that has been found, my lady,' he said coldly. 'You have told me that you have no knowledge of the dead man, yet, as I told you, others insist he was seen in the vicinity of your house.'

'Others may well have seen him,' she said grandly. 'My daughters and I did not.'

'I shall be making further inquiries,' Theo said.

Lady Clemence inclined her head.

There seemed nothing to be gained by our staying there. To my great relief, Theo bowed to the lady, bade her farewell and turned curtly on his heel. I followed him out of the room, across the hall and out into the fresh air.

'Could it be as simple as that?' I asked as we rode away.

'As what?' he replied angrily.

'As the outdoor servants who were letting their tongues run away with them in the tavern having seen the vagrant hanging around, while the ladies inside the house didn't.'

He made a sort of humphing sound that could equally have been agreement or rebuttal.

After a while he said, 'There's something going on in that house.' Silence. Then: 'Yes, Gabe, it could well have happened the way you say, but in my bones I know it didn't.'

'And your bones are recognized as reliable in law?' I asked.

He grinned. 'Oh, yes.'

I didn't argue.

I totally agreed with him.

Then I said, 'You're not going to be satisfied with her ladyship's somewhat brusque denials, are you?'

'Of course not,' he replied. 'I'm going to get Jarman Hodge to return to the tavern where the Wrenbeare servants go to drink and blabber about all the goings-on there, and I shall go with him.'

I noticed there was a light of excitement in his bright blue eyes. 'I'm coming too,' I said before I could think about it.

He grinned. 'Thought you might say that.'

We arranged to meet on the edge of the village later that evening. I'd been home in the meantime, eaten, then dug out the heavy cloak with a deep hood that I purchased a few years ago for protection when summoned out to attend a patient in foul weather. It has the advantage of covering me adequately well to disguise my identity, if necessary. I wasn't sure if I wanted it known far and wide that the doctor had been seen fraternizing in the tavern late at night.

Theo and Jarman were waiting for me just beyond the last village house. It was less than half a mile to the tavern, which was in fact not that close to the moor's edge and some way from Wrenbeare, and they were on foot. I dismounted and walked beside them. Reaching the inn yard, I tethered Hal and followed them inside.

On the way over, Jarman had seemed confident that the men we needed to talk to would be there, and so it proved. Once in the tap room, Jarman walked over to two men, one middle-aged, one a youth, sitting on a bench beside the hearth, mugs of ale in their hands, and, leaning down, muttered to the older one, turning to indicate Theo and me. 'The groom and the stable lad,' Theo said quietly to me.

Jarman straightened up and beckoned us over. Theo took some coins out of his purse and, handing them to Jarman, told him to fetch ale for us all. Then he drew up a second bench, he and I sat down and he said to the older man, 'My name is Theophilus Davey, and I'm—'

'You're the coroner, aye, so he tells us' – the man nodded in Jarman's direction – 'and you want to ask us to repeat to you what we told him a while back.'

'About the intruder at Wrenbeare, yes,' Theo said. 'Will you give me your names?'

The man hesitated, then, appearing to decide no harm could come of it, stabbed a thumb in his own chest and said curtly, 'Christopher Hammer, groom.' He jerked the same thumb at his companion. 'He's the stable boy. Name of Cory.' He didn't say whether the latter was a forename or surname.

'Thank you,' Theo said. He waited while Jarman put five mugs of ale before us. Then: 'You told my officer that you'd chased after someone who was loitering around Wrenbeare, and that—'

'Wasn't me blathering for all to hear, it was him.' Christopher dug an elbow into the ribs of the lad. He turned and glowered at him. 'Can't take his beer, this one.'

'Then perhaps you shouldn't let him drink so much,' Theo said pointedly. Addressing the lad, he went on, 'Cory, tell me what you saw.'

The boy looked very uncomfortable. 'We *both* saw it, master Coroner sir!' he protested.

Theo suppressed a sigh. I heard him mutter under his breath. 'Very well, then, you both saw this intruder, but only you talked about it? Is that right?'

'Er – yes,' Cory acknowledged. Picking up Theo's mounting impatience – which wouldn't have been hard as it was written all over him – he said, 'He came twice. First time, he was just hanging around, going round the house, peering in at the windows, but he didn't knock at the door nor nothing. Kit here asked him his business, and he legged it. We chased him for a bit – running away like that, he made us suspicious – but he was swift and we had work to get on with.' He gave a little self-righteous nod. 'Second time, it was late, and dark, and we reckon he must have got inside somehow, because he came hurrying out of the house as if the hell hounds were on his tail, and there was a lot of screaming – that was probably Mistress Denyse, she screams a lot – and then a bit of shouting, and then it all went quiet.'

'And did you chase him that time too?'

Cory shot a glance at Kit, who minutely shook his head. 'No,' he said.

I wondered if Theo too had the impression he was lying.

'Thank you,' Theo said. 'That's very helpful. One more thing: did either of you get a good look at this intruder?'

'We both did, first time he appeared.' Kit had taken over the account. 'And I reckon we saw enough of him, second time, to be sure it was the same man. Well, I say man, but he was skinny as a whip and not over-tall, and in appearance more like a young woman, or even a girl.'

'So how can you be sure it was a man?' Theo demanded.

Kit looked at him pityingly. 'I can tell a man from a woman,' he said.

'What else can you tell us?'

Kit paused to think. 'Dirty, with ragged clothes – a coat, I think it was he wore, but it was hard to tell. Barefoot, or as good as, with little slippers on his feet. Hair longish and unkempt, in a tangle round his face. Pale – I recall how his flesh was so white it seemed to glow, for all that he was so filthy. And—'

'You've not said nothing about the swellings!' Cory interrupted. 'He had—'

Kit put up his hand. 'I was just about to,' he said crushingly.

'Swellings?' Even in the single word, I could hear Theo's suddenly sharpened interest.

'Aye, on his face. Big lumps, nasty-looking, on his cheek, his nose, all over.' He shuddered, shaking his head. 'I didn't like the look of those lumps.'

Jarman Hodge bade us goodnight shortly before we reached Theo's house. I walked on with Theo. 'It has to be the same man,' I said, not for the first time.

Theo gave me a withering look. 'Yes, Gabe, so you insist on telling me.'

'And it's pretty certain he got into the house somehow,' I went on, 'if we're to believe Kit and Cory when they said they saw him being chased out, and so we're left with the original question: did he see something he shouldn't have seen, or take something the Fairlight women don't want to admit to having possessed?'

'The son-in-law might have been there the night our vagrant was chased off,' Theo said. 'Would any man, even a thin, girlish one, run away in such a panic if it was only three women after him?'

'Lady Clemence is rather well-built, as are her daughters,' I pointed out. 'And I imagine Denyse can be quite terrifying when she's really excited.'

Theo grinned. 'Yes, very well, but I'd wager that the husband, Avery Lond, was the main force behind our man's abrupt departure.'

'If he did indeed steal something,' I said, 'what happened to it? There was nothing on his body when he was found, not even a coin in his purse.'

'There was just that scrap of paper,' Theo said.

I'd forgotten about that. 'Did you examine it?'

'No. It's somewhere on my desk, amid every other piece of paper awaiting my attention. But I'll look it out in the morning. For now' – he yawned hugely – 'I'm off to my bed. Goodnight, Gabe.'

'Goodnight.' I mounted Hal and edged him off in the direction of Rosewyke.

*   *   *

Riding home, I decided that, if we were to discover what was behind Lady Clemence's denial of any intrusion by our dead vagrant, we needed to find out more about the family and their recent past. But it was all very well to come to that startlingly obvious conclusion; deciding how to go about it was another matter.

When I was turning into the track up to my house, I had an idea. Lady Clemence had said that Denyse had seen her father's body when she was ten years old. It was hard to guess her age now, but I put her at somewhere in the mid-twenties, which suggested her father had died about fifteen years ago. Whether it had been illness or accident – or even, I supposed, murder – I had no idea, but it seemed at least likely that a doctor could have been consulted.

When I had begun my physician's practice in the area, I'd feared at one time that an aggrieved predecessor was trying to discourage me. I found out his identity – he'd in fact been looking forward eagerly to retirement, and didn't resent me in the least – and we'd discovered that we liked one another. Since our first acquaintance, I'd ridden over to Buckland several times to see him, and he'd offered to try to help me over the flare-up of symptoms that I still get occasionally from the blow to the side of my head that brought my life at sea to an end.

His name was Josiah Thorn, he lived a short ride away, and he was, I thought, the most likely medical man to have attended the late Sir Thomas Fairlight. I would go over to see him in the morning and find out.

Back in his house at Withybere, Theo was not yet abed. Instead he stood in his office, a lantern illuminating his desk, going through the stacks of papers and documents that covered most of the surface. He was a reasonably orderly man, when he got the chance to be, but too often matters demanding his attention came in so swiftly that there was insufficient time to file away one set of papers before the next arrived. His staff were meant to see to the organization of the paperwork, but Theo knew he stood little chance even of finding items that he had personally put away and none whatsoever when someone else had done so.

He knew roughly where he'd put the torn scrap of parchment that had been tucked away inside the vagrant's coat, and, after quite a long time of hunting, he found it. He cleared a space on his desk and smoothed it out.

The feel of it beneath his fingertips told him it was heavy, high-quality paper, of the sort used by draughtsmen, calligraphers and artists. It was a soft, very pale golden colour. It was, he realized, a fragment of a larger sheet, for it had a tear going across it in a roughly diagonal line, and whereas the cut edges were sharp, the torn edge was slightly furry.

Theo stared down at it. Originally it had been about three hands' breadth across and perhaps five or six deep – helpfully, the fragment included three corners – but only the top right-hand third, or maybe nearer half, remained. Peering closer, the warmth of the lantern flame singeing his skin, Theo tried to make out the meaning of the dark marks flowing across the creamy-yellow paper.

There was an outline, roughly oval, and around it, very faintly indicated, a series of smooth lines, all running in the same direction. There were two deep holes each with a line close above it, and—

'Idiot! Imbecile!' Theo hissed at himself.

The image had suddenly revealed itself for what it was and, now that he understood, he couldn't understand why he hadn't seen it straight away.

It was a sketch of a human face.

And it had been done by a talented artist, for even in those few lines on the part of the page that remained, the mood of the model could be detected. No, Theo corrected himself, more, much more, than *detected*, for the face expressed such pain and suffering that it almost hurt to look at it.

'Who are you?' Theo whispered, running his fingers across the half-face as if by so doing he could assuage the agony.

Then he thought he knew.

And then it seemed like blasphemy, to have an image of Jesus Christ – and such an image – amid the clutter of papers, quills and ink horns on his desk. Picking it up carefully, holding it by the edges between fingers and thumbs, he put the image on a fresh sheet of paper, covered it with a second sheet and, opening a cedar-wood chest that stood against the wall, laid it inside. Then he rummaged around in the pot where he kept his keys for the one to the chest, locked it and removed the key.

Only then did he feel it was safe to abandon the drawing and go, at last, to bed.

FIVE

In the morning, I reorganized my day so that I could ride over to see Josiah Thorn as soon as I'd had breakfast, making a quick call on the way to make sure my patient with the broken leg was obeying my strict instructions not to put any weight on it for at least another week. I would be able to make a detour on my way home to see two more patients, and thus I could tell myself that I wasn't evading my responsibilities by riding off on a whim to chase after a ghost from the past.

My patient moaned that the flesh beneath the tightly bound and splinted leg was itching enough to drive any man mad, but I told him sternly to send his lad out for a suitably flexible stick and scratch away with that, since there was no possibility of the bandages being removed yet. He called me a name I haven't heard since my days at sea as I was leaving, but I put his testiness down to pain and frustration and decided to pretend I hadn't heard.

Josiah Thorn, so I was informed by the woman busy cleaning and tidying his house, was down by the river fishing. She was about to tell me how to find him but I stopped her, for I already knew. He'd taken me to his favourite fishing spot on a couple of occasions, and I was confident of remembering the way. I left Hal tethered in the shade outside Josiah's house and went on foot, down to the end of the lane and past a spinney of beech trees, then I turned off into a narrow little track overhung with honeysuckle and wild roses that led steeply down to the water.

And there, on a short stretch of pebbly beach overlooking a beautiful spot where ancient willows and alders shaded a deep pool formed by a bend in the river, sat Josiah. I wasn't sure he'd even cast a line, for his rod lay on the ground beside him. He had propped himself up against the broad trunk of one of the trees in a hollow that might have been made for him, and he looked supremely comfortable. He had abandoned the close-fitting black cap that he habitually wore over his long silver-streaked hair and now a shapeless old straw hat was pulled down over his eyes to shade them from the bright light off the water. I had an idea he might well be asleep.

I was happy to see him so content. He had lost his grand-daughter around the time that my sister had been widowed, and, for all that she'd been a troubled, wayward girl, still I knew he had mourned her sincerely. Life, however, was certainly more peaceful for him without her, and I hoped that this was proving to be a consolation.

I walked carefully over the pebbles, trying not to make too much noise.

'I'm not asleep,' said Josiah Thorn. 'I'm merely closing my eyes.'

'Ah, the perpetual protest of elderly men caught dozing in the middle of the day,' I replied.

He pushed back the straw hat and, seeing who had come to disturb him, his face broke into a broad smile. 'Doctor Gabriel,' he said warmly. He uncurled his long, thin body and reached out to grasp my hand. He gave me an intent look. 'The old injury troubling you again?'

When we first met, I had told him about the blow to the side of my head, just behind the right ear, that had laid me out for two days and left me with the legacy of unendurable seasickness; the legacy that had ended my days as a ship's surgeon. He had been both interested and helpful.

'No, but thank you for asking,' I replied. 'My head aches if I go on working too long at the end of the day, but then so do most people's.'

He nodded. 'Take the pain as a warning and obey it,' he said sternly. Then, in a much brighter tone, he went on, 'I was just deciding it was high time I fetched that flagon of cider out of the cool shallows and broached it, and fortunately I had the foresight to bring two drinking vessels. Will you join me?'

'I will. Moreover, since you look so very comfortable there, I'll fetch the flagon for you.'

The cider was excellent, and the river water had kept it pleasantly cool. When Josiah and I had silently done it justice, he said, 'Now, then, what can I do for you?' Before I could protest, he added, 'It is, as you have just pointed out, the middle of the day, and I know from long experience that you will have a dozen or more calls on your time, so I deduce that you have sought me out because you want my advice.'

I grinned. 'Quite right. But it may be a matter on which you cannot help me, since it concerns someone who I suspect was formerly a patient of yours.'

'Indeed? And you have inherited this man or woman?'

'Man. Well, not exactly, he's dead.'

'I see.' Josiah smiled. 'Not much you can do for him, then. Let's begin with his name.'

'Sir Thomas Fairlight.'

Josiah's face changed.

'Ah,' he breathed.

'Clearly you recall him?'

Slowly Josiah nodded. 'Oh, yes.'

'I believe he died some fifteen years ago?'

'Fourteen.' The reply came so swiftly, and was so precise, that I knew there was a tale to tell here.

'I should very much like to learn about him and his family.' I paused. 'It is not mere curiosity,' I added.

Josiah thought for quite a long time. Then he said, 'What exactly is the reason for your interest?' I told him, trying to be succinct yet leaving out nothing of importance. 'I see. And none of the three women, the widow and the daughters, is your patient?'

'No, and nor is the son-in-law. A man called Avery Lond, married to Agnes, the elder daughter,' I supplied, in answer to his questioning look.

'Ah. The marriage occurred since Sir Thomas's death, then, for the daughter was unwed then.'

'She's in the mid to late thirties, I estimate—' I began.

But Josiah shook his head. 'She is but thirty. She was born in 1574, her younger sister six years later.' He glanced at me, and I realized that his disturbed, angry frown wasn't because of anything I had said or done.

'That's quite a long gap,' I observed mildly.

'There were other pregnancies, but none to term,' Josiah said shortly.

'Poor Lady Clemence.'

He was shaking his head slowly and repeatedly. 'Oh, yes, indeed. Despite the harshness of her nature, she deserves your pity,' he muttered.

I was becoming very intrigued, and hoped he would elaborate. I knew only too well, however, the strictures that bound him. 'Is there anything you can tell me?'

He was silent for some time. Then he sighed deeply and said, 'Thomas Fairlight might have been wealthy, influential and, as a justice of the peace, of importance in the county, but he was a hard man, selfish, cruel and self-indulgent. His peers appeared to tolerate and perhaps even like and admire him, but he presented a very different face to those over whom he had power. Ah, I remember how that tubby little priest remonstrated with him . . . what was his name, now? Predecessor, or predecessor but one, to young Carew . . .' Then he shook his head, evidently giving up the search through his memories for the elusive name. 'Thomas Fairlight's was not a happy household. The burdens already borne by his wife and elder daughter were exacerbated with the birth of poor little Denyse. I give nothing away here that I should not,' he said with sudden vehemence, 'since these things are well known, and you tell me that you have seen Denyse for yourself.'

'I have,' I said. 'You imply, then, that her disturbances began when she was a child?'

'Oh, yes,' Josiah agreed. 'I attended Clemence Fairlight in both her confinements – she was not Lady Clemence then, Thomas not yet having been knighted – and neither of her daughters thrived. Agnes was a pallid, flaccid, yellowish baby, although she grew stronger as the years passed. But poor Denyse was lucky, or perhaps unlucky' – he shot me a swift glance – 'to survive.'

'What was wrong with her?'

'The bodily deformities which are surely still apparent in her were present from birth, and in addition she suffered from endless infections, rashes and fevers. She refused the breast, even though an experienced and capable wet-nurse was engaged, and only took milk when she was beside herself with hunger and had cried herself into exhaustion. Even from a few weeks, she appeared to fight all those who tried to succour and tend her, and I believe it is no exaggeration to say that her presence in the household was a permanent and devastating trial to all concerned.'

'Poor child,' I murmured. 'And the screaming?'

'Ah, you've experienced that, then,' Josiah said softly. 'It began as soon as she could utter a sound. I heard it within moments of her expulsion from her mother's body.'

I nodded. 'And what of Sir Thomas? He was surely not an old man when he died?'

'In the late fifties, if memory serves.'

I was surprised. 'So quite a few years older than his wife?'

'Twenty and more, yes.' He hesitated. 'Thomas Fairlight wished to marry, and Clemence Sulyard, as she was prior to marriage, was desperate for a husband. Although she was still young, suitors were not rushing to her parents' door.' He leaned closer, lowering his voice. 'You have seen her, Doctor Gabriel. She is a – ah – a *large* woman, and the length of her chin puts one in mind rather of a horse, does it not? With that coarse hair, and those pale, lashless eyes of hers, one is tempted to add that it is not a good-looking, or even faintly appealing, horse.'

'A little unkind, Josiah, but I am forced to agree.'

'Unkind,' he repeated, almost to himself. 'Yes, you are right to upbraid me, for the woman cannot help her looks.' He glanced at me from under his old man's wild, wiry eyebrows. 'But then she is not a kind woman, Gabriel. She—' But then he closed his mouth. Very firmly.

Silence fell, and for some time we sat back and listened to the music of the river hurrying past.

'I admit I am intrigued,' I said eventually. 'I sense I have more dealings with the Fairlight household ahead of me, for this matter is far from resolved.'

'I cannot tell you any more,' Josiah said. 'Already perhaps I have said too much.'

I thought back over his comments. 'You have told me when each of the family was born, which I could have found out for myself from parish records, and you spoke of two baby girls that you delivered. You expressed what I can only take to be purely personal opinions of those children's father and mother, and those I shall largely keep to myself.'

He was watching me intently. I had the strong impression that there was a great deal more he could say – that he urgently wanted to say – only the lifelong, binding doctor's oath of confidentiality stopped him.

I had, I decided, put an old man's peace of mind to the test quite enough for one day. I fetched the cider from the river, topped up our mugs and asked him how the trout were biting.

The next day was very full. I was called out to see no less than five young children who had all abruptly fallen very sick, with vomiting and diarrhoea and the resulting extreme listlessness that occurs when a small body expels almost all its liquids. I was able to reassure the parents that the symptoms were probably due to an unwise indulgence in under-ripe wild strawberries, and advised rest and plenty to drink. And a firm admonition to keep away from the hedgerows where the strawberries grow. There was also another visit to Gregory's old mother – she'd had a fall – and that took most of a morning, since it seemed poor Jane, the daughter-in-law, had reached the end of her rope and badly needed someone other than her husband on whose shoulder to have a good cry.

I also managed to spend an hour or so at my studies. When I had any spare time, I worked on the paper I was planning to present at the next meeting of the loose association of fellow physicians that we grandly call the Symposium. The three of us met when we were studying in London, at the King's College of Physicians, and, discovering many areas wherein our interests, our professional concerns and our natures shared common ground, we stayed in contact even when we returned to our own native areas of the land. One of the main views that unites us is our resentment of the tight restrictions which ancient and traditional medical practice still enforce on us. Even when we are all but certain that some long-employed method really doesn't work, it seems we are still called upon to use it. My own particular speciality is the doctrine of the humours, and I have been working on my rebuttal of it for years. The Symposium was due to meet again some time later in the year, in London, and I was determined to have something really powerful to present.

All of which temporarily distracted me from the matter of the dead vagrant and the resolute denial of the Fairlight women that, despite the firm evidence to the contrary, he had ever been seen at Wrenbeare.

Late in the evening I finally pushed my papers aside, stretched and, whistling to Flynn, went outside into the warm darkness to take the air before retiring to bed. Glancing up at the house, I noticed there was a faint glow from Celia's bedchamber. She was, I thought, probably at her sewing. She and I are alike in that both of us have the ability to concentrate on a task for long hours without allowing anything to distract us. It's a good thing that we are similar in this, because we understand each other and don't become resentful or annoyed at the preoccupation.

I strolled down the path to the road, my thoughts flitting here and there. I decided I'd call on Theo the next day, having abandoned him since our visit to the tavern. Then, hearing the sound of the river over to my right where it runs in its valley down to join the Tamar and the sea, I thought I might go and stand by the water awhile. I was on the point of heading over to where the narrow little path leads down to the river bank when I heard the sound of approaching footsteps.

Since setting up my practice I have become accustomed to being called out at night and, knowing it is my duty, I never complain. Sometimes, however, I do give an inward sigh at the thought of the long hours until I get back to my house and my bed. Now, when I was already weary, was such a moment.

But then it occurred to me that men coming to summon me – it's almost always a man when the call comes at night – usually run, or at least sound as if they're in a hurry.

These footsteps were measured, perhaps even hesitant, and it almost seemed as if whoever had come seeking my help was reluctant.

Turning away from the path to the river – Flynn took some persuading not to take it – I strolled down towards the road.

And, in the soft late twilight, I saw Jonathan Carew walking towards me.

'Is someone in the village sick?' I called out.

'No.' He stopped.

'Are *you* sick?' I was quite sure, in that first moment, that he was. He was even paler than when I'd seen him a few days ago, and the dark circles around his eyes had intensified. His eyelids looked puffy, and I knew without asking that he wasn't sleeping.

'Jonathan, let me help you,' I said. 'You can't continue like this, and I—'

'I do need your help, Gabriel,' he interrupted, 'but not on any medical matter.'

'But you're ill!' I protested. 'Tell me what ails you, and perhaps I can offer a remedy.'

'I am in no doubt as to what ails me,' he said sharply, 'and it is nothing that can be cured by prescribing this or that tincture or potion.'

'What other help do you ask of me, then?' I replied, equally sharply. 'I'm a doctor, that's what I do!'

He reached out and briefly touched my shoulder. 'I know, Gabriel. I'm sorry.' He hesitated. Then: 'Could we go inside? I do need to ask you something, but a measure of brandy would help me nerve myself to do so.'

He spoke lightly, but I sensed he was deadly serious. Turning, I led the way back to the house.

We settled in the library, which is at the front of the house on the left as you face it, and furthest away from Sallie's room, off the kitchen. I didn't want to wake her, and so, when I went to the kitchen to fetch the bottle and my heavy-based Venetian glasses, I moved quietly. Her snores continued undiminished and I decided I'd got away with it.

Jonathan and I sat down in chairs either side of the table,

and I poured out two generous measures of brandy. It was good stuff: a gift from a grateful ship's captain whose dislocated shoulder I'd put back with a minimum of discomfort and in time for him to catch the tide. I didn't ask him what cargo he was going off to collect, but I suspected the excellent brandy formed a part of it.

'Now,' I said, 'let me ask you again: how can I help you?'

Jonathan took a sip of brandy, then, with an appreciative glance, another. Then he said, 'I told you when you came to see me in the church the other day that I am haunted.'

'You did.'

He met my eyes. 'It is guilt that haunts me,' he said softly. 'Guilt at something that I did, several years back.'

'I'm not the one to help with that,' I replied. 'Shouldn't you refer it to the supreme authority?'

He smiled briefly. 'I've prayed, Gabriel. Believe me.'

Something in his expression told me not to pursue that line. 'Is this guilt one that can be assuaged by the taking of steps to redress whatever caused it?'

'I'm hoping it may be, yes.'

'And it's in this way that you require my help?'

He was silent for so long that I thought he wasn't going to answer. But eventually he said, 'I think I'm going to have to seek your assistance without telling why I need you to do what I'm asking of you.'

I shook my head. 'Jonathan, I don't understand. Are you saying you're going to ask me to do something but not explain why?'

'Yes.'

My first instinct was to refuse. If he wasn't prepared to trust me with the full tale, then he could manage without me. But then I looked again at his haggard face. Noticed how the weight had fallen from him. Remembered that I liked this man. And I heard myself saying, 'Very well, then. Tell me what you want me to do.'

He closed his eyes and I had the idea he might be saying a silent prayer of gratitude.

'Remember the lads who claimed to have found jewels in Foxy Dell?' he said.

Of all things, I hadn't expected that. 'I do.'

'And how the farmer – Rogeus Haydon – said he was sick of people trespassing on his land and was going to set his dogs loose, and then did exactly that?'

'Yes.' I'd seen the dogs a few days ago when I'd had cause to take the track beside the dell. They were terrifying. Their threatening presence, not to mention their physical condition, added to my dislike of Haydon. Like most of the village, I thought he'd beaten the two lads too harshly for what was only a minor misdemeanour. I didn't blame the boys' father for having fought him.

'I need to get into that dell where the lads had been exploring,' Jonathan said.

I was amazed. 'Whatever for?'

'I can't explain!' he exclaimed, exasperated. 'I just *told* you that, Gabriel!'

I nodded. 'So you did.' I crushed the various possibilities that were whirling through my mind, most of them unlikely and a few quite absurd. 'So, you want some suggestions as to how to deal with the dogs?'

His tense expression relaxed. 'Precisely so.'

I thought about it. 'He keeps them hungry,' I said after a while, 'which increases their ferocity. They are probably quite unacquainted with kindness, so there's no point trying to appeal to their better nature.' I thought some more. Then: 'We need to get hold of some pungent slabs of raw meat and a quantity of a powerful soporific. We'll lace the meat with the potion, throw it at the dogs when they hear us on the farm boundary and hurl themselves towards us to see us off, and pray that they find the meat more appealing than us. We then wait while they gulp it down and the soporific takes effect and, as soon as it does, we'll slip a length of rope through their collars and secure them, so that if they wake before we've done whatever you need to do in the dell, they won't come at us.'

Jonathan was staring at me. 'You sound very confident, Doctor,' he said dryly. 'Is this something you've done before?'

There had indeed been an occasion, a long time ago, when a similarly fierce guard dog had needed to be temporarily put out of action. Then it had been to allow me access to the private chamber of a very beautiful young widow whose father was somewhat strict about her visitors, especially male ones arriving without his invitation (although most assuredly with hers) during the hours of darkness. But I didn't think I needed to tell Jonathan the details, and in any case it was so long ago that I couldn't recall them with any accuracy. I simply said, 'Yes.'

'Will it work?' he asked quietly.

I shrugged. 'It depends on my managing to source a suitable soporific. I do not keep such medicines here, for they are dangerous in the wrong hands. But I have one or two ideas where they may be found.'

He waited. 'And?'

'I'll let you know if and when I succeed,' I said.

He must have picked up the reason for my pettiness. 'So, you're not going to give me a full explanation, any more than I gave one to you,' he murmured, but he was smiling. 'Well, I can't say I blame you.' He drained his brandy and stood up. 'Thank you,' he added.

'As yet I haven't done anything,' I pointed out.

'Yes you have,' he countered. 'You've said you'll try to help, and that alone may be enough to allow me to sleep tonight.'

I saw him to the door and watched as he walked swiftly away.

I went back to the library to fetch the glasses and put them in the kitchen. As, finally, I went up the stairs, I saw Celia standing in the gallery that runs right along the back of the house, quite obviously waiting for me.

'What did Jonathan Carew want with you so late?' she hissed. 'I *said* he was ill, didn't I?'

'He didn't come to consult me as a physician,' I said. 'He wants me to—' But I stopped. For one thing, I was pretty sure that our conversation had been confidential; for another, I still didn't *know* what Jonathan really wanted.

'*What?*' Celia demanded.

Knowing she wouldn't give up, I said, 'This is just between us, right?'

'Of course!' She looked stung that I'd even asked.

'I need to get hold of a strong sedative,' I said. 'It's not for Jonathan,' I added hastily.

'And you're not going to tell me who it is for,' she said resignedly. 'A sedative makes people go to sleep, doesn't it?'

'Yes.'

'Something such as poppy and mandragora?'

I stared at her in surprise. 'How did you know that?' I was quite sure she hadn't heard of it from me. I had used the combination in my days at sea for the worst of amputations, when it was a question of calculating the strength so as to keep the patient asleep while I cut and keep him unconscious – and unaware of the pain – for the first day or two of healing, yet not so strong that he never woke up. But it was dangerous and I was reluctant to risk it on human beings. There were other, less perilous ways of dulling pain.

Despite what I'd just said to Jonathan, I wasn't entirely sure about using it on dogs.

Celia smiled. 'Well, I didn't until a few days ago. But I just happened to call upon someone who was preparing a whole lot of remedies, including such a potion, and she told me all about it.'

Mentally I ran through a list of my sister's acquaintances but none seemed likely to possess the skill needed to handle mandragora and poppy.

Celia was watching me, a mischievous smile on her face. 'Oh, come on, Gabe,' she said softly. 'Think.'

'I am thinking!'

Then, out of nowhere, I saw a face in my mind's eye. Healthy, tanned skin, framed by thick, glossy black hair. Clear, bright eyes, blue-grey and very pale. Wide mouth and ready smile. Tall, elegant, with a figure to set a man's heart thumping. Strong, capable hands. I seemed to feel those hands, firmly holding my head as it pounded with the pain that is an aftermath of my injury; I felt the fingertips, travelling gently over my skull and easing the agony.

And, although she had helped me that day with touch alone and hadn't even offered a painkiller or a sedative, I knew who it was who made the mandragora and poppy potion.

'Judyth,' I breathed.

And Celia nodded.

SIX

I'd thought that puzzling over Jonathan's secretive and mysterious mission might keep me awake, but the day had worn me out and I went to sleep quickly. Very early in the morning, however, as soon as I was alert enough to think, my mind went straight to speculation.

The obvious reason for his wanting access to Foxy Dell was because there was something there that he needed. I thought about the place. It was right on the margin of Farmer Haydon's land, close to where the track from the village passed by. There was a large stand of very old trees – beech, oak, some slow-growing but vast holly – and they formed a sort of rough circle around a deep, rock-studded hollow in the ground. Local legend said this had once been a quarry, and from it had been extracted the stones that built St Luke's Church. If this was true, then the quarry was ancient, for the church dated to around the time of the Conquest.

In the depths of the hollow there was a thick carpet of dead leaves, in which grows a tangle of ivy, fern and mosses, interspersed with a few spindly holly bushes. The area was too overshadowed to permit much light to filter down, and only the shade-tolerant plants thrived. Beech trees clung to the steep sides of the dell, and there were holes and animal diggings among their roots.

Haydon's irritation with the lads was understandable, to an extent, for the villagers had long tended to treat the dell as if it were common ground. The encircling trees made it a secret place for lovers, and the massive trunks and branches of the trees were a natural playground for adventurous children. Mushrooms grew in the moist soil in the autumn, bluebells in the deep shade in spring, and villagers helped themselves to both.

But none of those activities or those bounties, I reflected, stretching, could be what Jonathan sought there.

The lads, I remembered suddenly, had been so excited

because they said they'd found jewels. I'd never thought that
was likely, although we weren't going to find out since whatever the boys had brought home with them, Haydon had
grabbed back. As was his right, I reminded myself, the objects
having been unearthed on his land.

And, even if it had been jewels, what would Jonathan want
with them, so urgently, so desperately, that he had sought my
help and was quite prepared to countenance the sedating of a
pair of powerful dogs?

Impatient suddenly, I threw back the bedclothes and got up.
Lying there trying to find the answer wasn't getting me
anywhere, and I'd be much better off starting my day and
knuckling down to what it held in store.

I'd hoped to slip out of Rosewyke unnoticed, but Sallie must
have been listening out for me and she set about making me a
generous breakfast. Then Celia arrived, still in her nightgown,
her long fair hair loose down her back, and wrapped in a gorgeous
silk garment that looked like a medieval monarch's robe.

'You're up a lot earlier than usual,' I greeted her as she sat
down and helped herself.

'Mm,' she answered. I noticed that she kept glancing at me,
suppressing a smile.

When Sallie came in with more hot rolls and a fresh pot of
preserve, she too started the surreptitious looks, and then she
and Celia would exchange a knowing glance and give those
almost imperceptible nods that women direct at each other
when they think they've spotted something invisible to the
lesser perception of a mere male. I always find it infuriating,
although I try hard not to show it.

Eventually, having wolfed down my food far too fast and
given myself wind, I got up and left the table. Celia said,
'Going somewhere nice, Gabe?' and I heard Sallie suppress
a chuckle.

I ignored them both.

I arrived outside Judyth's small and immaculate little house
so early that the dew was still sparkling on the colourful array
of plants growing abundantly all around it.

I tapped on the knocker – it was heavy, made of iron and in the shape of an angel – and peered in at the small, deep-set window beside the door. I could see along the dark little passage to the bright room at the far end, and all appeared ordered and tidy within. There was no sign of Judyth. I went round the side of the house, hoping to find her busy at some task in an outhouse.

When I'd visited her house before I hadn't seen the garden that adjoined the yard behind the house. Now, in the soft, warm sunshine of a late June day, the sight of it hit me with such impact on all my senses that I stopped still and simply drank it in. It was the smells, even more than the colours, the exuberant birdsong and the soft, buzzy sounds of industrious insects, that impressed, and even in those first moments I detected citrus, mint, sage, rosemary and cloves.

I sensed her come to stand beside me. Turning, I saw that she must have come out of the lean-to beside the rear entrance, for the door stood open. She said, 'Good morning, Doctor Gabriel. How can I help you, so early on a summer's morning?'

I heard the laughter in her voice, saw it in her shining eyes. I said, 'I hope I'm not disturbing you.'

'You are, but I don't mind.' She nodded towards the lean-to. 'I've been hard at work since soon after sunrise and it's high time I had a break.' She led the way up the brick path to the back entrance and stopped at the door into the cool kitchen. 'Sit down there, in the sun' – she indicated a wooden bench set against the rear wall of the house – 'and I will fetch a cool drink.'

She wasn't gone long. She returned carrying a tray laden with drinks – elderflower cordial – and some small golden biscuits. Despite my large breakfast, I took a couple. They were sweet and tasted of honey.

'Now then,' said Judyth. 'Delightful as it is to see you, I sense that there's something you want?'

'Celia tells me she came to see you recently,' I began.

Judyth nodded. 'She did. She looks well, Gabriel.'

'Yes. She begins, I think, to put the recent past behind her.'

'She has courage and determination,' Judyth said. 'Both of

which will help.' She studied me. 'But you're not here to talk about your sister, are you?'

'No, not really.' I took a mouthful of the cordial. 'She told me you were preparing potions the day she came here.'

'As indeed I am doing today,' she agreed. 'It's the season, Doctor. Everything in my garden is giving of its best, and I need to capture the essences while I can.'

'Yes. I think, too, you've been working with plants that do not grow in your garden. Mandragora, for example.'

'I have,' she said. 'A consignment of that and other plants arrived from the Mediterranean two weeks ago. I have purchased many items, and with them I am in the process of replenishing supplies of my stock remedies.' She raised her eyebrows. 'Do you require a strong soporific?'

'I do.'

She didn't speak for a moment or two. Then she said, 'I know it's not for me to warn you, and I'm sure you've used such a potion before and know its dangers, but the inclusion of mandragora among the ingredients makes powerful medicine, Gabriel.'

'I understand,' I replied. 'I have used mandragora, usually mixed with poppy, and sometimes such substances as henbane, hemlock and even lettuce and ivy when there was nothing else.'

'How do you use it?' she asked.

For a moment we were two professionals, discussing our work. It was a deeply gratifying experience. I would like to say I was temporarily unaware of how attractive she was and of how her presence so close beside me was making my heart beat faster, but I'd be lying.

'I blend the juices of the various plants and then dip in pieces of sponge to soak it up,' I said. 'I dry the sponges and store them, then when a soporific is needed, wetting a piece of sponge revives the potency of the juice and the resulting fumes usually succeed in making the patient insensate.'

She was listening intently. 'You do not fear that unconsciousness will slip into death?'

'Of course. It's very difficult to achieve the correct strength, and patients differ in their tolerance of the narcotic.'

'Yet still you risk it?'

'I haven't used it since I left the sea,' I said quietly. 'In my previous life, I frequently treated injuries so terrible that men would cry out to me to end their life and their agony. In such cases, worrying about whether my soporific would be a little too powerful wasn't the first concern.'

'I see,' she said. Then, very quietly: 'I didn't mean to sound as if I was criticizing you.'

'No, I know.'

'So, why, if I may ask, do you now require mandragora?'

I paused. I thought about it, questioned myself, then decided there was no reason not to tell her. 'It's for a couple of dogs.'

She started to laugh, and the sudden easing of the tension made me join in.

'Dogs,' she repeated.

'Very big ones.'

'You plan to perform some surgical procedure?'

Looking at her, seeing the laughter still dancing in her eyes, I was aware she knew full well I wasn't planning any such thing.

'No, Judyth. I need to put them to sleep.'

'And I don't suppose for a moment that you're going to tell me why.'

'I would,' I said swiftly, 'but it's not really my secret.' *And besides*, I could have added, *I don't really know.*

She smiled, and I knew she understood.

She got to her feet. 'Come into my still room,' she said, 'which, as no doubt you've observed, is an elegant name for that little lean-to, and I'll decant some of my preparation for you.'

The still room was cool and the fragrances and scents within so strong that I felt my head reel. Judyth took a stoneware jar down from a dark shelf high up under the roof and took it to her workbench. As she poured some of the mixture into a small bottle, she told me how much to use.

'You don't want to kill these very large dogs, do you?'

'No, of course not.'

'Then I'd advise no more than four drops. You're going to use meat as the carrier?'

'I thought so, yes.'

'Not fresh meat,' she said thoughtfully, 'better something that's on the turn and with a strong smell. But of course you'll have thought of that.' She considered, her head on one side, looking down at the bottle in her hand. 'Maybe five drops, if these dogs really are big.' She met my eyes. 'I'd hate to think of one or both of them waking up too soon and taking a chunk out of you.'

'So would I,' I muttered.

She handed me the little bottle. She was still looking at me, her expression very serious. 'I've never given this remedy to any other healer, midwife, barber surgeon or physician,' she said gravely. 'It is potentially lethal, Gabriel.'

I took it from her. 'I know, Judyth,' I said gently. 'I'll be very careful, you have my word.'

She went on looking at me for a moment. Then, nodding, she turned away.

Back at Rosewyke, I couldn't stop thinking that we were in late June, when the days are longest and people tend to stay up late into the night, the urge to sleep postponed by the endless twilight, and that there couldn't have been a worse time to plan a secret night-time mission. Nevertheless, I took the precaution of slipping into the pantry when Sallie wasn't looking and removing two big slabs of belly pork from the platter-full that she'd set aside for salting. I put them out on a window ledge in the full sun and let the heat do its work.

Late in the afternoon, however, clouds started to build up in the south-west. At first they were big, white, fluffy and innocent-looking. Blown in off the sea, however, they held moisture. Then the wind veered right round, but still the clouds – turning dark and sinister now – continued their steady progression. They were driving up against the wind, a sure sign that a storm was on its way.

I asked Sallie to serve me an early supper, muttered a remark to Celia about going to discuss something with Jonathan – the truth, if not the whole truth – and, collecting my old black cloak, set off as the first drops were falling. Celia, intent on a complicated and very beautiful piece of embroidery, took little notice but to question my sanity. Sallie was already tucked up in her room. She hates storms and has been known to hide under the big table in the kitchen when thunder rolls over us. Samuel was scurrying towards the yard as I left the house, and I nodded to him and called out, 'Terrible weather!'

I had decided to walk down to the village. If I wanted to be unobtrusive, it made no sense to ride my big black horse. My boots were of good leather, well greased against the wet, so at least my feet would stay dry.

By the time I was huddling against the old stone wall of Jonathan's cottage, banging on the low oak door, my feet were about the only part of me that *were* dry. But the night was warm, and the hard walk, added to the thrill of the mission, had set my heart pounding. I was sweating, and glad that I was wearing only a shirt and breeches under the cloak.

Jonathan opened the door, recognized me with a faintly surprised glance, then quickly ushered me inside and shut the door again. The faint light from within had spilled out for no more than a few moments. Had anyone been watching – and why should they? – they would barely have noticed, and I'm sure they wouldn't have identified the vicar's visitor.

We stood in Jonathan's comfortable little room. 'I think I know why you're here,' he said with a half-smile.

'It's a very dark night and there's a storm,' I replied. 'Both factors will make people keep indoors.'

He nodded. 'Not dogs, however. Well,' he amended, 'a dog with any sense would stay in its kennel this evening, but I don't imagine Farmer Haydon's mastiffs are given that option.'

'Neither do I.' I reached beneath my cloak and took out a cloth bag. 'I've brought some meat,' I said. 'It was sitting on a sunny window ledge for some time earlier today, as no doubt you can detect.' The smell was, indeed, quite ripe.

'Irresistible to a pair of large, under-fed dogs,' Jonathan observed.

'So I'm hoping.' I delved inside the purse on my belt and extracted Judyth's little bottle. 'And this, I'm also hoping, will lay them out.'

For a moment doubt crossed the vicar's face, but he banished it. 'Thank you, Gabriel,' he said. 'I have a length of rope.' He crossed the room to the coat hooks beside the door, taking from one of them a bulky coil of fine rope. He handed it to me, then removed a dark cloak similar to mine, wrapped it round him and picked up a horn lantern, handing a second one to me. Then he met my eyes. 'I don't think there's anything to gain by waiting,' he said. 'Shall we go?'

I nodded.

He set off down a narrow path that led away behind the church and took us on a roundabout route to the track that encircled the bulge of Rogeus Haydon's land. It would have been half the distance if we'd gone straight through the village, but that would have meant passing several houses and an inn. As it was, we arrived at the stretch of track that passed closest to Foxy Dell without having seen a soul.

Jonathan peered in beneath the trees. 'Is it worth going straight in and hoping the dogs won't hear us?' he asked in a low voice.

I was just about to say I didn't think so when his question was answered far more emphatically. There was the sound of something large hurtling through undergrowth, a deep-throated growl, one sharp bark, and then the horrifying shape of a wide-eyed, muscular and very large black dog came bursting through the trees some fifty paces away.

I had the meat ready and now, trying to keep my hands steady, I took the stopper from the bottle with my teeth and allowed four drops to fall onto the first piece. Guessing that the fumes from the freshly administered potion might well act on the dogs even before they'd gulped down the meat and ingested the drug, I hadn't wanted to treat it until the very last moment. Now, with several stone of very angry dog racing towards us, I wished I had done. The bottle was still in my hand, so I added a fifth drop.

Then I flung the piece of meat at the dog.

You could see its dilemma in its eyes. Its purpose in Farmer Haydon's household was to patrol his boundaries and repel intruders, as savagely as it liked. To this end, I didn't doubt, the farmer kept it penned up in some filthy kennel when it wasn't on guard duty and only gave it food when he really had to. Now the dog was out among the sweet and intensified scents and smells of a warm, rainy night, doing what it did best, and, as if that wasn't enough, someone had just thrown it a big slice of slightly rancid and powerfully pungent meat.

You couldn't blame the dog. Even as the pork flew through the air towards it, I'm sure it had already decided. It made a very agile, twisting leap – extraordinary in such a large dog – and its jaws closed on the meat before either meat or dog had a chance to hit the ground.

I thought at first, for a few awful moments, that the mandragora potion wasn't as strong as Judyth had claimed, that she'd made it all wrong, that I hadn't used enough: in short, that it wasn't going to work. The dog was slavering and slobbering, gulping at the meat as if it hadn't eaten in living memory, and already half of it had disappeared down its gaping throat. And, as if that wasn't cause enough for grave anxiety, now there came the sound of distant barking swiftly becoming louder: the other dog was on his way.

Jonathan grabbed hold of my arm and said, 'We should go! It's far too dangerous to stay if—'

But just then, with no warning whatsoever, the first dog collapsed. Just like that. It was as if all strength in its legs had suddenly gone, so that it fell on its knees and then, quite gently, rolled onto its side. Its eyelids drooped, then closed. Its jaws, at first still feebly working, became motionless.

The other dog was almost upon us. I did exactly what I'd done before, and laced the second piece of meat with five drops of Judyth's potion. The dog had stopped barking and, head down, he was aiming straight for us like a cannonball on a flat trajectory. I had a moment of misgiving – *this one's brighter and he's not going to be seduced into taking the bait* – but I threw the meat anyway. The dog saw it, watched it arch closer.

And came on.

But then some blessed little snake of a scent trail must have reached its flaring nostrils. It turned its head – so quickly that I was surprised it didn't damage its thick neck – and fell on the pork.

This time, the mandragora worked even more rapidly. The

second dog was slightly smaller and, besides, I thought it had
inhaled more of the fumes. Just as its companion had done,
it subsided into a still, silent heap on the wet grass.

Jonathan had the rope ready. He looped one end through
the first dog's collar, tying it very firmly. I almost offered to
check the knot for him since I know a bit about such matters,
but decided he wouldn't have welcomed the interference. Then,
swiftly, he wrapped the long tail of the rope round the trunk
of the nearest tree, again tying a solid-looking knot. The second
dog was closer to the tree, and in no time Jonathan had fastened
the rope to its collar. Straightening up, he turned to me. 'How
long will they stay asleep?'

'I can't say precisely,' I said. I'd once known a large sailor
stay unconscious for the best part of three days when I'd given
him mandragora, but that had been an extreme case (I'd had
to remove a piece of jagged timber blasted off the ship's deck
from the side of his head, relocate his jawbone and sew up
quite a lot of his face, and when he finally woke up the pain
was so excruciating that he begged me to put him out again).
'Long enough.' *I hope*, I might have added.

Jonathan nodded. 'Come on, then.'

He slipped in between the trees and into the dell, and I was
right behind him.

The deep dell was some twenty paces across, steep-sided,
enclosed by deciduous trees in the full glory of their summer
foliage, their branches reaching out to join up over our heads.
It was safe for Jonathan to strike a flint and put a flame to
our lanterns. The soft golden glow illumined the dell and,
under any other circumstances, would have made it a place of
enchantment. But even under the present circumstances it
wasn't too bad. The storm had moved off, the thunder now
grumbling away up over the moors, and, although it was still
raining lightly, the trees protected us.

I stared around me. 'You know, I presume, what you're
looking for?' I asked. Jonathan nodded briefly. He was clearly
preoccupied. 'Hadn't you better tell me so I can help in the
search?' I added mildly.

He gave a *tsck* of irritation, but I knew it was with himself and not me. 'Sorry,' he muttered. 'The lads said they'd found jewels, and—'

'Jonathan, we've already agreed they did no such thing!' I protested. 'You surely can't believe that—'

'Be quiet and *listen!*' Jonathan said in a sort of suppressed shout. 'We're looking for something that two unsophisticated village lads might have *mistaken* for jewels.' He was already peering at a portion of the steep bank beneath a beech tree, reaching down to investigate a hollow where some animal, fox or badger, had been digging.

There didn't seem any option but to copy him.

We worked our way slowly around the circumference of the dell. There were many holes and dips, some deeper than others, and it was clear that a variety of wildlife used the spot. Some of the excavations looked recent, some had vegetation growing around the openings and clearly hadn't been used for years.

Then I came to a place where something had been digging vigorously and, from the sight and the smell of fresh-turned earth, within the last two or three weeks. It looked as if there had been a depression in the side of the bank – it was very steep just there and a series of hollows undermined a big old beech tree whose roots were exposed – and the soil was soft and easy to dig. Whatever – whoever? – had been digging had apparently enlarged the entrance to the pit, or tunnel, although for what purpose I had no idea.

But it was worth investigating.

I began to shovel earth away with my hand. Almost immediately I felt a sharp pain, as if a thorn had been driven into the soft flesh on the side of my palm. Turning to catch more of the light from the lantern, I tried to see what I'd done. The wound was full of earth, so I bent down and washed it on the wet grass. The cut was bleeding profusely – *good, that'll clean it*, I thought – but it was shallow and wouldn't need stitching. I took off the kerchief I'd tied inside my collar to stop the rain dripping down my neck and wrapped up my hand, tying the fabric tightly.

I noticed that Jonathan was looking at me, his eyes wide, his expression frozen. 'It's all right, it's not serious,' I said. 'Not a bad cut, merely a lot of blood.'

He didn't answer. I noticed then that in fact it wasn't me and my wounded hand that he was staring at so fixedly.

It was something beyond me, on the slope at the foot of the bank beneath the hole I'd just been enlarging.

And, as I looked down, I saw it too.

The light from the lantern was shining out brightly, catching on what lay there on top of the reddish earth and sparking from it the most beautiful array of colours: red, blue, violet, yellow, green.

Jonathan and I dropped to our knees.

In that entranced moment, it really did look as if a secret hoard of jewels had tumbled out of its hiding place. As if rubies, sapphires, amethysts, citrine and emeralds were spread out, ours for the taking.

Jonathan was first to recover. Straightening up, he proceeded to continue what I and my unknown predecessor, animal or human, had begun, reaching inside the hollow and pushing aside the earth, swiftly and with no care for the possibility of cutting himself as I had done. I was about to issue a warning, but then I saw what he was uncovering.

There was something wrapped in sacking, roughly rectangular in shape and the longer side around the length of my forearm and hand, and the object, or objects, had been thickly padded round with straw. Then as Jonathan went on digging I saw that there were two sacking parcels . . . no, three, for there was a smaller one lying between the two larger ones that hadn't been visible at first. Carefully, cautiously, Jonathan pulled them out of their earthy vault and laid them reverently on the floor of the dell.

'These are what we came for?' I whispered. The mood was such that whispering seemed appropriate. Jonathan nodded.

I waited for him to speak – to perhaps give some sort of explanation, for such was very much in order – but he didn't. He just stood there, head bowed, staring down at the sacking parcels.

So I said, rather more firmly than I'd intended, 'We should go, Jonathan. Those dogs may not be able to come at us with their mouths wide open in anticipation of our flesh, but if they wake up they'll start such a riot of barking and howling that sooner or later – and probably sooner – someone will alert Farmer Haydon.'

Jonathan started, and I had the feeling he was coming back from some far-distant place. 'Yes, right, of course,' he muttered. But he was still wide-eyed, abstracted.

'You take this one' – I handed him the heavier of the two larger parcels – 'and I'll bring these two.' I picked them up, noticing as I did so that on one of them a corner of the wrapping had rotted or been chewed away. I closed the gap as best I could, tucked one parcel under each arm and took a firm grip, then led the way up and out of the dell.

The dogs hadn't moved. However, both were clearly still alive; one was making a soft, whining sound and the other was snoring.

With a brief exclamation, Jonathan put down his parcel and untied the rope, coiling it and looping it across his body. There was a small piece of meat left beside the second dog, a stringy piece of fat beside the first one, and he picked both up. 'Be careful,' I warned, and he nodded, holding the meat at arm's length. He picked up his parcel and we hurried away.

Halfway back to his house, I called out to him – he was walking ahead of me – and nodded towards a deep ditch running beside the track. 'There?' I suggested, indicating a rat hole just above the water level.

'Yes, it'll do,' he muttered. Climbing down, bracing himself so as not to fall into the water, he shoved the remains of the meat deep inside the hole.

Then he picked up his parcel and we went on.

Back in the sanctuary of the Priest's House, we threw our wet cloaks on the floor and wiped the water and mud off our hands and faces. As I stood transfixed by the sacking parcels, carefully placed on the stone floor of the tiny vestibule just inside the door, Jonathan fetched brandy and glasses. He poured out generous measures, handed one to me and, raising his own glass, said, 'Thank you, Gabriel, for what you did tonight. Apart from the fact that it was you who found them' – he gestured towards the parcels – '*and* provided the sedation, I couldn't have done this without you, and you have my eternal gratitude.'

He downed his brandy in three or four gulps, and I did the same. As I felt its burn go down my gullet, Jonathan put his glass down, squared his shoulders and muttered, 'We'd better see what we've found.'

SEVEN

Jonathan and I knelt side by side on the worn stone flags of his room. I realized all at once that the storm was long gone, the rain had ceased and the wind had dropped. There was barely a sound from the deep, still darkness outside. Jonathan had fastened the shutters and barred the door, as if what we were about to do had to be kept at all costs from the eyes of anyone but the two of us.

He had lit a fire in the hearth, for, although the night was quite warm, both of us had got very wet. The heat was welcome, as was the light of the flames. In addition, several candles burned around us, set in a rough circle. Although I was in the company of a man of God – a priest in holy orders – I had the strongest sense that there was something there in the snug little room with us that wasn't anything to do with God at all.

Jonathan had a small penknife in his hand and, leaning over the first of the parcels, he slipped it under the string that had been used to stitch the sacking together and hold the parcel tight. Whether by accident or design, he had selected for the first parcel to be opened the one that had a hole in one corner. He cut the string in several places and then drew the contents out of the sacking. Then he unfolded the sacking, spreading it out on the floor, and began to bundle up the straw. I helped him, and soon the contents of the parcel were revealed.

I wanted to stop and stare, for even that first rapt glance had enchanted me. But Jonathan was busy with the second of the large parcels, working more swiftly now, tearing at the sacking in his impatience and shoving the straw aside.

On the remains of the sacking and straw that had concealed and protected them lay five glass panels, about a foot across by a foot and a half high. The glass was set in lead, and the top of each panel formed a pointed arch. One of the panels had been damaged at the lower right-hand corner; it was from the first parcel, whose wrappings had been disturbed. By an inquisitive animal or by human hands?

But then Jonathan lifted up one of the panels and held it against the candlelight, and there was no room in my mind for anything but wonder.

It was old; anyone could have seen that. It was the work of an early medieval artist, and it had all the charm, vitality and quirkiness of the very best stained glass. The central image was of a man in a close-fitting white coif stooping over someone lying propped up in bed, both figures smiling and looking rather cheerful for a doctor and patient.

For that was what they had to be.

The image was bordered with a deep band of flowers and plants, as if to illustrate the raw materials from which the physician had made whatever medicine he was spooning into his patient. And the colours were so brilliant that they dazzled the eye.

Jonathan laid down the first panel and picked up the second. The same deep, wonderfully coloured border – I spotted corn liberally dotted with poppies, lavender, a vine heavy with deep purple grapes – and within it, a trio of plump, red-cheeked nuns in white veils and black gowns busy gathering blooms and putting them in wide, flattish wicker baskets. The third panel was devoted only to flowers, and its images were the most stunning of all. It was the damaged one, and the corner where the glass had been shattered was filled with a posy of the most flamboyant of garden blooms, in every conceivable colour.

I understood how it was that the lads who had been nosing around in Farmer Haydon's dell had believed they'd found precious jewels.

Jonathan held up the last two panels. One depicted the doctor in his coif again, this time bent over what looked like a mortar and pestle and presumably grinding some ingredient to powder. I'd done the same myself, countess times. The last of the five showed the same man, but this time he stood a little behind the central figure, which was that of a slender man dressed in a golden robe holding out for the viewer's consideration a bunch of lilies.

My eyes met the clear, intelligent gaze of the slender man and instinctively I bowed my head. The style of this early glass work might be simple, rustic and naive, but the artist's love for the Son of God must have guided his hand when he made the image, for the calm face shone with powerful compassion.

'Our Lord,' came Jonathan's quiet voice. Even though he spoke so softly, I detected profound love and reverence. '"Consider the lilies, how they grow; they labour not, neither spin they, yet I say unto you, that Solomon himself in all his royalty was not clothed like one of these."' He met my eyes. 'The Gospel according to St Luke,' he added. He laid a hand lightly on the repeated image of the doctor. 'And here he is, standing at the Saviour's side.'

I already knew.

I'd already recognized the man as a doctor, doing the very things I did, and in the context of sacred stained-glass panels in a church named for him, he could only be St Luke. And I'd realized as soon as I saw the shape of the panels where they belonged. 'They were made for your side chapel.'

'St Luke's Little Chapel. Yes, they were.'

'And at some point in the recent past, the power in the land told the people that all such images were blasphemous, evil and wrong, and had to be collected up for destruction,' I went on. Perhaps, I reflected, it had happened when the boy king, Edward, succeeded the giant figure of his father, at which time the iconoclasts had forcefully insisted that so much of beauty must be destroyed because the miracles, the *feigned stories*, as they'd had it, depicted in the old stained-glass windows were no more than religious superstition. 'But someone couldn't bear that fate for these five panels, so they removed them and hid them.'

Jonathan nodded.

I waited for him to speak, for I was certain he knew far more about the matter than I did.

But he was silent. As I watched him, I saw some strong emotion working in him. His expression was one of deep sorrow – of grief – and, as if he couldn't bear my scrutiny, he turned away.

I wanted only to distract him from whatever was troubling him. Without even pausing to think what significance there could be to the last parcel – the smaller one that had been pushed in between the other two – I drew it forward and said, my voice sounding so falsely cheerful that I was embarrassed, 'There's one more! Go on, open the final one!'

Jonathan seemed to make a big effort to return from wherever his sombre thoughts had taken him. With a sigh, he carefully packed away the first five panels and then took the last parcel from me. This one had been wrapped in much the same way, although possibly there was more straw; it certainly did a better job of padding out what lay hidden within.

Even as Jonathan uncovered the image, it struck me that this was the sixth image, and there were only five empty apertures high up in the wall of St Luke's Little Chapel . . .

And then I heard Jonathan's muttered exclamation of amazement.

And I too looked at what the last parcel had concealed.

It was quite clearly work of a much later date than the first five images. The lines of the lead were straighter and simpler, and the process by which the panel had been made was altogether more sophisticated. The five earlier panels were beautiful, vibrantly colourful, and, enchanting in their naivety, they brought a smile to the face.

The image in this sixth one didn't bring a smile.

It – *communicated*, was the only word I could think of, but the emotions it invoked were very far from the delight, the reverential love and the simple happiness of the first five panels.

It had a power that seemed to leap out from the inert glass and lead from which the panel was made and smack the viewer right between the eyes. It was as if – I struggled to analyse the strong emotions – as if uncovering it, exposing it to the human gaze, had unleashed some latent force with which it was invested that now surged impatiently into life . . .

In silence, Jonathan and I tried to take in what we were staring at.

It was an angel.

He was slender, his naked body elegant, perfect. His shoulders were square, his chest deep, his pectoral muscles well defined. His torso narrowed to the waist and the straight, boyish hips, and the legs were long and graceful. The genitals had been depicted in great detail – the penis was uncircumcised – and a first glance looked out of proportion; too large for the body.

The head, shoulders and upper body were framed by the wings, large and curving, drawn with such care that each feather could be clearly made out.

The angel's hair was bright gold and he had blue eyes.

His face was so beautiful that it took the breath away.

On hands and knees at his feet, elbows resting on the ground and hands clasped before the face, was a man. He was of the middle years, bearded, his face lined, his expression full of love, of adoration, of total prostration before the object of his worship. He too was naked.

After what seemed a long time, I said, 'This, surely, is no holy image.'

'No,' Jonathan replied.

'It's – he's—' But I didn't know how to go on.

'I have no idea what this is or where it came from,' Jonathan said. 'I was certainly not expecting to find it hidden away with the five panels from the chapel.'

'It's not from the chapel?'

I regretted the question even as I heard myself pose it.

'Of course it isn't!' Jonathan said scathingly. 'For one thing, there are only five clerestory openings. For another, can you really believe this is a sacred image?' He was still staring at the last panel, his eyes fixed to it as if he couldn't bear to look away.

'No,' I said shortly. Then: 'It's erotic, isn't it? It has . . . power.'

'Yes,' Jonathan said shortly. Then suddenly he grabbed a big bundle of straw and spread it over the image. He folded the sacking back into place and then began searching for some string. I pulled a long piece from the sacking that had been round one of the bigger parcels and silently handed it to him. He wrapped it round the sacking and tied it.

With that angel covered once again, the atmosphere in Jonathan's room changed.

It was as if we'd been bathed in some fierce, dazzling light, and its source had abruptly been cut off.

I wasn't sure if I felt relieved or dismayed.

Theo too had been busy over the last two days.

He had talked at length with Jarman Hodge about the visit to Wrenbeare and the suspicious divergence of evidence concerning the dead vagrant. They agreed that the outdoor servants' version was far more credible but, as Jarman had said in some frustration, 'Bugger-all we can do, chief, if her ladyship swears there never was any intruder.'

In the rare moments when he was alone in his office with nothing very pressing to do, Theo would open the cedar-wood chest and have another look at the torn sketch. On one occasion, as he was tidying up for the day prior to joining the family for supper, his daughter Isabella caught him staring at it and, clambering up onto his lap for a cuddle, asked who the man was. 'I don't know, sweeting,' he had to admit.

She leaned against him and he stroked her long, soft, blonde hair. 'He's sad,' she said. 'Can you make him happy again?'

Theo sighed. 'I don't know that, either.'

In the morning of the following day, Theo had a visitor.

He was shown into Theo's office by a member of the staff who habitually sat in the outer room and whose purpose was to filter out enquiries that didn't really need to be referred to the coroner himself. As Symon tapped on Theo's door and muttered, 'This one insists on seeing you. Sorry, chief, but he won't take no for an answer,' he looked decidedly nervous and Theo noticed with a smile that, backing away, he gave the visitor a wide berth.

Theo studied the man. He was huge. He was probably a head taller than Theo, who was by no means small, and so broad that he gave the impression of only just managing to

squeeze his shoulders through the doorway. He was dressed
in an ankle-length coat, tattered and not very clean, which
bulged here and there as if all manner of unlikely objects were
stored beneath it. He had close-cropped hair of a nondescript
mid-brown sprinkled with grey, and he was unshaven: on first
sight, he was wild-looking. But his brown eyes, set deep in
the folds of his anxious face, were soft and kind. His mouth,
wide and, as he hovered on the threshold of Theo's office,
quivering into an uncertain smile, was well-shaped. It stuck
Theo irrelevantly that, before the years of hardship wore him
down, the man might once have been fine-looking.

Theo waved a hand towards the chair in front of his desk.
'Sit down,' he said.

The big man glanced apprehensively at the chair and, very
gingerly, did as he was bade. The chair gave a creak of protest.

'What can I do for you?' Theo asked.

The man eyed him for a few moments, then said, 'You are
the coroner?'

'I am. Theophilus Davey is my name.'

The man nodded swiftly as if he already knew that. He
raised a hand and, pointing a none too clean hand at his vast
chest, opened his mouth as if to announce his name in return.
But then, with a sudden violent shake of his head, he let the
hand drop and closed his mouth with a snap.

There was another, longer, pause, and then he said, the soft,
tentative voice at odds with the big, wild body, 'I am hunting
for someone.'

Theo was trying to place his accent. He didn't sound like
a native English speaker. But then the words the big man had
just uttered penetrated and suddenly Theo was on the alert.
'Who?' he rapped out.

The big man seemed to shrink away. He held up both hands,
palm outwards, as if to ward off an attack.

'I apologize if I sounded sharp,' Theo said more gently.
'Please, tell me who it is you seek and why you think he may
be known to me.' He paused, wondering how to explain delicately to this frightened, worried man that in general people
only came to the coroner's notice once they were dead.

'I seek my friend,' the man said after an even longer pause.

'He was with me, I cared for him, making him eat when he wasn't hungry, finding a warm place to sleep when he was cold and exhausted.' He hesitated, glancing up at Theo from beneath unkempt and bushy eyebrows. 'When he was sick,' he added in a whisper.

'Your friend?' Theo prompted as the silence extended.

The man nodded violently. 'My friend, yes, yes, of course, since we were not much more than boys. I was the big one, the strong one, and I looked off for him . . . that is right, no?'

'Looked out for him,' Theo corrected.

'Thank you,' the man said, giving a polite little bow.

'And why do you think your friend came here?'

The big man frowned. 'I believe it is so,' he said simply. 'Jannie told me what he was planning, and I—' But then all at once all colour left his face. He put both hands up to his mouth as if to stop any more words getting out and, abruptly standing up with such force that the chair fell over, he blundered for the door and wrested it open.

Theo leapt up. 'Wait!' he yelled. 'Stay and tell me more – there's nothing to fear, and maybe I can help you . . .'

He trailed off. There was no point in continuing, for the big man was already out of the front door and running away up the road.

Returning to his office, Theo reflected that there wasn't very much *maybe* about whether or not he could help the big man find his missing friend. Admittedly, one half-starved vagabond looked much like another, but when one of the species turned up dead and another came searching for a missing one, the laws of logic suggested strongly that it had to be one and the same man.

But at least, Theo told himself, he had learned something.

The dead man's name was Jannie.

And, even if he had died cold, sick and alone, there had been at least one person in this hard world who cared about him.

That evening, after the children were abed and Theo had enjoyed a particularly toothsome supper with Elaine, the realization came to him that he wasn't going to sleep that night unless he'd discussed the big man and his missing friend with somebody. The somebody he had in mind was Gabriel Taverner, and, for the whole day since the big man's visit, Theo had been half-expecting to see the doctor present himself in his office.

But he hadn't.

Elaine, yawning and already muttering about it being sensible to have an early night as they were both tired, was surprised, not to say quite cross, when Theo announced he was going out. When he told her he was heading for Rosewyke, she gave him a perceptive look as if to say, *Of course you are*, and said no more.

The late evening air had the particular sweetness that comes after rain. As Theo rode off, he reflected to himself that he probably wouldn't have bothered if the fierce storm that had struck earlier was still raging. A night of little sleep was preferable to a soaking.

The sky cleared as he covered the few miles to Rosewyke. Approaching the house up the long path from the road, he was surprised to see it in darkness. Gabriel, to the best of his knowledge, was not a man to retire early to his bed.

Theo dismounted and, trying to be quiet – no need to wake the household if the master wasn't there – made his way to the yard at the rear. Peering over the wall, he could see right into the stables. Celia's grey mare was in her stall, and Gabriel's black horse was dozing in the neighbouring one. Hearing a sound from behind him, Theo turned to see Gabriel's outdoor man standing watching him warily.

'Oh, it's you, Master Davey!' the man said with relief when he could see Theo's face. 'I heard a noise and came to investigate.'

'I am sorry if I woke you, er—'

'Samuel,' the man said. 'No need for apologies, sir, I wasn't asleep. After the doctor, were you?'

'Yes.'

Samuel shook his head. 'Then I fear you've had a wasted journey. He went out, and in the midst of the worst of the storm, too.'

'And I don't suppose you have any idea when he'll be back?'

'None whatsoever,' Samuel said cheerfully.

It was in the nature of a doctor's profession, Theo reflected morosely as he rode home again, to be called out at night. But why, he thought tetchily, did it have to be *this* night?

Theo was thinking once more about Gabriel Taverner the next morning as he sat in his office, staring grumpily out at the bright sunshine drying the puddles from the previous night's storm. *I shouldn't have to seek the bloody man out*, he said to himself. *Who's the coroner here?*

He knew his irritation was irrational, which somehow only intensified it. The doctor owed him no particular allegiance and certainly wasn't any more bound to help him identify the dead vagrant than any other local resident. And why, Theo asked himself, did he want to see Gabriel anyway?

To talk to him, was the only satisfactory answer.

And then, as if the wish had summoned up the man, Symon from the outer office put his head round the door and announced that the doctor had just arrived and wondered if he could have a word.

Theo's immediate thought, as Gabriel came into the room, was that he looked furtive.

'What can I do for you, Gabe?' he asked, his tone deliberately neutral.

'I meant to come and see you before,' Gabriel answered, 'only the past couple of days have been very full and I didn't have the chance.' He waited, but when Theo made no comment, went on, 'I was wondering if you've made any progress with the identity of the dead man.'

I have studied the scrap of paper that was folded up and tucked away inside his coat until I see that half a face in my dreams, Theo could have said, *and yesterday a very large man with a strange accent called on me to ask if I'd seen his companion, and I'd wager a small stack of coins on it being our dead man he's searching for, only he ran away before I learned nearly enough.*

But he just said shortly, 'Perhaps.'

'Oh!' Gabriel was looking at him doubtfully. Then he said, 'Is anything the matter, Theo?'

'I called on you late yesterday evening, after the storm,' Theo said. 'You weren't there.' *Good God*, he thought, angry with himself, *I sound like some love-lorn suitor lurking round his beloved's door for a sight of her.* 'No doubt you were summoned to attend a patient,' he added brusquely.

'I had indeed been called out,' Gabriel said calmly, 'only not to anyone needing my medical skills.' He smiled briefly. 'Jonathan Carew required my help.'

Theo stared at him. He had the strongest sense that there was a lot more to the matter, but that Gabriel was intending to keep it to himself. *And why shouldn't he?* he thought.

All the same . . .

'Was this help that was needed anything to do with our dead man?' he asked.

Gabriel shook his head. 'As far as I can tell, nothing whatsoever.' He paused. 'It was something that clearly affects Jonathan deeply, although he did not explain why.'

Theo didn't answer. Gabriel put up with the silence for a few moments, then his expression darkened. Approaching Theo's desk, he leaned down, resting his hands on it. 'Theo, I'm sorry I wasn't there when you called, and also that I don't feel any obligation to explain my whereabouts to you on what was a private matter and nothing to do with you, either personally or professionally. But I'm here now, I've come to offer any help I can, so will you stop looking at me so suspiciously and tell me if you've any news?'

Theo stared up at him. Gabriel was a big man, as tall as himself but not as broad, and there was, as he'd thought before, something dangerous about him. Out of nowhere came a memory of the events of the previous year, when Theo had been quite certain there was more to what had happened than he'd been told; than he was ever going to be told . . .

Nothing but speculation, he told himself.

'It is possible that we now have a Christian name for our dead man,' he said.

And briefly, crossly, he told Gabriel about the big man's visit.

EIGHT

I was still thinking about Theo's reticent visitor as I rode on my way. As Theo had pointed out, the obvious conclusion was that the huge man had been asking about the dead vagrant. The obvious conclusion, although not necessarily the correct one.

With some effort, I turned my mind to other matters.

I was on my way to visit a patient who lived a mile or so beyond Rogeus Haydon's farm, on the road out to the moors. She was an elderly woman, and she'd been attacked by someone hiding behind her henhouse when she had gone out the previous day to collect the eggs. I'd visited her already and she wasn't badly hurt. She'd been very frightened when the man, or woman, or boy – she hadn't got much of a look at the thief – had leapt out at her, and furiously angry that he'd made off with a capful of eggs. The only damage, however, was a bruise on her shin where she'd fallen as her assailant rushed past her in his panic to escape.

There was no real need for my second visit. The old woman's husband was already grumbling that she had no right to be sitting in her kitchen with her feet up and why wasn't she getting on with her chores? Did she expect him to do everything himself?

'Yes,' had been her answer to that. She'd caught my eye behind her husband's back and winked at me.

This morning, the bruise was coming out and the front of her skinny leg was mottled black and purple. 'Pretty, isn't it, Doctor?' she asked with a grin.

'Gorgeous,' I agreed. I examined the leg, turning it this way and that, then laid it carefully back on the stool on which it had been supported. 'Another day of rest,' I pronounced, 'and then, provided it doesn't pain you too much, I think you might be able to return to light duties.'

As her husband stomped off in disgust to feed the hens, the old woman whispered, 'Thank you, Doctor.'

Having seen my patient, I now felt free to attend to the real business that had taken me out on that particular road: Farmer Haydon's mastiffs.

I had believed Judyth when she said they would suffer no permanent harm from being drugged. But, having seen the rapidity with which the mandragora had stopped them in their tracks, I couldn't stop the doubts niggling away at me. While it had been of prime importance to send them to sleep while Jonathan and I explored the dell, I certainly wished them no permanent harm. They were splendid animals and only bad-tempered and fierce because the farmer had made them so.

I rode along the road that wound round Farmer Haydon's acres. I slowed down, began a one-sided conversation with Hal, and even whistled a tune or two. No sign of the dogs.

I was now approaching the track that turned off towards the farmhouse. Still no dogs. I was fearing the worse when a loud voice yelled out, '*Oi, you!*'

I drew rein. Turning, I saw Rogeus Haydon stumbling down the track towards me. 'Did you call?' I said politely.

'Yes I did!' he cried. His cheeks were bright red, he was puffing hard and sweat was pouring down his face. As he ran, the flesh of his chest and belly wobbled like a jelly. 'You wait there, I need you!'

I waited until he had run right up to me. 'Are you sick?'

'Me? No, I'm never sick.'

You may well be soon, I thought, *if you continue to eat and drink so much that you make yourself swell like a cow in calf.*

'Then someone in your household needs my help?'

A crafty look crossed his face. 'Yes,' he replied.

I turned Hal's head. 'In that case lead on and I'll follow you up to the house.'

The farmhouse was set a short distance back from the road. The yard was filthy, and I tied Hal to the gatepost so that only one of us need enter it. I was about to head over to the door, standing ajar, but Haydon said, 'Not that way.'

Thinking that his outdoor workers probably lived in their own quarters off the yard, as indeed mine did, I let him lead me over the muck, mud and the foul, rotting straw of the yard to an enclosure on the far side.

Haydon pushed the door aside and said, 'What do you make of that, then, eh?'

The two dogs looked up at their master and me. One gave a soft bark, one cowered away. They looked dazed, sleepy, and puzzled – if a dog can look puzzled – although they were without doubt alive.

But it was not the time or the place to demonstrate my relief.

I said, 'I'm a physician, Farmer Haydon. My patients are human, not canine.'

He waved a dismissive hand. 'Ah, but it's all one, isn't it?'

The answer to that was either very simple or impossibly complex. Since I didn't have the patience for the latter, I simply said very firmly, 'No.'

'You're here now,' wheedled the farmer. 'Can't you have a quick look and tell me what's happened to them?'

I should have said no. Most of me wanted to say no, but then the larger dog gave a little whine, and shook its head as if mystified at its own weakness, and guilt at having caused its distress overcame me.

I knelt down on the straw – fairly fresh and quite clean, I was relieved to find – and held out a tentative hand to the larger dog, who extended his nose to sniff it. 'He'll not hurt you,' Haydon said. 'I'm here, see, and he knows you're no threat.'

It was reassuring. I leaned closer and ran my hands over the dog's huge head. I fondled his ears, and he pushed himself against me, almost knocking me off balance. He was panting now, and his tongue looked dry.

'Have they been sick?' I asked.

'Not in here,' Haydon replied. 'Why?'

'I think they've probably eaten something that disagreed with them,' I said, which was as close to the real diagnosis as I was going to give. I ran my hand along the dog's body, feeling the ribs beneath the short coat. Then, looking up at the farmer, I said shortly, 'Your dogs don't get enough to eat.

Kept hungry, they're far more likely to consume things best left alone.'

'They need to be hungry if they're to do their job,' Haydon countered. But he couldn't meet my eyes.

I went over to the second dog and had a good look at him too. 'You asked my advice and I'm giving it,' I said curtly. 'Feed your dogs properly. Keep them fed and watered – both of them need water right now – and treat them with a bit more compassion.' Haydon gave a snort, which he quickly tried to disguise as a cough.

It suddenly occurred to me to wonder if he knew about the removal of the panels from Foxy Dell; if, indeed, he'd even been aware they were there. Still making a pretence of examining the dogs, I said as casually as I could manage, 'Does their presence stop trespassers as efficiently as you had hoped?'

He gave a self-satisfied chortle. 'Oh, yes indeed! Those lads won't dare come back, and nor, I'll warrant, will anyone else.'

'Not even for jewels?' I persisted. It was risky, but I had to know.

'*Jewels?*' Now the scathing laugh was full-blown, so much so that it prompted a coughing fit. When he had recovered, Farmer Haydon said, 'The boys got a beating for nothing. What they found was just a couple of bits of old broken glass, and I insisted on taking them back purely to make a point. They were my property, after all, found on *my* land.' He threw out his chest and thumped it. 'Chucked them on the midden when I got home.'

I gave the dogs a last pat, waiting until I was sure my relief wouldn't be obvious.

Then I got up, brushing straw from my hose and jerkin.

'Are they going to be all right?' Haydon demanded, nodding at his dogs.

I stared at him. 'Yes.'

I strode back across the yard and untethered Hal, mounting and nudging him with my heels. 'How much do I owe you?' Haydon called after me.

'Nothing,' I said over my shoulder. 'As I told you, I treat humans. It wouldn't be ethical to charge for advising on the health and wellbeing' – I stressed the word – 'of dogs.'

He was saying something as I rode off, possibly expressing his thanks.

I wasn't at all sure, however, that I'd earned them.

It was approaching noon when I got back to Rosewyke. I was hungry, and the exertions of the previous night were catching up with me. I'd hoped to call in on Jonathan as I passed by the village, but he was neither at home nor in the church. It occurred to me that he might be avoiding me – or, more accurately, avoiding my inevitable questions, of which I had so many – but I suppressed the thought.

Sallie served a cold spread of bread, cheese, meats and pickles, accompanied by a jug of ale, and explained the lack of a hot dish by announcing that she hadn't had the time since she'd been busy all morning making rose water and intended to go straight back to it once Celia and I had eaten.

'You'd almost think,' Celia remarked quietly as Sallie bustled in and out, a preoccupied frown on her face, 'that our unreasonable demand for a midday meal is something of an inconvenience.'

I grinned. 'Undoubtedly it is,' I said. 'But she does make excellent rose water.'

When we'd finished, and Sallie had raced to clear the table and wash the crocks, Celia and I went through into the library. It faced south-west, and the afternoon sun was pouring in. We settled in chairs set either side of the hearth, and the sweet smell of stocks and roses floated up from the arrangement Celia had placed in the empty fireplace. I felt very sleepy.

But, just as I was starting to doze off, Celia said, 'You were back very late last night.'

'Yes,' I said noncommittally.

'And don't tell me it was to see a patient,' Celia went on very softly, 'because, for one thing, I didn't hear anybody come calling for you, and, for another, you didn't take your bag.'

'Oh.' She had checked, then.

'You don't need to tell me if you don't want to,' my sister went on magnanimously. 'I just wondered, that's all.'

I was about to say I had no intention of telling her, but then, thinking about it, I wondered if that first reaction wasn't perhaps too hasty.

Because after what I'd seen last night there were so many things buzzing round in my head, and, in the absence of Jonathan, nobody with whom to discuss them.

And Celia, I reminded myself, was no unsophisticated illiterate. Our grandmother, the redoubtable Graice Oldreive, had believed fervently that everyone should be educated, girls as well as boys, and, Celia's and my parents being too busy to find much time for the task, had taken it upon herself to introduce my siblings and me to the wonders of the world. Celia, who had remained at home long after I'd gone away to sea, had been the main recipient of our grandmother's teaching, our elder brother Nathaniel having also abandoned the schoolroom at around the age I did, in his case for the life of a farmer.

Could I tell Celia about last night? It was obviously a mission that no one was meant to know about. Jonathan and I had hidden our identities under enveloping cloaks and gone out in a storm, under cover of darkness. It was hard to think of anything else we could have done to ensure nobody saw us.

But the person I was thinking of sharing it with was Celia.

My sister and I had always been each other's confidante. Although I was much closer to my brother Nathaniel in age, and the same sex into the bargain, he and I had never been in sympathy in the way Celia and I were. Perhaps Nathaniel had only been doing what was natural in the eldest child, but I'd always felt he was more like a third parent than a brother. Even from when we were very small, long before Celia was born, I had been the one to want to explore, to push the boundaries set by our parents and grandparents, to break the rules if the end result seemed worth the risk. Nathaniel, however, never went along with it. I can still remember the adult expression on his small face as, greeting yet another of my wild ideas for a thrilling adventure with a disapproving frown, he would say, 'I do not think that is very wise, Gabriel.'

I'd grown to adulthood believing he disapproved of me. Although I love him, I'm never sure that I actually like him.

The arrival of Celia into my world, however, brought the

sibling that I'd longed for. Although I was nine when she was born, we understood each other from when she was old enough to understand anything. We were two of a kind; I once heard an old family retainer, long since dead, remark to a friend when she thought I wasn't listening that Celia and I must be old souls; the instant and easy closeness between us meant, in her view of the world, that we had loved each other in another life.

I don't know what to think about that.

But I do know that Celia and I had always defended each other, told lies for each other and automatically, whatever the point at issue, sided with each other. And, in the course of the dreadful events of last year, we'd been privy to each other's greatest and most terrible secrets.

Of all people, my sister knew how to treat a confidence.

So I told her where I'd been the previous night, who I'd gone with and what we'd brought away with us.

When I'd finished my tale, for a few moments she didn't speak. She was frowning, and I guessed she was amassing her thoughts.

Which indeed she was.

'The first time people had to protect their stained glass was, of course, when King Henry changed the nation's faith and destroyed the monasteries,' she said.

'Of course.' I nodded sagely as if I'd known that all along.

'Which was' – my sister shot me a sharp glance that told me she wasn't fooled for an instant – 'from 1536 onwards. It wasn't just the glass that the king's vandals destroyed,' she went on, and I heard Grandmother Oldreive's old resentments and anger in her voice, 'it was everything that reflected the Catholic religion, so statues, icons, relics, reliquaries and everything else popish went the same way.' She paused for breath. 'Then when the old king died and his son Edward came to the throne – and that was in 1547 in case it had slipped your mind' – another pointed glance my way – 'the rules were pretty much made by the adults who advised him, since he was only ten, and the iconoclasts who were howling for stricter reform made the most of it. There was a royal injunction that said shrines, pictures, paintings and anything at all depicting miracles were henceforth against the law, and all the beautiful old stained glass had to be replaced with plain panels.'

My grandmother, I reflected, must have felt the hurt deeply. For a moment I wondered if she'd actually known the beautiful St Luke panels I'd seen last night; it was possible, although she and the rest of my family hadn't habitually worshipped in the church at Tavy St Luke's, their home, Fernycombe, being some distance away. But might not the rumoured beauty of the panels have attracted visits from the curious?

'There was of course a powerful Catholic revival when Mary came to the throne,' Celia was saying, 'but her reign only lasted five years, and the preoccupation of the queen and her ministers was burning heretics rather than redecorating the churches in the Catholic style, and then, with the coronation of Queen Elizabeth in 1558, Protestantism was made the state religion and that was that.'

'I thought Grandmother Graice was a great admirer of the late queen?'

'Oh, indeed she was,' Celia agreed. 'When Elizabeth made her famous comment about not wanting to open a window into men's souls, in effect telling her people that what they believed was up to them as long as they didn't make a fuss about it, Grandmother said it was the wisest thing a crowned head had ever said.' Her eyes took on a faraway look, and there was a faint smile of reminiscence on her face. 'The Romans took the same view, you know,' she said. 'You had to worship the official state gods, because those who held the power believed the empire would fail otherwise, but you could worship any other god or goddess you chose in addition.' She turned to me. 'Sensible, weren't they?'

'Mm.' But I wasn't really thinking about the Romans, or even about the late queen. I was thinking about the hours my sister must have spent in our grandmother's company; about how, although Celia was so lovely and, on the surface, possessed the required womanly skills and virtues, there was so much knowledge stored away inside her head, and she had the intelligence to benefit from it.

'So you reckon the five panels came from the little chapel

in Jonathan's church and were probably put in around the time that the church was built?' Celia asked.

'Yes. Well, that's what Jonathan thinks, and I could see for myself that the glass is early medieval.'

Celia nodded sagely. 'Ah, yes, Gabe, you always were the expert,' she said softly.

I ignored that. 'But the other one – the one with the beautiful angel—'

'The beautiful *naked* angel,' she reminded me.

'Yes. That one's quite different.' I paused, thinking how to put my impressions into words. 'The figures in the medieval glass – St Luke appears more than once, and there are some nuns and an image of Christ holding the lilies of the field – they're very appealing, and the colours are wonderful, but the faces are a bit like a child's drawing. You can tell what they're feeling, but in a very simple way. St Luke, for example, when he's pounding herbs, he's clearly enjoying it because he's got a big smile on his face.'

Celia nodded. 'But the angel panel is different?'

'Yes! His face – it's like the most skilful, detailed painting. He's stunningly beautiful, but he's so sad. His expression goes straight to your heart, and you can't help but think he's seen what happens in the world and he grieves for it. That he's been terribly hurt, and he's suffering some pain, either emotional or physical, that will never end.'

Celia was looking at me in astonishment. 'You really were affected, weren't you?' she breathed.

'Oh, yes. Jonathan was, too. He – when we were back in his house looking at what we'd discovered, there was a power coming off the angel image – honestly, Celia, I'm not making this up – and it was a very uneasy power. We both felt it, and when Jonathan gathered up a handful of straw and covered it up again, it was a great relief.'

She was still watching me, and I knew exactly what was going through her head. She wanted to see the panels – particularly the angel panel – but she didn't think Jonathan would let her, and she desperately wanted me to try to persuade him.

But she didn't voice her thought. With admirable restraint,

she said, 'We should now ask ourselves where the sixth panel came from.'

'Very well,' I agreed.

'I would imagine,' she went on calmly, 'that once it became clear that Queen Elizabeth wasn't going to be the religious tyrant that her half-sister had been, some of the old Catholic families began to wonder if they might quietly re-introduce some religious stained glass in their houses, and probably their private chapels too, although I think that would still have been frowned upon. But—'

'But if nobody had been making sacred stained glass for a generation because it was outlawed,' I interrupted, 'then who would they turn to?'

'Precisely,' she agreed. 'The craft had virtually been outlawed, and there were no craftsmen and artists left. People wanting to commission a new work would have had to search abroad, and the first place to enquire would probably have been Chartres, where masters in the art had long congregated.' She looked at me, frowning slightly. 'Possibly that's another reason why the sixth panel looks so different; because the man who made it had been taught his craft in France rather than following on in the ancient English tradition.'

I nodded. It was logical.

As silence fell, I felt again the intensity of her desire to see the panels. I said, 'I'll ask him, Celia. I promise.'

'In exchange for the wealth of information I've just imparted to you,' she said with some asperity, 'none of which you had any idea of before, so don't even try to say you did, I think that's the least you can do.'

Theo had had a long, hard day and was looking forward to shutting up the office and heading upstairs to sit in his comfort-able chair, enjoy a glass of wine to sharpen his appetite for whatever Elaine had commanded to be cooked for their supper, and summon his three children for a goodnight cuddle before Elaine rounded them up and packed them off to bed.

But such domestic delights had to be postponed, for just as he was getting up from his desk, Jarman Hodge slipped into the office.

'Can it wait till morning, Jarman? No it can't.' He answered himself before Jarman could, for he had seen his agent's expression. 'Come and sit down.'

Theo sat back heavily in his chair and Jarman perched on the bench on the other side of the desk.

'It may be nothing,' Jarman began, 'but it set me to thinking and wondering, and I reckon I should share it with you.'

'Go on.'

'The stable lad – Cory – from Wrenbeare came to see me. Christopher Hammer, the groom, sent him.'

'What did he want?'

'He didn't *want* anything, he came to tell me something. There's been another intruder. Or, I suppose, it could be the same one, if we're wrong about the original one – if he existed – being our little dead vagrant.'

Theo let out a deep sigh and muttered an oath. 'I suppose I'd better hear the rest.'

'It's a garbled sort of a tale if ever there was one,' Jarman went on, 'but it seems there's a young, simple, walleyed little scullery maid they all call Tatty – and before you ask I've no idea what her real name is – and they tend to take her mutterings with a pinch of salt. Anyway, she got really frightened a couple of nights ago when she went out to use the privy before bed, saying she'd seen a scary black wolf lurking behind the wall, and she was weeping, wailing, shuddering and the rest. They all told her there were no wild wolves in England and hadn't been for hundreds of years, so then she changed her tune and said it was a ghost, or a bad spirit, or even Old Nick himself, and in the end one of the other women made her a strong soporific and put her to bed. According to Cory – who hasn't really much right to call others simple-minded, when all's said and done – Hammer and the other servants reckoned you ought to be told because you'd been asking about the other incident.'

'But this girl – Tatty – said she'd seen a wolf. Isn't it far more likely it was some big, hungry stray dog after kitchen scraps?'

'Yes, probably,' Jarman said laconically. 'Anyway, there it is.' He got up to go. 'Kit Hammer sent Cory to tell me, and now I've told you, so I'll leave you to your evening and head away home.'

'Yes, very well,' Theo said absently. 'Thanks,' he called out as Jarman closed the door out onto the road.

If Jarman heard, he didn't reply.

Still thinking, Theo got up, closed his office, locked the outer door and at last went upstairs to join his family.

NINE

The next morning, the countryside around Rosewyke was hidden under a soft white pall. Over to the west, where the Tavy ran in its valley, the mist was particularly thick. There was barely a whisper of breeze to blow it away, and it would probably not dissipate until the sun in its waxing power rose high enough to dispel it.

Such early conditions always presaged a hot day.

Celia and I went down to the village to seek out Jonathan as soon as we'd had breakfast. We found him as he was leaving the church and on his way home, and, with a smile, he invited us to go in with him.

'I have a fair idea why you're here,' he said.

I was going to make some comment about Celia being no more likely to leak the news of the discovery than either he or I, but Celia got in first.

'Gabriel told me what you were doing the night before last,' she said, walking close beside him and speaking very quietly. 'I would love to look at the panels, if you don't object.'

He stopped, looking down at her with an unreadable expression. I thought at first he was angry, but then he said, 'It will be my pleasure to show them to you. As for objecting, it's not for me to say who may or may not look at them.'

We had reached his house and he opened the door, standing back to let us precede him inside. We went through into his little room, and he waved us to the two chairs beside the hearth. Then he disappeared, returning in a few moments with one large sacking parcel, which he placed on the ground. Then, one by one, he held up each of the stained-glass panels so that the morning sun pouring in through the window lit them from the back.

Celia simply gazed at them.

As Jonathan laid them gently down upon the straw and the sacking, she said, 'They are magnificent, and how right that you have dug them up from their hiding place.' She stared straight at Jonathan. 'What are you going to do with them?'

My sister is nothing but forthright.

'They definitely came from the wall of St Luke's Little Chapel,' Jonathan replied. 'I've made quite sure – I tried putting one in place yesterday evening and there's no doubt about it. So I'm going to put them back.'

'You're certain that's wise?' I asked. 'It's possible there may be a risk, for we do not yet know quite where King James stands on the subject of religious images, and it might be better to find out what he—'

Jonathan turned to me. His green eyes held some strong emotion, stopping me in mid-sentence, but when he spoke his voice was calm.

'The St Luke panels have been hidden away for far too long already. Their concealment has caused terrible anguish' – for a moment his pleasant expression slipped – 'and now they should be purified by being on display for all to enjoy.' He paused, then added softly, 'Washed with the warmth of the sun and empowered by the enchanting power of the moon and stars.'

It was a strange thing to say, quite unlike the usual speech of our vicar. Celia, who clearly thought so too, shot me a swift glance, but managed not to comment.

For some time we simply drank in the beauty displayed before us. Celia, I noticed, had a soft smile on her face. Looking at Jonathan, I saw with faint surprise that there was pain in his expression. At one point, his lips moved as if in silent prayer.

Presently he collected up the panels, handling them with great care, and went out to return them to wherever he was storing them. As it became plain he wasn't going to show her the sixth one, Celia called out, 'May I not see the last panel too?'

He stopped in the doorway, his back to us. For a moment he didn't reply, and then he said, 'It is not like these five.'

'I know, Jonathan,' Celia said. 'Gabe told me.' She hesitated, then said in a matter-of-fact voice, 'If you're worried that the depiction of a naked man is unfit for female eyes, let me remind you that I was married, and the sight of the human body, be it male or female, is not something that will make me swoon with horror.'

Jonathan made a faint sound that might just have been a suppressed laugh. He went on out of the room and along the narrow hall, and when he came back he had the last panel in his hands.

As he had done with the others, he held it up to the sunlight.

Seeing it in such circumstances rather than in the candlelight as I had done the first time, I found that its power increased tenfold.

And now the sight of the beautiful face and body of the angel, his gorgeous feathered wings, his desolate blue eyes, affected me in quite a different way. The night before last, I'd seen it as an erotic image, but now somehow it seemed . . . purer.

'Is there a Bible story for which this could be an illustration?' I asked Jonathan. 'Seeing the angel again, I am wondering if it may after all have been designed for a sacred purpose.'

Jonathan, too, was staring at the image. 'The angel, I agree, bears no taint of the profane,' he said. 'I would be tempted to think you could be right, but look at the man on his knees.'

I did so, and immediately wished I hadn't.

The bright sunshine revealed his expression with a clarity I hadn't noticed the first time.

His hooded eyes had a look of calculation; of cruelty.

And his slack mouth appeared to be drooling.

Celia made a sound of disgust. 'He's *slavering* over that boy,' she said. 'He's quite desperate to—' Abruptly she stopped. She didn't need to go on, for I was sure we all knew what the kneeling man had in mind.

Jonathan turned to her. 'I think you're right,' he said softly.

'Put it away!' she said. I sensed a brief struggle in her: she wanted to look away, but the power of the image held her.

Jonathan did as she bade, and, as the bright colours disappeared beneath straw and sacking, once again there was the sense that the mood in the room had subtly changed.

Celia was quiet for the first stretch of the short journey back to Rosewyke. But then abruptly she said, 'Gabe, there's an aspect of this that goes much deeper than the finding of some beautiful medieval glass that's been robbed of its rightful place and hidden away in a hole in the ground for decades.'

'What do you mean?'

She sighed. 'I concede that people with a sensitivity for good art and a fine eye for great craftsmanship can probably get very irate when they see masterpieces like those panels bundled away out of sight so nobody can enjoy them any more. But whatever's affecting Jonathan is far more profound than that. When he said that stuff about the panels washed with sunshine and bathed in moonlight, I'd swear he was quoting the words of someone else.' She paused to think. 'Something's troubling him badly. It's – it's almost as if he's guilty.'

'Guilty? But what's he got to feel guilty about? Surely *he* didn't hide the panels away?'

'No, of course not. They've been missing for years, haven't they? And Jonathan only came to Tavy St Luke's . . . Actually, when *did* he come?'

I thought about it. 'He was here when I first came to Rosewyke, in '97, although I was still worshipping with Mother and Father then and didn't meet him until later.' I tried to recall what Jonathan had said about his recent past when we had first met. As memory served, he said he hadn't been at Tavy St Luke's for long, having come from a brief stint in London and, before that, Cambridge, where he had studied canon law at Trinity Hall.

'Well, it's not worth trying to puzzle it out now as he wouldn't even have been born when the iconoclasts were smashing up the windows and the relics,' Celia said dismissively. 'He certainly wouldn't have been prising the St Luke

panels out of the wall and hiding them away in Foxy Dell.'
She turned to frown at me. 'So why is he guilty?'

'I'm not sure I agree with you,' I said. 'He might just have
been—'

But she interrupted me, irritation in her voice and the
very way she sat on her mare, her body tense. 'He's in
torment, Gabe! I sat there in that room of his and I felt
waves of anguish coming off him. Dear God, I was wishing
and *wishing* I knew him better, that I was his good friend,
his sister, whatever, because then I could have knelt down
on the floor beside him, put my arms round him and tried
to *comfort* him!'

I looked at her, amazed. Seeing my expression, she shook
her head and turned away, but not before I'd seen tears glis-
tening in her eyes.

'His emotion touched you, I see,' I said gently.

She smiled swiftly, a quick quiver of her mouth, there and
gone again. 'It did,' she agreed.

I thought carefully before I spoke. Then I said, 'He may
not be a close enough acquaintance for you – for us – to
impose comfort on him.' *For that requires a degree of intimacy
that I believe may be all but impossible to achieve with
Jonathan Carew*, I could have added. 'But nevertheless he is
our friend, and I do agree with you that something troubles
him deeply.' I paused as something struck me. 'It's – it's almost
as if he's on some sort of crusade, or mission,' I said hesitantly,
realizing the truth of it even as I put it into words. 'As if
something very powerful is driving him. So we shall do as
friends do,' I went on, trying to lighten the sombre mood, 'and
keep an eye on him.

Celia looked at me as if to say, *Is that the best you can
come up with?* But, after a moment, she nodded. Then she
kicked the grey mare to a trot, then a canter, and we rode
home.

The day delivered the heat that the early mist had promised,
and then some more. I had a call to make to the north of
Rosewyke and as I returned, longing for a draught of cold
water and a bucket of the same to plunge my head and face

into, I was summoned urgently to a little community close to the river. Some children had gone too near a bee swarm and several had been badly stung.

I'd almost anticipated someone being stung today. I'd heard the bees, I'd even seen them fly overhead as I rode out. There must have been thousands of them, forming a dense, dark, sinister little cloud, and the noise of their combined buzzing had been so alarming and eerie that I'd felt goose pimples break out on my skin, despite the heat.

I tethered Hal and rushed into the cool kitchen where the parents and a couple of other older people – grandparents perhaps – were trying to calm the frantic children. The old woman was holding a large earthenware bowl and there was a very strong smell of urine. Day-old, no doubt; I recalled the sovereign country remedy for bee stings.

The mother, wrestling to hold a little boy of about five still while she tried to extract one of the stingers on his forearm with the end of a spoon, gave me an anxious look. 'He's got two, her over there's got one' – a little girl weeping pitifully, sitting on her father's lap with his big, tanned arms round her – 'and the lad in the corner' – she jerked her head towards a boy of eight or nine, cowering under the table and trying to make himself as small as possible in the hope of being over-looked – 'has three, or maybe more.' She shot the lad a furious stare. 'Won't let me look, little sod!'

I knew full well that her anger came from her distress. 'I'll see what I can do when I've looked at these two,' I said, keeping my voice low and calm.

I knelt down before the child being held by his mother. I had already taken my long, pointed tweezers out of my bag and now, hoping that involving the little boy in what I was doing might catch his interest and lessen his panic, I showed them to him. 'I'm going to grasp that nasty sting very firmly and with one quick twitch, I'll have it out. I'll do the same with the other one – don't worry, I'll be so fast that you won't have time to feel more than a brief little burning sensation – and then your grandmother there' – I looked enquiringly at the older woman holding the bowl and she nodded eagerly – 'will put some of that wee on them.' The little boy made a face. 'I know, it's not a very nice thought, is it? But it'll help stop the stinging, you'll see.'

The operation was carried out much as I'd predicted, other than having to take a brief pause to wipe my streaming eyes when the grandmother advanced with her bowl of piss. Noticing, she looked at me apologetically. 'I'm sorry, Doctor, it reeks, doesn't it?'

'Just a bit,' I agreed.

She leaned closer. 'It's one of old Black Carlotta's remedies,' she confided in a whisper.

I might have known.

Black Carlotta was what, in a less paranoid and fearful age, we would probably have called a hedge witch. Nobody, ever, called anybody a witch nowadays. But I had met Carlotta and I admired her; I'd even say I liked her, except that she was so strange and so different that liking or not liking her seemed irrelevant and also slightly disrespectful.

'It's a good one,' I said now to the worried grandmother, who appeared to have realized a little too late that mentioning one medical practitioner to another one – who, moreover, just happened to be treating your grandchildren – wasn't exactly tactful. 'Most households can lay their hands on urine, and there's no doubt that something in it seems to ease the pain of bee stings.'

'Vinegar does the same if it's a wasp,' the grandmother told me helpfully.

I smiled. 'So I've heard.' She missed the mild irony.

I turned my attention to the little girl, then managed to persuade the lad under the table to come out and be as brave as his younger siblings.

When I'd seen to him and the kitchen and all of its occupants, including me, stank of stale piss, the father said apologetically, 'While you're here, Doctor.'

He held up both arms, on which I could see at least seven stings without even looking very hard.

With an exclamation – 'Why didn't you tell me straight away?' – I got to work on him.

He was clearly in considerable pain. He had a sting on his brow as well, up under his hair, and that one took me some time to extract. I went to treat it with the urine, but he waved my hand away. 'So close to my nose, Doctor, I reckon I prefer the pain,' he said quietly.

His wife, watching with eyes full of love and pride, said, 'He went racing over when he heard the children screaming. Went right in there amongst those blasted bees, batting at them and trying to beat them off while the little ones ran for home.'

'Well done,' I said quietly to him. I stood up straight, stretching my back. 'Keep up the bathing, only you could probably exchange urine for cold water quite soon.'

He gave me a quick grin. 'That'll be a relief.'

The family offered me water, ale, something to eat, but I declined. Declaring that they all needed a bit of peace and quiet after the excitement – it would have been tactless to say I couldn't even contemplate food or drink when the stench was still so strong in my nostrils – I made my farewells and rode home.

The heat intensified as the sun reached, and passed, its zenith.

Rosewyke was cool and quiet. Samuel and Tock had disappeared somewhere, probably to the shady spot by the river where Samuel claimed he liked to fish, although I was pretty sure the main attraction was the proximity of cold water and the soft, cooling breezes that rose up off it. Sallie, after serving Celia and me with a light midday meal – nobody was hungry – had retired to her room. I was in fresh clothes, and my attire of the morning was outside in the yard, steeping in a bucket of cold salted water.

Celia, too, had gone to her room, and was undoubtedly already asleep.

I strolled through the house, staring out at the blazing sun, the overheated land, the total stillness.

I could work, I thought. I had papers to write, notes to make up.

But then, yawning, I decided that work could wait. I climbed the stairs, went into my bed chamber and, heeling off my boots, lay down.

I was asleep in moments.

*   *   *

At Wrenbeare, Denyse Fairlight is out of sorts.

Despite the heat, her mother, Lady Clemence, has visitors. She sits in her once-opulent but now shabby room, holding court. Her elder daughter and her son-in-law, impatient with the ritual, long for the visitors to be gone so that tight, formal garments can be loosened and they can begin to cool off.

Denyse is hiding again. She is *too hot*. She has been made to wear one of the heavy robes that her mother insists upon when the rich ladies come calling. The robe is a little too small for Denyse, who has grown plump, not to say fat. The maid-servant had to haul on the strings of the stays in order that the gown should fasten. Denyse is sweating underneath all the clothes. She hates sweating.

After an interminable time, the visitors get up and they go.

Denyse sits on the wide window ledge, hidden behind the curtain, watching as the big woman on the bay mare and the two younger, smaller women, one on a roan, one on a black horse with a star, ride away.

Denyse doesn't like visitors. She doesn't like strangers of any sort. She doesn't much like anybody, and she barely tolerates her mother, her sister and her sister's husband. She is wary of the servants and she thinks there are far too many of them. They are always watching, watching, *watching* her with their narrowed, chilly eyes, muttering about her behind their hands, reporting to her mother the things she does and the wild, stray comments that fly out of her mouth before she can stop them. (She can't stop them. That is the trouble.) Then she is summoned before her mother to *give an account of herself.* How Denyse loathes that phrase, with its assumption, even before she's had a chance to explain, that she's in the wrong and has been *unacceptably naughty* again – another phrase she detests – and has earned herself a punishment.

Her mother's punishments are inventive, varied and always dreadful.

Denyse closes her hands into fists and beats them on the window sill.

She always hides when outsiders come. Her mother receives people in the big room, and there are plenty of places where Denyse can conceal herself. There are three big windows for a start, each of which has heavy, full-length curtains. Today when she heard horses coming up to the house she jumped up onto the window sill below the little window in the alcove beside the fire, then crouched down low behind the big arrangement of flowers sitting on it. The flowers make her sneeze, but she has taught herself to suppress the noise of a sneeze. Sometimes doing that makes her nose bleed and that is frightening. Blood, pouring from her nostrils and soaking the bosom of her gown. But the ability to silence a sneeze is useful, nevertheless, since so often she needs to be absolutely quiet.

Somehow the rest of the hot, scorching, airless, windless day passes.

Denyse is called to eat her supper, but she won't. She clamps her jaws together and, when the big woman in the kitchen tries to prise them apart to push in a smelly piece of cold meat, Denyse bites her finger.

Then Denyse's sister's husband is summoned and he speaks to her *very sternly*. 'You will eat,' he says in a cold and toneless voice. 'Your mother has decreed it. You know what I shall do if you refuse.'

Denyse does know. She emits a tiny whimper: she can't help herself. She unclamps her jaws and eats. A mouthful of meat – *ugh!* It tastes like it smells – and some bread. Some of the vegetable mess, slimy on the side of the platter, even slimier in her reluctant mouth. A hunk of bread with some cheese.

Finally her sister's husband nods, turns and stalks away.

Everybody is too hot, thinks Denyse. They are scratchy, irritable, and even nastier than they usually are.

She is called, washed, undressed, put in her nightgown and sent to bed. Sometimes Mary lets her go back downstairs to say goodnight.

But they are in a hurry tonight – her mother, her sister, her sister's husband – and Denyse knows they want to talk about *secret matters*. She has heard her sister mutter, 'We have to have a talk about the secret matters!'

She's not sure what these matters are, because every time

she tries to creep up close and eavesdrop, somehow they always know and they haul her out of her hiding place and eject her from the room, very often hurting her. Sometimes they hurt her quite badly.

Her sister's husband quite often hurts her on purpose. He beats her. So does her mother. Beatings are, however, more acceptable than the punishments that her mother inflicts on Denyse's most serious misdemeanours.

We have to have a talk. Denyse hears her sister's hissed words inside her head. She repeats them aloud, but in a soft and almost inaudible whisper. She knows – although she doesn't understand *how* she knows – that these secrets they want to discuss are bad things.

So many bad things seem to have happened here.

Denyse doesn't understand, but she is scared all the same.

She has been scared for much of her life.

She falls asleep, despite herself.

She wakes. She doesn't know what time it is. It's cooler, and it's dark.

She remembers that they – her mother, her sister, her sister's husband – were going to *Have a Talk.* She gets out of bed, tiptoes past the door to Mary's room – Mary is deeply asleep and snoring softly – and creeps downstairs.

The big room is empty.

Moonlight shines in through the three long windows. Somebody must have forgotten to draw the curtains.

Denyse goes on into the room.

It's not empty after all.

There's someone asleep on the rug in front of the fire.

Oh, oh, how funny! It's her mother!

Denyse starts to giggle, but puts her hands over her mouth to stop the sounds.

She can smell something . . . It's not very nice. It smells like the privy after she's used it for more than pissing.

She stands very still.

Her mother is in her nightdress. It's white, with embroidery on the yoke.

But the embroidery, Denyse knows full well, is blue and green. It's meant to be bluebells in a chain.

So why is there red all over the front of the nightgown?

Has her mother suppressed a sneeze and given herself a nose bleed?

Denyse creeps nearer. She doesn't want to – she wants to run, run, run back to bed and shut the door, bury her head beneath the covers – but she can't seem to help herself.

She stands over her mother.

She takes a swift look at the face and then thinks with relief, *It's not Mother, for that can't be her face. She never looks like that.*

But why, then, is this person wearing Mother's nightgown with the bluebells on it?

And *what's that smell*?

There are two smells now, the horrible privy stench and something that reminds her of when a pig or a calf is slaughtered. Denyse is not meant to watch and they have no idea that she does, but she has hiding places elsewhere than in the big room.

She bends forward.

Some bad person has torn the front of the bluebell nightgown. There's a huge rip, gaping at the edges.

And there's a hole in the body underneath, too.

It looks to Denyse, as her eyes widen and she has the first glimpse of the truth, as if someone has slashed a hole in the chest and reached in for the heart.

It looks as if the heart has been burst, crushed, destroyed.

Denyse's damaged, broken mind sheers away from the terrible sight.

And, still with her hands over her mouth, she starts to scream.

Her hands muffle the sound.

Which is why it takes some time for her sister's husband, a lighter sleeper than his wife, to perceive at last that there's an odd noise coming from downstairs and realize reluctantly that he ought to go and see what it is.

He sees his mad sister-in-law in the main room. She's in her nightdress, the generous folds of the back, gathered from a yoke, caught up unattractively between her large, floppy buttocks. He can see one of her pale, fat, hairy legs. The thigh has a huge, blue-black bruise spreading across it.

He reflects, yet again, how much he loathes her.

'Come along now, Denyse, stop that silly noise,' he says with a long-suffering sigh. 'You know you're not meant to be down here in the middle of the night.' He sighs again. 'Where the hell is Mary?' he mutters. 'She's meant to watch out for your night-time wanderings.'

He steps forward to take hold – reluctantly – of Denyse's arm.

She is squat and wide, and her sturdy body has been hiding what lies before her on the hearthrug.

But then the stink hits him, so forcefully that he heaves and dry-retches.

And then he sees the body.

Avery Lond, unlike Denyse, is not a young woman with a broken mind, and it is his mother-in-law, not his own mother, who lies brutally slaughtered at his feet.

Neither of which factors prevent him from opening his mouth and, with no terrified hands to suppress the noise, howling far more loudly and penetratingly than Denyse.

TEN

I knelt on the floor, avoiding the blood, and stared down at the corpse.

In my life at sea I'd seen horrors. Men in disbelieving agony with parts of themselves ripped away. Men screaming with fever, crawling with alien parasites, crushed and broken by falls, accidents, mishaps: ships are not safe places, even when they're not engaged in combat. Men weeping because they've endured more than they can stand.

But I'd never seen anything like Lady Clemence Fairlight lying before her own hearth in a pool of her own body waste with the heart ripped out of her body.

Theo, crouching beside me, said in a voice I hardly heard, 'Was it an animal attack? The serving maid did say she'd seen a large wolf lurking outside.'

I shook my head. 'Unless a wolf can wield a knife, then no.' I pointed to the long gash that stretched from just beneath the collar bone, widening to gape open over the broken ribs and ending a hand's breadth above the navel, sunk deep in rolls of flesh. 'That cut was not done by claws or teeth.'

I heard Theo suppress a groan and swallow a couple of times. When he spoke again, however, he had controlled the nausea and his voice was steady. 'Human agency, then.'

'Yes.'

'A man.'

I wasn't sure if it was a statement or a question. I replied anyway. 'Not necessarily. A strong woman with sufficient resolve could have sliced open the flesh of the chest and upper abdomen, provided the knife was sharp and long enough' – for the cut went deep – 'and could also have smashed the ribs with another implement such as a mallet so as to give access to the heart.'

Theo swallowed again. 'Is it not very difficult to—'

But he didn't seem to be able to go on.

'To extract a heart? No, not if you have in your hand the knife that made that cut. Basically the heart is held in its place by blood vessels and a tough sac of membrane that is attached to the skeleton and the diaphragm. You just have to slice away the—'

Theo made a retching noise, and I realized I was telling him far too much.

I twisted round to look at him. It was only when I turned from staring down at what had been done to Lady Clemence that I appreciated how I'd been fixated upon her. I made myself blink, and knew from the sharp little pains in both eyes that it was a while since I'd last done so. 'Has the knife been found?' I asked. 'And the mallet, or whatever it was? And the . . .'

He knew, of course, what I referred to. He shook his head. 'They're searching, but nothing yet,' he said tersely. 'I've sent for more men to come and join in as soon as it's fully light.'

I nodded. 'I'll need to see – er, whatever is found,' I said.

He was frowning, I noticed; I guessed he had a question to ask. 'Would you – would the person who did this have to be a surgeon, or a physician?' he said presently.

'No,' I replied. 'Many if not most people know where the heart is. Think of how many folk slaughter their own animals.'

'But this isn't a pig or a bull calf!' he protested violently.

'I appreciate that.' I tried to make my tone soothing. I could see how distressed he was. 'But pigs, cows and sheep all have a heart too, and its anatomy and function differ little from that of a human being.'

Abruptly Theo stood up. He looked furiously angry, and I guessed it was at the horror of what had been done here. Quite often, I've noticed, when terrible things happen, the mind somehow becomes confused and displays the wrong emotion. I've seen the bereaved who are broken at the death of a loved one wail at them in a fury of accusation, as if it's their own fault they're dead.

'"Tis a vile thing to die, when men are unprepared and look not for it,"' I muttered.

Theo nodded. Mastering his emotion, he said, 'She can't have expected this. To die by such violence, in her own home.'

'She can't,' I agreed. Then, for I sensed he needed the reassurance: 'I think it would have been swift. The very brutality suggests to me that this was done with great passion, and the killer would not have wished to linger.'

He gave a sort of snorting laugh. 'Some compensation, I suppose.'

I'd forgotten about the pair of Theo's officers whom we'd left standing out in the hall, either side of the foot of the staircase, and when one of them now came into the room, cleared his throat and spoke, it made me jump. Judging by the abrupt way Theo spun round, I guessed it was the same for him.

'Begging your pardon, Master Davey, Doctor Taverner, but what should we do about that?'

I stared at the young man, only then realizing it was the thin, pale youth – Gidley – who had been present when the vagrant's body was recovered. I felt sorry for him. If that earlier discovery had made him vomit, what must this one be doing to him?

'About what, Gidley?' Theo asked, not unkindly.

The pale youth's eyes widened in amazement. '*That*, sir!' he said in a sort of hissed shout. 'That racket!'

And then, shocked that I'd been so absorbed with the corpse and its terrible injuries that I'd managed to block everything else out, I heard it.

Somewhere not far away – not nearly far enough – someone was screaming. Rhythmically, repeatedly, incessantly, and at a pitch that, now I was attuned to it, I understood must be all but unbearable for anyone nearer. Gidley, for example.

'It's the daughter, sir, the one that found her,' Gidley said anxiously. Then, his natural diffidence when speaking to his superiors overcome by horror, he blurted out, 'It's not natural! They're saying she's possessed, that she was found with a knife in her hand standing over the body, that she's always loathed Lady Clemence and did her in!'

'Don't listen to the wild gossip of frightened servants,' Theo said, going over to the lad and putting a kindly hand on his shoulder. 'All we know for sure is that it was Mistress Denyse who discovered the body, and that her screams alerted her brother-in-law, who sent for us.' Gidley was watching him intently, eyes wide with alarm. 'Anything else is nothing but speculation, and you, as an officer of the coroner' – Gidley visibly stood up straighter at the description of himself, which had clearly been precisely Theo's intention – 'have a duty to remain above such talk.'

'Yes, sir,' Gidley said, a firmness in his voice that hadn't been there before.

'As for what we shall do about the noise,' Theo went on, 'we shall try to stop it.' He glanced back at me. 'Doctor Taverner has finished with the body for now' – he raised his eyebrows at me and I nodded – 'and so arrangements will be set in place for its removal to my cellar, leaving the doctor free to go to Mistress Denyse.'

I stood up and, overcoming a sudden profound lassitude that had little to do with having been dragged from my bed before dawn and summoned to this carnage and everything to do with my deep reluctance to face the madness that I knew awaited me, I picked up my doctor's bag and did as the coroner bade me.

Everyone fears madness.

Those who have the courage to tend and care for the sad unfortunates among us who have lost their minds and their reason manage to find a way to cope with their fear, and they have my sincere admiration. I've encountered madness a few times in my life and in my medical career, from poor, simple Tock – harmless but pretty much witless – to the ship's carpenter whose brain appeared to melt in the ravages of delirium, making him believe that he was a monkey who had been made a saint, or perhaps even a god, and that the rest of his shipmates, officers and ship's surgeon included, had to crawl on their bellies to worship him. He died, fortunately for everyone including him, but the group of sailors who were foolish enough to indulge in the fiery, fiercely alcoholic and highly toxic drink prepared by a band of natives on an island off South America weren't so lucky. Their madness endured all the way back across the Atlantic. The captain – on advice from me – had no option but to lock them up in chains in the hold, for their own and everyone else's safety, and the howls, screams, oaths and terrible sounds of crashing violence that we all endured for seven weeks have stayed with me ever since, not to mention the stench of five men constrained in a small space, their food hurled in and not let out to piss, shit or wash. The last I saw of the doomed sailors was as they were carted away, hooded, bound, still fighting, to the care of the monks.

I did not expect any such horror in the bedchamber of Denyse Fairlight.

Which goes to show how wrong you can be.

Her room was right at the far end of a long corridor, and just before it was the open door of another, larger room, the two chambers clearly defined as a separate space cut off from the main body and life of the house. As I walked past the larger room, a tall woman emerged. It was Mary, and she no longer looked calm.

'Thank Jesu you have come,' she breathed when she saw who I was. 'She's been at it for hours and appears unaware of all attempts to comfort her. In here.'

I followed her into the room at the far end. It was small and ill-lit, the one little window concealed by heavy curtains and, to judge by the smell, firmly closed. The screaming was by now deafening and for a moment, shocked into silence and immobility, I stood and stared at the woman who was making it.

I would scarcely have recognized her from the previous time I'd seen her. Then, despite the mania in her eyes and the illogicality of the peculiar things she said, she'd been decently dressed, washed, tidy. *Normal.* The word slipped into my mind before I could censor it.

Now she looked entirely different.

The voluminous nightgown was bloodstained and, as if aghast at the sight of the bright red on the fine white linen, she had tried to rip away the soiled parts. The modest neckline gaped, revealing heavy white breasts resting on folds of belly. She sat on the bed with her legs wide apart – I noticed bruising – and the rolled-up skirts of her nightgown displayed her pubis. Her long hair was tangled and disordered, torn from its night-time plait probably by her own frantic hands, and hung around her face in heavy, greasy hanks. She was deathly white apart from two patches of hectic colour on her cheeks.

Her eyes were wide open, the whites showing all around the pale irises. Her mouth, too, yawned gapingly, and there was a small cut to one side. I could see the rotten teeth at the back of her jaws and the red, pulsing throat. There was a rhythm, I noticed, to the screaming: it would rise in a crescendo in five repeated bursts of sound, and then there would be a sixth, louder and longer. Then there would be a silence – my ears throbbed when it came – and just for a moment the thought would come, *Thank God, it's stopped.* Then it began again.

Mary and I stood close together in the doorway. At first Denyse gave no sign that she'd noticed us. Then I thought I saw a quick flick of her eyes, to Mary, to me. Just for an instant the screams abated. The they started again, if anything louder and more intolerable than before.

Perhaps it was the pain in my ears; perhaps the aftermath of being roused from deep sleep to ride several miles as fast as I could to stand over a mutilated, brutalized body was making me a little short. Whatever it was, I acted without thinking. I strode across the room to the bed, sat down beside the screaming woman and said loudly, kindly and very firmly, 'That's enough, now. You will do damage to your poor throat.'

Denyse stopped in mid-scream. She had turned to stare at me, and now a strange, twisted smile crossed her face. Tears filled her eyes, spilling out to run down the plump, dirty cheeks. Then she said, 'My throat already hurts badly.' And, before I could stop her, she flung her arms round my waist and dropped her head in my lap.

I had no idea what to do. Acting on instinct had at least stopped the screams, so I did it again. Raising a hand, I began to stroke the harsh, disordered hair. I kept the action smooth, soothing, and I started to talk softly to her. 'What a shock,' I said gently. 'What a dreadful thing, to find your poor mother dead.' There was a horrified gasp from the doorway. Mary was staring at me, her face aghast.

Looking up at her, I said, 'There is no purpose to pretending it hasn't happened. Nor, indeed, that Denyse did not witness the body.'

'But we never speak of such things before her! We always keep her ignorant of—' Mary began. Then, folding her lips on whatever else she'd been about to say, she dropped her head and fell silent.

I returned my full attention to Denyse.

I knew I had to be careful. I'd just assured Theo that a woman was capable of having done the carnage downstairs, and, as we'd been told, Denyse had been found right beside her mother's body. It was possible, I had to admit – even, perhaps, likely – that she'd carried out the killing.

Even if she had, I reasoned, she was in deep distress and her mind was clearly disturbed. All the time; not just now, because of what had just happened. I was a doctor, and I had taken a binding oath.

'You must rest,' I said softly. 'Mary shall find you a clean nightgown, and bathe your face and your sore eyes. You shall have a warm drink and something to eat. What do you like best?'

'Cake,' came the instant, muffled reply. 'Cake with currants and spices.'

I glanced again at Mary and, nodding, she slipped away.

I went on stroking Denyse's hair.

It seemed wrong to sit there on the bed with her while so much of her body was revealed by the torn and rucked-up nightgown, and I reached out for the blanket that lay folded across the end of the bed and spread it over her. It was coarse and hairy, and not very clean. I'd noticed other signs of neglect in the room: the floor was stained, with a drying puddle of something brown and noxious beside the far wall. The curtains were torn, hanging off the pole at one end. Denyse's damaged nightgown was far from new and didn't fit her very well. It was, I'd have bet, a cast-off of her mother's or sister's.

She gave a soft little sigh and snuggled closer to me. Then she said, 'I saw a dead body before.'

'Yes,' I agreed, 'so you told me.'

She sighed again, more deeply. 'Everybody dies,' she said.

'But you—'

I was going to tell her she wouldn't die for a long time because she was still young, but she interrupted. 'I wanted to hear what they were talking about,' she said suddenly, in an urgent whisper. 'Everything is horrid here and they are all so anxious. They bite their lips and grow pale with anxiety, and nobody has even the tiniest bit of patience with me when I get things wrong in my head and make them cross. Mother beat me even harder than usual, and Avery said I must be shut in the cellar in future when people visit, at least until I learn to curb my tongue.' She stopped, and I felt her plump body shake as she sobbed. 'He stopped up my mouth as a punishment and he left me like that,' she whispered. 'He said it was to teach me to guard my words.'

She had, I reflected, just explained both the heavy bruising on her legs and the cut in the corner of her mouth.

'I thought they'd be having their secret talks when it was dark, down in the big room,' she went on, her voice all but inaudible, 'and when I woke up in the night, I went down to see if I could listen at the door. I often do that,' she confided, 'and I have very many places to hide so that they don't know. But when I went down, I couldn't hear them. I went on into the room, in case they were speaking really softly, and then I saw . . .' She stopped.

'I know what you saw,' I said. 'I saw it too, and it was dreadful.'

She nodded, the rough head rasping up and down against my belly. 'There was blood on her nightgown,' she muttered. 'And a big *hole* in her.'

'Yes,' I agreed.

You still could have killed her, I was thinking.

There came the sound of hurrying footsteps, and then Mary was back. She had a bowl of steaming water in her hands and a clean nightgown over one arm. She took in the sight of her charge, lying down quietly with her head in my lap, and nodded; with approval, I thought.

'That's right, Mistress Denyse,' she said soothingly, 'nice and peaceful.' Meeting my eyes, she said, 'Food and drink are coming. I'll wash her now, and prepare her for bed.'

She came up to the bed, and took Denyse in her arms. It was with relief that I relinquished her. I felt a kindness in Mary; whatever brutalities were meted out to Denyse from her family, the woman who had the care of her seemed to be different.

As Mary stripped off the soiled nightgown and squeezed out a cloth in the hot water, I turned away and reached into my bag. I still had some of the potion that Judyth had given me to sedate the dogs, and I didn't think a small dose would go amiss now. I waited at the door for the kitchen maid bringing Denyse's cakes and warm drink, taking the tray from her. I put it on the floor, there being no table of any description in the room, and carefully put two small drops of mandragora into the drink.

Presently Denyse, washed and dressed, her hair brushed so that some at least of the tangles were gone, was in her narrow bed, propped up on pillows. I handed the coarse pottery mug to Mary. 'I've put a sedative in it,' I said very quietly to her. 'Your charge needs sleep now.' And so do you, I thought, taking in her pallor and the deep lines round her eyes, with their look of strain.

She nodded. Sitting down on the edge of the bed, she held the cup to her charge's lips and waited while, greedy as a child, Denyse gulped it down.

I didn't wait to watch her scoff the little cakes.

Theo and I rode slowly in the wake of the cart bearing the body of Lady Clemence. We were heading home for food, a brief rest and a change of clothing; both of us were soiled with blood and body waste. Theo would be returning to Wrenbeare later. Two of his officers had been left at the house, still pursuing the hunt for the murder weapons and the heart and, now that the sun had risen, with a great deal more urgency. Halfway back to Theo's house, three more men hurried past us in the opposite direction. They paused to hear Theo's instructions, then raced on.

Some time after they'd gone and breaking quite a long silence, Theo said, 'There's no reason it can't have been Mistress Denyse who did it, for all that you clearly feel sorry for her.'

'You're quite right,' I said calmly.

'About what? That she could have done it or that you feel sorry for her?'

'Both.'

He made a sort of *hrumph!* sound.

I'd told him what had happened up in Denyse's bedchamber. What I'd observed, what she'd told me, the tentative opinions I'd formed. Was still forming. 'She's suffered greatly, I believe,' I said now. 'Beatings, imprisonment, and I'm sure there's—'

'Look at it from their point of view,' Theo interrupted harshly. 'She's pretty much out of control, or so it appears, and they have the care of her each and every day.' He paused, then added more reasonably, 'People get tired, Gabe.'

I was about to protest that Denyse was clearly out of her wits and couldn't help herself, and that her family should show more patience and compassion, but I stopped. Theo was right: I should have considered the situation from Lady Clemence's viewpoint, and that of her elder daughter and son-in-law. She had been the wife and was now the widow of a man of wealth, a man of importance and standing; a justice of the peace, admired, looked up to. The members of his family surely weren't to be condemned for wanting to retain a little of his glamour; for hoping to garner a little of the respect that Sir Thomas had been held in for themselves. And there was poor, unattractive Lady Clemence, sitting stiff and haughty, pathetic in her desperation to cling to her dignity and her position while her fat, ugly, mad daughter danced around giggling inappropriately, making up to men, displaying far too much of her sad, malformed body and talking about dead bodies.

So instead I said, 'Yes, I suppose they do.'

Theo turned to me, the surprise in his face suggesting he hadn't expected such meek agreement. Recovering swiftly, he said, 'So, do you think she did it?' When I didn't imme- diately reply, he went on, 'She'd have had cause, perhaps. The mother beat her, treated her unkindly, kept secrets from her, handed her over to the care of that other woman.'

'Mary is kind to her,' I interrupted.

'But others are not,' Theo replied swiftly. 'Lady Clemence. The sister's husband. Avery Lond. He's not kind.' There was a pause. 'D'you think we ought to warn him to be careful?'

I wondered if he was joking, but a quick look at him told me he wasn't. 'He's not a large man, and perhaps hasn't a great deal of fortitude, but I think he'd be able to fend off Denyse,' I said.

Theo and I had met Avery Lond when we'd arrived at Wrenbeare. All had been in turmoil, with Denyse's screams shattering the night silence and the various wails, moans and sobs of the servants like some ghastly chorus in the background. Mistress Agnes had fainted and was being tended in her chamber by her maid. Her husband – thin, narrow-shouldered, bloody- handed, face as white as chalk and the smell of vomit surrounding him like a miasma – had been slumped at the foot of the stairs, barely able to speak for shivering. 'She was just *standing* there,' he kept saying. 'She had blood on her nightgown, and her hands pressed to her mouth, and she was making these noises . . .' He paused, his teeth chattering. 'Then I saw – I saw *it*.' He raised his head, wide eyes staring unseen around the hall. 'The blood, the gaping hole in her, and, oh, sweet Jesus, the *smell*.'

All of us – Wrenbeare servants, Theo's men, Theo and I – had taken a hasty step back as Avery Lond threw up again.

'He was in deep shock earlier,' Theo now remarked fairly. 'Still, he knows, none better, what Denyse's capable of, so he'll probably—'

'Theo, that's a huge assumption,' I protested. 'As yet we have no grounds whatsoever for believing she's any more than the unfortunate person who found the body and raised the alarm. And' – something which I hoped was convincing had just occurred to me – 'surely she wouldn't have had time to hide the weapons and the heart, since Avery Lond found her screaming right over the body?'

'She could have hidden them first and then gone back to the body and started up the racket,' Theo replied.

I muttered, 'Bollocks.'

He heard, I was sure of it, but, other than to give me a long, assessing look, he didn't reply.

ELEVEN

Back at Rosewyke, the day had begun. Celia had already breakfasted and, dressed smartly, was clearly on her way out. Sallie, tutting over my filthy tunic and hose, told me robustly to get the garments off so that she could put them in to soak. 'There's water waiting for you in your room, Doctor, and I'll have food ready when you come down again,' she called out after me as I headed for the stairs.

Celia followed me up to my room, discreetly remaining in the long gallery outside the open door as I stripped to my skin and washed. 'Do you want to tell me where you've been?' she asked, in a casual tone that didn't fool me for a moment. My sister has always had a lively curiosity and, after the events of the recent past, she is very alert to the whisper of violence.

There seemed no reason not to tell her, for the news of

Lady Clemence's death would swiftly spread through our small community. Since, in my mind at least, the murder just had to be connected in some way with the rumoured presence at or near Wrenbeare of the dead vagrant, I told her about that too.

'Something's most definitely amiss at the house,' I said as I towelled my head and face dry. 'Mistress Denyse told me everything was horrid – that was the word she herself used – and her family were anxious and troubled. And Lady Clemence and her elder daughter—'

'That's Agnes, married to Avery Lond, you said?'

'Yes, that's right. She and her mother both lied about the vagrant, which is suspicious, surely?' I dragged on a fresh chemise and hastily donned the rest of my clean clothes, then went out to join Celia in the gallery. 'I keep asking myself, what did the vagrant see, or take away, that the family didn't want revealed?'

Side by side, Celia and I descended the staircase. She was frowning, clearly puzzling over the matter. 'Maybe you should also ask yourself whether he was simply a desperate, hungry thief who broke in looking for food and was killed because, by sheer bad luck, he saw what he shouldn't have done.' She paused, glancing at me. 'Or not,' she added enigmatically.

I didn't stop to dwell on that. 'But he wasn't killed, was he? I told you, I believe he died of natural causes. Starvation, the depredations of long illness.'

A flash of understanding it her eyes. 'He was the one you thought might have had leprosy!'

'Yes, but he didn't. There's no need to worry.'

She shook her head in irritation. 'No, I know. I wasn't worrying, I was *thinking*.' She paused, then went on slowly, 'He went *twice* to the house.' She turned to me, clearly expecting this remark to mean something.

It didn't. 'So?'

She clicked her tongue in annoyance. 'Come on, Gabe! I know you've been up half the night dealing with a brutally murdered corpse and got yourself befouled as well, but *think!*' She waited, as if to give me the chance to redeem myself with some startlingly pertinent and intelligent reply, but very soon her impatience got the better of her. 'If he'd simply been hunting for food, wouldn't being chased away the first time have warned him off and made him go for an easier target next time?' Before I could comment, she rushed on. 'It's what I was hinting at just now! If it wasn't just bad luck that the vagrant broke into a house where there was something terribly secret that he shouldn't have seen, then we need to think about what else it was.'

We stood at the foot of the stairs, staring at each other, and now I knew what she meant. Her eyes were sparkling and her bright, intelligent interest seemed to fizz off her. In the midst of my preoccupation with the murder and the link to the vagrant, a small thought surfaced with a cheer of joy: *my sister has all but recovered.*

I reached out and drew her to me, hugging her tightly. 'Yes, I've got it,' I said into her smooth, fragrant hair. 'But you say it.'

She disengaged herself and stood grinning up at me. 'If it wasn't just mischance that took the vagrant to the home of the Fairlights, then we have to conclude that he knew the house, or the family, or both.' She stopped to think, then added, 'There was something at Wrenbeare that he wanted very badly, to the extent of risking returning even after he'd alerted them to his presence, when it was far more dangerous for him because they'd be on their guard.'

We went through into the morning parlour, where Sallie had set out a gut-stretching breakfast for me to which I was pretty sure I'd do full justice. I sat down, reaching for warm bread rolls, butter and honey, and Celia, despite having already eaten, pulled out a second chair and joined in.

'So what was it?' I asked through a mouthful of bread and honey. 'What was he looking for so determinedly?'

'And did he get it?' Celia added. 'Was there anything in his possession or on the body?'

'No.' There had been that scrap of paper, but it was surely not relevant.

'But then if someone from Wrenbeare had followed him and murdered him, they'd have taken it back, wouldn't they?' Celia said. 'That was the whole reason for killing him; to stop him revealing whatever secret they were guarding!'

'But he wasn't killed,' I repeated. Another thought struck me, and I voiced it. 'I wonder if the failure to obtain whatever he wanted so badly at the house of the Fairlight family was a factor in his death? Whether it affected him so badly that he simply gave up and died?'

Celia didn't respond. Watching her closely, I realized she probably hadn't taken in my last suggestion; she was still totally focused elsewhere.

She looked at me in silence for a moment. Then she said, 'Are you absolutely sure the vagrant wasn't murdered?'

It was now about a week since the vagrant had died. His body was still in the crypt of the empty house, and the last thing I wanted to do was to return to it.

I called in on Theo first. He too had washed and changed, and he had the look of a man in a desperate hurry to be somewhere else.

'Make it swift, Gabe,' he greeted me. 'I'm away back to Wrenbeare as soon as I've seen to this.' He waved a hand over the papers strewn on his desk.

I outlined the main points of my conversation with Celia and as I went on, he began to nod his understanding. 'Go on, then,' he said before I'd finished. 'I don't envy you, mind, but if you're right, we need to know. It has to be done.'

I turned to leave. 'Take one of my men with you,' Theo called after me. 'You'll have a much better light for spotting tiny details if you take the corpse upstairs into the sunshine. There's a courtyard behind the house where you won't be overlooked.'

I nodded. 'Good idea.'

I didn't take anyone with me, however. I reckoned I could carry the body alone, and I prefer to work without someone leaning over me.

The empty house was dark, forlorn and, despite the warm weather, felt more than a little damp. The smell wafted up even as I strode along the hall. I ran down the stone steps to the crypt and went to the body. I noticed something on the flagged floor beneath the trestle and, momentarily hopeful that it might be some previously overlooked object that had dropped from the corpse's clothing, bent down to pick it up. But it was nothing of interest; merely part of a honeysuckle flower, now limp and dying, and no doubt trodden in unheeded on the sole of one of Theo's or my boots.

Without letting the thought of what I was doing get through to my conscious mind, I picked up the body – it was indeed a light burden – and carried it up to the hall and out through the rear door into the sunny little enclosed yard. Roses and honeysuckle ran out of control over the walls, their fragrance fighting with the stench of decay.

I laid the body on the stone flags.

If there are no marks on a corpse of violence or poison, and murder is suspected, then one very likely possibility is suffocation.

Angling myself so that the full light of the early sun shone down on the dead man's face, I peered into his mouth and nose.

And, eventually, purely because I went on looking even when at first there was nothing obvious, I saw what I'd missed on my first two examinations.

I was furious with myself.

The nostrils were difficult to investigate because of the lumpy swellings at the end of the nose, but that was no excuse. For when I drove myself to force a way in past the fleshy growth and poke up inside the left nostril, I found some very fine filaments of fluff. When I repeated the procedure with the right nostril, there they were again. They were tiny, and I'd never have spotted them in the dim light of the crypt, no matter how many lanterns I'd lit.

I looked now at the mouth. It was hard to be sure but, now that I knew what I was looking for, I thought there might be bruising on the inside of the lips, as if they'd been pressed hard against the teeth. Finally I raised the lid of the remaining eye and peered very closely at its white. There were a handful of minuscule red marks on it.

The vagrant had been smothered to death.

I straightened up and, bending down over the dead man, said softly, 'I am very sorry. I should have made these discoveries sooner, but, now that I have done, I will do my best to uncover what happened to you.'

I went on kneeling there for a few moments, then got to my feet, picked up the body and returned it to the cool, dark crypt.

Theo had gone by the time I returned to his house.

While I very much wanted to race after him to Wrenbeare, there were other matters awaiting my attention. For one thing, I had patients to see, at least two of whom were in a state requiring my daily ministrations. For another, I needed to carve out a space amid the overwhelming demands of this day to think about the implications of what I'd just discovered.

I scribbled out a message for Theo and one of the youths in his outer office said he'd ride over presently and deliver it. Thanking him and telling him to make it sooner rather than later, I hurried away.

It was fortunate for the three patients I attended that morning that none of them was seriously in need of my full range of expertise and the best of my professional skills, because they didn't get either. Two had been sick with high fevers but were now convalescing; the third merely needed stitches to be removed and a fresh dressing.

I had time, riding between the three households, to let my thoughts fly back to the dilemma of where to go from here. Most crucially, I decided, I needed more information, and primarily about the household at Wrenbeare, since it appeared to be at the very heart of this strange business. The prime source was, of course, the household itself. I hoped very much that Theo shared my conclusion; he was there, right now, and as coroner he had the authority to demand answers to all the questions he cared to ask. Jarman Hodge had not been around when I'd been to Theo's office, so I was also hoping he had gone to Wrenbeare too. He'd already managed to extract a few confidences from some of the servants, and surely he too would feel the urgent need to find out more.

I'd wondered about approaching the present justice of the peace for our area. Lord Underhay, Cosmo to his friends, was a quietly intelligent, fair-minded and studious man who, so those in the know said, had studied law at Cambridge and practised in London and, later, Bristol before retiring to his own county on inheriting the estate and the title from his late father. He would surely have been able to provide information about Sir Thomas Fairlight and his family, assuming I could provide a good enough reason for demanding it. But it would, I believed, have to be an extremely good reason, for he was a man of the law, trained in reticence and diplomacy, firmly in the habit of guarding confidences with the rigidity of a suit of armour. Why on earth should he feel the need to gratify a country physician's curiosity?

As at last I left my final patient behind me with nothing worse to complain of than a somewhat lighter purse and the smarting of the flesh of his left buttock where I'd taken out nine stitches, I realized that there was no need to bother Lord Underhay when there was someone else I could approach, closer at hand and, or so I hoped, more likely to be amenable.

And I turned Hal's head to the north, and rode off for Buckland.

The day had turned humid and overcast after the bright morning and there was rain on the way. I didn't think it likely that Josiah Thorn would be out on the river bank, and so I rode instead to his house.

It took him a few moments to answer my knock at the door and, as he ushered me along the dark little passage to his room, I noticed that his hair was ruffled on one side and that his face was flushed with sleep.

'Don't go telling me this time that you were only closing your eyes,' I said as we sat down either side of the hearth, I on a settle, he in his chair, 'because I won't believe you. And I'm very sorry for having disturbed you,' I added.

He waved aside the apology. 'No matter. It was high time I woke, anyway. If I sleep for too long after the midday meal, I don't get off at night.'

After the midday meal. With a start, I realized how late it was. The remains of Josiah's meal sat on a platter on a small table beside him, and the sight of the heel of bread next to the large chunk of golden cheese flooded my mouth with saliva. Perceptive man that he was, he noticed.

'Eat it,' he said with a smile. 'Make sure you have some of that pickle. It's excellent.'

I reached for the platter. It would actually be fairer to say I grabbed it, then fell on the food. He was right about the pickle. 'I forgot to have dinner,' I said lamely as soon as I could speak.

He nodded. 'I remember how it is,' he said kindly.

He got up and went out into the scullery, returning with a mug of ale. That, too, was excellent.

'Thank you,' I said when I'd finished. 'Your generosity makes it all the harder to broach the reason for my presence, because I'm here to press you on a matter I raised last time I saw you.'

'Are you, indeed,' he murmured. 'I had a feeling you might be.'

'I'm afraid that, first, I have some deeply distressing news,' I went on. 'Lady Clemence Fairlight was found dead in the small hours of this morning.'

His face went very still. After quite a long pause, he said, 'I see.' I saw his lips move and I imagined he was praying for her.

Before he asked, I said, 'It wasn't a natural death.'

His eyes flew to mine. 'No?'

I shook my head. 'She was murdered.'

'*Murdered.*' He looked horrified.

I didn't think I needed to tell him the details unless he asked. 'Mistress Denyse found the body,' I said. 'It seems from what we've been told that she tried to muffle her screams, but the son-in-law, Avery Lond, heard her and went down to see what was the matter. He said to us he didn't suspect any such horror as the sight that faced him, for Denyse often wanders in the night and then starts to sob, moan and scream when she forgets why she got up and can't find her way back to her bed. Or so I was told.'

'That poor, poor woman,' Josiah breathed.

I wasn't sure if he was referring to Lady Clemence or her strange daughter. Perhaps it was both.

Then he said anxiously, 'Do they – is it thought that Denyse might have killed her mother?'

I shrugged. 'It's crossed people's minds,' I replied honestly. He paled a little more, but he didn't comment.

There was a pause. Then I said, 'It's not the first dead body that Denyse has seen.' I looked at him, but his head was turned away. 'I'm told she saw her father's.'

Now Josiah shot me a swift glance. 'Yes.'

He wasn't going to elaborate unless I pressed him, I reflected. 'You would have been in attendance, Sir Thomas having been your patient.' I made it a statement and not a question.

'Of course.'

'And presumably the sight was sufficiently disturbing for Denyse still to dwell on it, fourteen years later.' He was shaking his head. 'She does, for I have heard her. *Dead bodies!* she said, and she told me she'd seen a dead body, then she shouted, *Dead, dead, dead!*'

'Yes,' he said quietly.

'You knew,' I murmured. 'You've been consulted about her, haven't you? They've asked you more than once if you can do anything to help her, to control her wild moods, to restrain her, and—'

'I was the family's physician,' he interrupted sharply. 'Naturally they asked for my help. But—' He stopped.

'Was she insane before she saw her father's body?' I demanded starkly. 'It's my belief that she was.'

'You know nothing about her!' he flashed back.

'Then tell me! That's why I'm here, because I need to know!'

I heard the echo of my loud voice, and knew I'd made a mistake; I'd left myself wide open to the response I'd have given myself, had I been in Josiah Thorn's position.

'And what right have you to be provided with such knowledge?' he asked silkily. 'You are not their doctor, so why should I believe your interest in the matter is anything more than prurient curiosity?'

It seemed that the only slim chance I had of persuading him to confide in me was to tell him the whole story, describing the moment when Theo and I found out that there had been an intruder at Wrenbeare of whom the family denied all knowledge, that this intruder had been found dead – murdered, I now knew

– and that he had seen or knew something about the Fairlight household that they preferred kept secret.

And now Lady Clemence too had been killed.

When I'd finished, Josiah was quiet for a long time.

Eventually he sighed deeply and said, 'I begin to understand your interest, Gabriel. You have been involved, it seems, through no fault of your own and, indeed, at the invitation of the coroner.' He sighed again, then put up his long hands, stained with age spots, and rubbed his face. 'While I must retain the right not to share with you, or indeed with anybody, private matters concerning members of the Fairlight family who are and were my patients, I will tell you as much as I can.' He hesitated, frowning. 'As much,' he amended, 'as I judge you would be able to learn from other sources.'

'Thank you,' I said.

He glanced at me sharply. 'It is with extreme reluctance that I do this,' he warned. 'But now you tell me that Clemence has been murdered, in her own house, and I am bound to help in any way I can. If revealing to you matters from the past that I would far rather were left there will assist you and Master Davey to find the truth of her death, then it seems I have little choice.'

He leaned back in his chair. He closed his eyes, as if perhaps the better to recall the past. I waited. Then he began.

'It starts, of course, with Sir Thomas Fairlight,' he said, his voice already sounding weary. 'He was born in 1533 into a wealthy family with several titled men among its ranks.'

'Yes, Wrenbeare is an old house, and there's evidence that once it was fine, and the house of the wealthy and powerful,' I observed.

Josiah nodded. 'Yes. There were some fine men – and women – among Sir Thomas's forebears.' His eyes opened and he stared straight at me. 'But Thomas was not fine; not in any way.'

'So you told me.' He'd hinted at this when I'd asked him before. 'He was cruel, selfish, self-indulgent, I believe you said.'

'All of those,' Josiah agreed. 'All of them and more, for he developed a strong sexual appetite when he was not much more than a boy, and his youthful sexual encounters were legion.'

'Serving maids, tavern wenches, innocent young servants?' I suggested.

But Josiah shook his head. 'No. Thomas could not make himself approach girls or women. *I* know this not because I listened to the gossip, you understand, but because Thomas himself told me.' He paused, and the expression in his eyes suggested he was back in his own past, listening as his patient spoke to him. 'He was *proud*, I believe, when he told me of the fumblings with little maids and servants, of how he even tried to force himself on one poor lass. He wanted to be able to brag of his conquests, you see, but in truth there weren't any. And then he began to realize where his true appetite lay, and by the time he was . . . oh, about fourteen, I suppose, his sexual nature was firmly established.'

'He preferred boys,' I said quietly.

'He did. For the next decade and more, he indulged himself to the full, in all the places where his family's aristocratic lifestyle, wealth and position took him. London and Paris were his preferences. He once told me there was more variety in Paris, and he went there whenever he could.'

'Did his father know why he wanted to go?'

Josiah shrugged. 'I cannot say. Mortimore Fairlight was a decent enough man, but he was withdrawn after the death of Thomas's mother, and I believe he preferred to ignore unpleasant matters and tell himself they weren't really happening.'

'Yet even a man such as he must have wanted his son to marry and have children,' I said. 'Wrenbeare is, or could be, a fine inheritance, and surely he'd have wanted the family line to go on?'

'Indeed he did, and by the time Thomas was in his early thirties, Mortimore had roped in all sorts of aunts, uncles and cousins to help him persuade Thomas to do his duty by marrying, and marrying well.' He gave a wry laugh. 'A Fairlight wife had to be the right sort of woman.' Slowly he shook his head, his face infinitely sad, as if the pains of the world were just too much.

Presently, though, he recovered, and went on.

'By the time Thomas was thirty-six, he too understood that he wasn't going to advance as he so fervently wanted to unless he had what everyone in his family was now persistently and clamorously persuading him to acquire: a normal family life. And so, with Thomas reluctantly dragged along, the great bride hunt began.'

'And they found Clemence.'

'They did,' Josiah agreed. 'One of Mortimore's sisters knew her kin – she was a Sulyard before she married, an old Devon name – and was aware there was a daughter who was hanging on hand, as the vulgar would have it.' He smiled, but there was sorrow in his expression. 'Clemence was sixteen when she married Thomas, and he was thirty-eight. In truth, she was not a beauty. She was hefty, horsy, pale-fair with almost colourless eyes and eyelashes. She was ungainly and unattractive, poor girl, and nobody had asked for her hand before, nor indeed shown any interest in her whatsoever. And once married, she had to face the fact that she didn't appeal to her husband at all.' He was shaking his head again. 'She was as ignorant and as innocent as most maidens going to the marriage bed, and cannot possibly have known that it wasn't just her: that no other woman would have aroused Thomas either, since he had married against his inclinations.'

'And so she suffered in miserable silence,' I said.

'She did. Matters might have improved had she turned out to be good breeding stock and given birth to a succession of big, healthy babies – that was after all why Thomas had been encouraged to marry her – but she couldn't even achieve that, and there was never the longed-for son.'

For a while there was silence in the cosy room. I was thinking about Clemence, pity and deep sympathy filling my mind, and I dare say Josiah was too.

Presently Josiah went on with his account.

'It wasn't until 1574, three years after the marriage, that Thomas and Clemence's first child was born, and, as I believe I have already told you, I attended the birth. Agnes was small and sickly and at first she failed to thrive, although she improved as she grew out of childhood.' He fixed me with a stare. 'You tell me she is married?'

'Yes. She appears to be in good health at present.'

'Good, good,' he muttered. But his attention seemed to have turned inwards, and I think he had spoken without really thinking what he was saying. He remained quiet for some time.

'And then Denyse was born?' I prompted.

'Hmm?' He looked up. 'Yes, although there was a gap of six years following Agnes's birth, during which time Clemence had at least two miscarriages. And then,' he pressed on before I could comment, 'she managed to carry a second child to term, and Denyse was born.' He stopped, almost as if he was cutting off his own words. 'And Denyse,' he added after a moment, 'is as you have observed her.'

I waited, but he didn't go on.

'I asked you just now,' I said carefully, 'whether Denyse lost her reason as a result of seeing her father's dead body or if the condition had existed before.' I was sure of the answer, but I wanted him to tell me.

'You did, you did,' Josiah said wearily. 'And you already know, Doctor Gabriel, don't you?'

'Yes.'

'It became evident very soon after her birth that Denyse was sick in her mind,' he said. 'We – I – tried everything, but there appeared to be no remedy. She was—' But words failed him. 'Seeing Sir Thomas in that terrible state when she was ten didn't help, of course, and it is no surprise to hear that the sights, smells and sounds of that dreadful day still haunt her.'

'He was murdered, then? He died by violence?'

'No,' Josiah said heavily. 'Like his younger daughter, he lost his mind. He died crying out at the top of his voice, tied down on his bed, thrashing about in his own filth and bleeding profusely from the mouth where he'd bitten his tongue. He'd been raving for three solid days and the sudden silence when at last he gave up the fight and died was like a blessing from heaven.' He paused. 'I thought I'd gone deaf,' he whispered. 'I could still hear the echoes of him screaming at me, telling me he was going to get himself free and chase after me to cut me in pieces, sobbing that the devils of hell were coming for him and he was going to cut them in pieces too and hurl them into Satan's fire. Then his heart burst and it all stopped.' He paused, deep in the past. 'He was a horrible sight,' he added softly. 'His face was purple, his eyes were staring, his mouth wide open in a great yawning howl.'

Then he flashed right back into the present, glared straight at me and said, 'And that was when I realized that little Denyse, ten years old, was standing just behind me.'

'Dear God!'

'It was *their* fault! Lady Clemence, the older sister, the woman who cared for her! They should have been watching her!' Josiah protested, as if even after fourteen years he still felt the need to exonerate himself. 'She was meant to be shut up in her room far away from what was going on in her father's chamber, but the whole household was like a broken wasps' nest. Everywhere people were hurrying and bustling about, whispering in corners, trying to peer into Sir Thomas's room, trying to find out what was happening, and most of them just longing to hear the old man was dead, since he was all but universally loathed and feared, and only Denyse had any affection for him, poor little lass.'

'What did she do when she saw he was dead?' I asked.

Josiah gave a bitter smile. 'What do you think? She began screaming, and she didn't stop.'

TWELVE

I rode away from Buckland with my mind a muddle of images, stray thoughts and weird, unlikely ideas. I'd gone to see Josiah Thorn looking for something in the Fairlight family's past; something which already known about, or accidentally discovered, by someone else had been grave enough to cause that person's death.

I'd found out that Sir Thomas Fairlight, knight of the shire, justice of the peace, had preferred boys in his bed to girls or women. When I'd first heard this, in Josiah's own words that had still carried the echo of his deep distaste for the man, it had seemed shocking. Now, as I rode back towards Tavy St Luke and home, the soft rain a great deal more wetting than it looked so that already I was soaked, I thought about it all again and I realized it wasn't as bad as Josiah's telling of it had made it sound.

Thomas Fairlight was far from being the only man of wealth, power and position whose sexual habits didn't bear close scrutiny. He'd been dead for fourteen years. Would the exposure of these habits now really be so terrible for his family?

The upright, plain, solid Lady Clemence would be embarrassed, yes, but—

With a start I recalled that Lady Clemence wouldn't be feeling such an emotion, or indeed emotion at all, any more.

The rain came down harder. Daylight had faded as the heavy clouds built up, dark grey turning to black. It looked as if a storm was coming. Hal's head drooped and I tried to hunch my shoulders in a futile attempt to protect myself.

We were almost at the village, which I would pass on my left as I rode on home. I looked down at it in its little hollow. Just at that moment there was a sudden flash of soft yellow light from the church. Jonathan – it was probably he – must have opened the door briefly, perhaps to peer out and see how hard the rain was falling and how wet he was going to get dashing back to his house.

The light disappeared. I could make out no sign of a running figure, though, and I guessed he had gone back inside.

I pictured the interior of the church. The aisle, the simple altar, the tiny chapel separated from the main body by its sturdy wall, with the empty spaces at the top where the beautiful panels had once been.

Without really thinking about it, I turned Hal's head and, kicking him to a trot, went down into the village.

There was a long rail behind the church for the hitching of horses and I led Hal beneath the steeply pitched roof that covered it, tethering him then removing his saddle so that I could brush the worst of the rain off him. There was water in a trough, and despite the rain, the air temperature was still warm. I reckoned he'd be all right there for a while. Then I ran across to the church door.

I didn't see Jonathan at first. A candle had been lit on the altar, and in the storm-clouded darkness its light seemed very bright. As my eyes adjusted, I noticed there was a second light source, and I walked up the aisle and across to the low doorway that led into St Luke's Little Chapel.

I went in.

It lived up to its name. It was some five paces long, three or four wide. Its stone walls were bare, and a large, unadorned stone served as the altar. On it was a plain wooden cross. Three small rush lights had been lit at its foot, and there was a little pottery jar containing wild flowers. There was, I thought, beauty in the simplicity.

'I'm glad you're here, Gabriel,' said Jonathan's voice. 'I'm about to begin replacing the panels, and the presence of somebody else would be reassuring.'

I turned. Jonathan was standing at the foot of the dividing wall, and in deep shadow.

The turmoil in my mind gave a last flurry of pointless activity and then slowly came to a halt. Realizing that helping somebody in a manual task – and a challenging one at that – was exactly what I needed, I rolled up my sleeves. 'No doubt you've worked out how to do it,' I remarked. 'Tell me how I can help.'

He smiled briefly. 'Mainly by holding the ladder steady and passing things up to me as I require them.'

'Ladder?'

He nodded down towards the base of the wall. I made out a roughly made wooden ladder, with eight crude rungs set quite widely apart. I looked back at Jonathan, mentally adding his height to that of the ladder. 'You're sure it's long enough?'

'Yes, if I stand on the top step. Which is why I'm pleased to see you,' he added. My doubts must have shown in my face, for he said with some impatience, 'It's all right, I shan't fall. And for sure you can't go up it, since you're a much bigger weight than I am and, in addition, I've already been up and I've worked out how to put the panels in.'

He was quite right about our respective weights. 'Very well,' I said.

He raised the ladder against the wall beneath the first gap and swiftly climbed to the top rung. My calculations had been out, for now I saw that his head and shoulders easily rose above the sill at the base of the space. He took a small hammer from where he'd stuck it through his belt and, without turning, he said, 'Pass me the first panel, please.'

He'd arranged them along the base of the wall, side by side. The damaged one, I noticed, had a new piece of glass to replace the broken one. 'When you say first,' I said, 'are we speaking right to left or left to right?'

I was sure I heard him sigh. 'It doesn't really matter, since we cannot know the original placement. Right to left.'

Very carefully I picked up the panel and held it up to him. It was the one with the image of the doctor – St Luke – bending over the bedridden patient. Jonathan reached down and took firm hold of it, then placed it in the empty space.

It fitted perfectly.

Jonathan was busy with the hammer and what looked like a handful of wooden pegs, but it wasn't clear what he was doing. 'If it wouldn't distract you, do you want to describe how you're attaching it?' I asked quietly. The last thing I wanted to do was speak loudly and make him jump. He wasn't exactly wobbling, but his perch up there certainly looked precarious.

'There's a narrow strip of dowelling at the bottom of the gap,' he said, 'and it seems to me that its purpose is to hold the glass firm, since the space between it and the stone is just the right size.' He paused and there was the sound of tapping. He gave an *ah!* of satisfaction. 'Then, to prevent the panel toppling forward, there's a series of small wooden pegs that have to be hammered into the corresponding holes in the surrounding wall.'

'Where did you get the pegs?'

'They'd been left tucked safely away behind the strip of dowelling.'

As if, I thought, *whoever had removed the panels knew full well that, one day, someone would replace them.*

There was more tapping, quite a lot of it, and then he was coming back down the ladder.

He was smiling broadly. 'What do you think?'

I stared up. Although I could see the difference – that the gap was no longer a gap – that was about all. 'There's not really enough light,' I said apologetically.

He too was staring upwards. 'No, you're right.'

He hurried off into the main body of the church. After a moment, the light of the one candle on the altar began to increase. And then, for the first time in more than half a century, the beautiful image in bright glass of St Luke ministering to the sick man, in its gorgeous border of flowers and foliage, shone out once more like a handful of jewels in the noon sunshine.

'It's a wonder,' I said softly. 'Well done.'

Jonathan was silent, but, observing his lips moving, I guessed he was praying. Then he picked up the ladder, moved it a few feet to the right and, hurrying up it, said, 'Next one.'

I'm not sure how long we worked. Not all the panels went in as easily as the first one, and we spent quite some time trying them in different spaces until we achieved the best fit. In the penultimate space there weren't enough pegs, and after quite a lot of discussion – not all of it very amicable – Jonathan decided to go back and remove a peg from each of the previous panels to make up the deficit.

He was nothing if not a perfectionist.

I'd been on the point of suggesting we wait until the morning, when a call on one of the village carpenters would swiftly supply what we needed, but I held back. Jonathan was driven; I could sense the fierce determination coming off him. The job had to be finished *now*.

Finally it was done. He came down the ladder for the last time, and I breathed a silent sigh of relief. I'd noticed a crack beginning to snake its way along the second to top rung, and it was creaking ominously every time Jonathan put his weight on it. I'd mentioned it to him, but he'd ignored the warning.

He set the ladder down along the base of the wall and we stepped back, looking up at the five panels. For quite some time we were content just to gaze and admire, but presently he said, 'I've been trying to decide which one I like best, and I think I know. But you first.'

I didn't hesitate, for I'd made up my mind when I'd first seen them. 'I admit I have a great fondness for the three jolly nuns picking flowers, especially the one who looks as if she's just sneezed, but my favourite is the doctor with his patient.'

Jonathan grinned. 'I thought it might be. He reminds you of yourself.'

'He doesn't look like me,' I protested.

'He does. He's a tall man, broad like you, and he looks as if he'd having to fold himself to fit in that tiny bedroom.'

'Oh, all right, he does a bit. But that's not why I chose it. It's because I've felt just like he's feeling.'

I didn't think I'd explained what I meant, but Jonathan knew. 'It's all in his expression,' he said. 'He's hoping that what he's doing is going to help, but he really isn't sure.'

I nodded. 'It's so often the way of it,' I agreed. 'To convey that, in a small piece of stained and painted glass . . .' I was lost for the words to describe how it was affecting me.

I felt Jonathan's brief touch on my shoulder. 'All that skill,' he murmured, 'and these panels had to be wrenched from the place where they belonged and hidden away in order that they shouldn't be destroyed.'

He had spoken softly, but nevertheless I couldn't prevent the swift look around. 'Careful,' I breathed.

He turned to me in surprise. 'I don't believe we are over-heard. And it is the truth. Would it matter if we were?'

I shrugged. 'Who can say?' Then, for the atmosphere was suddenly less easy, I added, 'But you haven't yet declared your favourite.'

He looked up again. Without hesitation he pointed to the central panel. With the candle flames from the altar in the main church now illuminating it, the image was even more impressive than when that calm, perceptive gaze had first looked out at us in Jonathan's house three nights ago. There was St Luke, still in his coif, this time no longer in the central position but a little to the rear. Before him, capturing his entire attention – and his love, just as the image would surely capture that of everyone else who looked at it – was Christ. His golden robe glowed, his light auburn hair shone like a halo, his eyes, hooded and bearing a depth of sadness and a wealth of compassion, stared down. The lilies that lay across his outstretched arms and the long, graceful hands as yet innocent of their terrible wounds were perfect in their beauty.

I might have guessed that this would be Jonathan's choice.

As we extinguished the rush lights and the candles and prepared to leave the church, Jonathan told me of the unveiling ceremony he was planning. Interrupting him, I said, as I'd said before, 'You're sure about this?'

He paused in the act of opening the door. It was raining even harder now, and he'd already invited me to go back to his house to wait until it eased before I rode home.

He smiled faintly. 'I've told you *how* I plan to reveal the panels, Gabriel,' he said. 'I haven't said *when*.'

'But you've just replaced them! Do you really think nobody's going to notice?'

'I left the ladder there, didn't I?' he said. 'I'm having five simple wooden shutters made. They'll be ready tomorrow, and I'll put them in place as soon as I have them.'

'Why didn't you hold back till then to replace the glass?' I demanded.

He looked sheepish. 'I couldn't bear to wait any longer.'

In the cosy comfort of his little room, we towelled off the worst of the wet and then he fetched pewter cups and a bottle. 'Not as fine as your brandy, but it's not bad.' He poured out two good measures and passed one to me. I sipped it. It was rum.

The other night he'd given me brandy. Had he finished that, then, in the loneliness of his sleepless nights?

I waited until Jonathan was settled in his chair. Then I said, 'Have you heard the news from Wrenbeare?'

'I have.' His face was grave. 'Although I did not know her well I have met Lady Clemence Fairlight several times, for she used to attend service at St Luke's and she would frequently stop to have a word about the sermon. It's always refreshing, and a sop to the vanity, when a member of the congregation shows that he or she has paid sufficient attention to take issue with a point or two.' He paused. 'I am distressed to hear of her death; even more at the manner of it.'

'It was brutal,' I said.

'So I was told. And the younger daughter, they say, is thought to have done it?'

'That rumour was not spread by me,' I said quickly. 'The only evidence against her is that it was she who found the body, and that there was blood on her nightgown.'

'Which surely could have got there when she crouched over her mother,' Jonathan observed.

'Quite so.' I paused, then decided that, bearing in mind who I was talking to and the wide range of human experience he'd have come across because of his profession, it was all right to continue. 'Had she been responsible for her mother's fatal injuries, I'd have expected her to have blood on her hands. A lot of blood. Even given that undoubtedly weapons were used – a knife and something akin to a mallet – the killer must have been covered in blood. And she'd have to have hidden them before doing anything to attract attention.'

'I see,' Jonathan said. 'A knife and a mallet,' he murmured. 'A frightful way to die.' He shook his head as if in denial of such brutality. 'In addition to our compassion for the victim, however, I believe we should also spare a thought – many thoughts – for the daughter.' He hesitated, then said delicately, 'She is not right in her mind, I believe.'

'She's not,' I confirmed. 'Just at present, I imagine she's as *wrong* in her mind as it's possible to be.'

'Is there any clue as to the identity of the killer?'

I liked the way he had utterly taken my word for the fact that it wasn't Denyse. 'Not that I know of. Theophilus Davey and his men have been at the house today, however, and may have discovered fresh knowledge.' If not Theo himself, I reflected, then Jarman Hodge might well have winkled out something helpful.

'And what about motive?'

I told him about the vagrant and the theory that he had stumbled across some desperate secret. Jonathan was a very good listener, and I found myself going on to describe my visit to Josiah Thorn and the information about Sir Thomas Fairlight's dubious habits.

And, echoing my own thought, Jonathan said, 'Is that enough

to kill for, given that Sir Thomas has been dead for well over
a decade?'

'He died in 1580,' I said. 'Yes, I'm wondering the same
thing.' I studied him. 'You weren't here then.'

'No.'

Then I remembered something that Josiah Thorn had said,
on the first of my recent visits. He'd revealed a little about
Sir Thomas's nature, and there was something he'd said that
was nudging at the edge of my mind . . . He'd said that Sir
Thomas's equals seemed to quite like him, or perhaps he'd
said *tolerate*, but that it was a very different matter with his
subordinates, and I'd had the clear impression that the man
had been a bully.

*I remember how that tubby little priest remonstrated with
him.*

I heard Josiah's voice quite clearly.

'Can you tell me anything about your predecessor here at
St Luke's?' I asked Jonathan.

He reacted as if I'd stabbed him.

'What do you mean?' The words were breathed rather than
spoken, and barely audible.

'I'm afraid I don't know exactly when you came to the parish,'
I said, trying to pretend I hadn't noticed his peculiar reaction
and keep my voice pleasant and conversational, 'although I
believe it was during the years I was studying in London.'

'I came here in 1598,' Jonathan said tonelessly.

'Ah yes, I was indeed away from the county then.' I smiled
at him but his face remained frozen. 'So who was here immediately before you? Who precisely did you replace?'

I thought he relaxed infinitesimally as I elaborated the
question.

'My predecessor was a man named Philip Snell,' he said.
Still he looked wary.

'And he was a tubby little man?' I repeated Josiah Thorn's
description.

Jonathan smiled faintly. 'No, quite the opposite. He was very
tall and thin, aesthetic looking, stooped with arthritis. This was
his last incumbency and he died here, which was when I came
to replace him.'

'He'd been here a long time?'

'No, less than a decade, and . . .' But suddenly he stopped speaking. Whatever strong emotion had had him in its grip just now had returned, stronger than before, and Jonathan had gone so white that I feared he was on the point of collapse.

I swiftly got up and poured another measure of rum, silently handing him the mug. He took it without looking at me, swallowing it in one draught. I returned to my seat, watching him closely. Some colour returned to his face, but the strange inward look remained.

After some time he seemed to recover.

He raised his eyes to look at me and attempted a smile, although it was a mere phantom of his usual expression. 'Thank you,' he said, indicating the mug. 'I felt strange briefly.' The smile slowly became slightly more genuine. 'The excitement of replacing the panels, not to mention clambering up and down a very crude ladder with a creaking rung about to give way any moment, must have overcome me.'

I went on looking at him, although I didn't speak.

I didn't believe his explanation for his odd turn; not for an instant. He was fit and strong, not more than a year or two older than I was, and climbing any number of ladders was highly unlikely to have affected him so profoundly. As for the excitement of putting back the panels, he was a man in his prime, not a nervous spinster given to palpitations and fainting fits.

Something profoundly distressing was troubling Jonathan Carew.

But if he didn't want to tell me what it was, if he preferred to make silly excuses that he must have known I wouldn't swallow, that was up to him.

I drained my mug and put it down on the small table beside me, rather too forcefully. I stood up. 'The rain seems to have eased a little, or, at least, not got any heavier,' I said. 'I'll make for home now, I think.'

He too rose, and saw me to the door. As I stood on the threshold, he said, 'Gabriel, I—'

I turned. 'What?'

But he shook his head. 'Nothing. I just wanted to thank you for your help.'

'Thank *you* for the rum. Good evening, Jonathan.'

I strode off up the path and went to find my horse.

Alone in the safety of his room, Jonathan closed the door, checked that the window was fastened and sank back into his chair. For some time he simply sat there, waiting for his pounding heart to slow down.

When Gabriel had asked that question, when he'd been blind to Jonathan's extreme reluctance and pressed and pressed with his questions – *tell me about your predecessor, when did you come here? had he been here a long time?* – Jonathan had required all his strength and more to overcome the all but irresistible temptation to flee or to cut off Gabriel's innocent enquiries with a fist in his mouth. He had succeeded, but only just. And then Gabriel had asked if the predecessor had been a tubby little man.

Jonathan groaned aloud. Blindly stretching out his hand, he reached for the rum and, not pausing to find his cup, put the bottle straight to his lips.

Then he leaned back in his chair and, at last letting the tide of memories overwhelm the mental barrier he had erected so long ago to keep them at bay, he waited for them to hit him; to bring back to the forefront of his mind Martin Oude, his youth, his long life, and what had happened to him.

He knew that it would be painful; much more than painful.

But it seemed that he had no alternative.

Martin Oude was born in East Anglia in 1520. As a very small boy he understood the love of God as if God were a warm, caring, immanent presence who was permanently aware of every living member of his creation, present in their daily lives and concerned with all that affected them. When the three-year-old Martin fell over and skinned his knees, he believed he felt God's kindly arms helping him up, God's lips putting a gentle kiss on his forehead to comfort and reassure him. As he grew out of childhood, those around him who had believed his faith would mature as his body and mind did were disappointed, for with a few more years to his name Martin began to perceive Jesus Christ as his saviour, as the exemplar for anyone wanting to live a good life, and as the perfect, shining, glorious embodiment of love. And as a steady, ever-present companion walking right beside him.

Entering a monastery as a young novice was the obvious, the only choice for the twelve-year-old Martin. Despite the hardships, the privations, the discipline, Martin was as happy as a human being could be, for he had been told that every discomfort and pain was an offering to God and his beloved son. Kneeling on the hard stone floor, Martin would hold up his arms as if his hands supported an imaginary golden platter on which he had laid his hunger, his aching limbs, his frost-bitten toes, his back that stung from the lash and the occasional piercing stabs of homesickness. In his mind, the age-worn hands of God and the wounded hands of Christ – the two images seemed to flow and mingle in his mind – would stretch out and receive his gifts, and he would sense a loving smile bestowed upon him from the heavenly realms. Then all the sacrifices of his hard life would be worthwhile – oh, so much more than that, for he would have given himself ten times over if he could – and he would sense perfect peace, perfect love, descend on his sore shoulders like a warm, soft shawl.

But it was not long before the idyll came to an abrupt and violent end.

For Henry VIII, King of England, had fallen in love – in lust, anyway – and in order to marry the woman he didn't seem to be able to live without, he had amputated his realm and everybody in it from the Church of Rome. Henry was now the head of the Church of England and those who refused to accept this, who refused to take the solemn oath of fealty to their ruthless, selfish, violent egotist of a monarch, were put to death. Some died by the axe, some died in the flames. But all died.

In a few short years, Henry tired of the woman for whom he had changed the entire religious life of England. She too was killed, and the only small mercy shown to her by the man who once would have walked through fire to bed her was to summon an expert swordsman from France to cut off her head. This Frenchman was reputed to be so swift in his decapitations that it did not hurt, but who could possibly say?

The same year, 1536, the dissolution of the monasteries began.

Martin's small community lasted longer than some, for they had no treasures, their buildings were dilapidated, and their vow of poverty genuine. But in the end they too were thrown out onto the charity of others, and charity was hard to come by just then.

Martin did not really understand the concept of the change of religion that was being forced upon the population of England. Was God not still God? he asked his superiors. Was his love, and that of his precious son, not still as all-encompassing, as ever-present? Yes, of course, they replied shortly. And can I not still love God just as I have always done? Martin would press them. Yes, they said, patience fast running out in the face of far greater problems looming ahead than the anxieties of one innocent and naive young ex-monk. Problems such as homelessness and starvation, and how to support a community of unworldly men when you yourself were all but on your knees with distress and hunger-induced sickness.

But Martin's guiding light remained strong and it did not waver. He knew that the sole purpose of his life was to serve God and, if he could no longer do so as a monk in a religious order of the Church of Rome, he would learn how to perform the same service under the new religion. Over the course of many years – for he was shy, scared and diffident about asking for help and advice in this new world he didn't understand – at last he emerged from long, puzzling and arduous training as an Anglican vicar.

He had told his new masters that he came from Suffolk and would quite like to go back there. Either they didn't take it in or they decided, for their own good reasons no doubt, not to indulge him. He was dispatched to Devon, to the pretty Norman church of St Luke's in the tiny village of Tavy St Luke's.

Martin swallowed his disappointment meekly, as he always did, and set about throwing himself into his new life. God's love was still holding him up, filling him with joy and driving out his moments of doubt, sorrow and pain, and he felt it was only fair to do his very best in return. And, indeed, it was not hard to become happy in Tavy St Luke's, for the village was charming. To one used to the wide spaces and the huge skies of East Anglia, the landscape was alien at first: the village lay in a fold of soft green hills, with steep, wooded slopes leading down to rills, streams and rivers, and looming up to the east like a stern, protective barrier there were the moors.

The little Priest's House seemed like ultimate luxury to one such as Martin, who had never slept in a room on his own before. He knew how to scrub, clean and cook – the monks had trained him thoroughly – and also how to dig over a likely looking patch of earth and plant vegetables and fruit bushes. Everything grew for Martin Oude, and quite soon after his arrival he was exchanging surplus produce for those items he could not provide from his own little garden: milk, butter, cheese, and very occasionally a piece of meat. Fish he sometimes caught for himself in the sea and more often in the many waterways of the area. Eggs he obtained from his own hens, which he kept in a carefully fenced-off patch behind the house and locked up at night in a henhouse on stilts. His neighbours scoffed at first, muttering about hens not needing such elaborate arrangements. They changed their tune, however, when they began to understand just how prolifically Martin's hens laid for him and how, when there was a fox lurking, only Martin's little family of fowls survived unscathed.

Martin was kindly, loving, generous, and he never turned anybody away. In a very short time, his parishioners started to wonder how on earth they had managed before he came to them. He was able to give so much because whenever he felt his mental strength waning, he could restore it simply by going into his church. He had loved the little building from first seeing it, and that love grew with each day.

The body of the church was utterly plain, its windows made of pieces of thick, greenish glass set in a maze of lead. The altar was a heavy slab of oak set upon two stone supports, and the cross was as simple as everything else. The true glory of the church was in the five stained-glass panels set high in the wall that divided off the little chapel, dedicated to St Luke the Healer, from the main church.

Martin knew he had seen images of his Lord before, but they had fled his mind and his memory the moment when he first saw the panel depicting Christ holding out the lilies of the field. He had gazed up into the deep, mysterious eyes and something in him – in his soul, perhaps, or maybe his heart – had fluttered up out of him and winged its way to the still figure above him. When finally he managed to tear his eyes away – he had no memory of just how long that had been, although his aching bladder told him it must have been hours, perhaps – he had noticed there were four more panels. They too were exquisitely beautiful, and Martin fell in love with them as well.

As he crept hunched and bent out of the church – he had been on his knees for far too long, and even a young man can grow stiff and cramped under such circumstances – he began to understand why he had been sent to Tavy St Luke's. Silently, unheard by anyone but God, he vowed to give everything he had, including his life if need be, to look after those panels.

For the year was 1547, the old King was dead, and his son, the boy King Edward VI, sat on a throne all but hidden by the swarm of advisers.

It was the time of the iconoclasts.

The young king was vulnerable, and it seemed that those who pushed to the front and shouted the loudest got their way over matters of policy. The Protestants were determined to make ground, and when they suggested to Edward that it was time to rid the country of the outer trappings of popery, Edward agreed and issued a royal injunction to the Church that his father had founded to destroy the shrines, the pictures, the paintings and everything else that smacked of 'feigned miracles', so that there could be no reminder of these in the walls and the windows of churches and private houses.

Martin hoped at first that the King's Commissioners might be very slow in reaching his little corner of Devon. Optimist that he was, he even wondered if they might pass him by

altogether, and he spent many hours on his knees praying that
this would be the case.

Of course, it wasn't.

When he knew for sure that the stern-faced, ruthless men
were on their way, he went into his church late one evening
for one last look. He whispered aloud, 'How can they believe
it is right to destroy such beauty? Such old, precious things?'
He knew by now that the panels were several hundred years
old, and the work of one of the very best of the medieval
masters.

He looked for a long time at the panel with the flowers, the
one with the three happy-faced nuns, the ones of St Luke
grinding his herbs and ministering to the sick man in his bed.
Lastly, as always, he turned his eyes to Christ.

Then, with a heavy heart, he fetched his ladder.

It was easier than he had thought to remove the five panels.
The delicate, expert craftsmanship of the hands that had made
them extended to the fitting of them in their slots in the wall,
where each one stood firm against the slightly smaller confines
of its space, held in place by a length of dowelling and a series
of pegs hammered into neat little holes in the wall. Martin
laid the pegs carefully on the sills of each space. He knew
deep in his heart that, one day, the panels would be put back.

It was the one small spark of light on a very dark night.

He had prepared a hiding place. After much searching and
the rejection of everything else, he had settled on a hidden
little dell on the edge of the village, surrounded by a copse
and with beech trees growing out of its sloping sides. To the
best of Martin's knowledge, nobody went there. He didn't
think anybody owned the land; certainly, nobody farmed it,
for it was useless for agricultural purposes. Generations of
foxes had dug into its earthy sides and it was riddled with
tunnels and holes. It had been a straightforward matter to dig
out a large enough space for the five panels and, that night,
all Martin had to do was wrap them carefully in two thick
waddings of straw and then tie them into two lengths of
sacking.

He carried the two parcels – they were a great deal heavier
than he'd expected – out to the dell. He prayed constantly as

he hurried and stumbled along, and his prayers were answered because no one saw him; no one called out a greeting; no one demanded to know what he thought he was doing.

As he slid the second parcel into the hiding place, he put a gentle hand upon it. It was the one that contained the Christ panel.

'Forgive me, Lord, that I must treat your precious image thus,' he whispered. 'It is not for lack of respect, as I hope you know, but to keep safe this great beauty until the time of danger is past. I will not—'

But then, emotion and stress finally too much for him, he found he couldn't go on. Thrusting the parcel into the bank and backfilling the hole, he could barely see for the tears streaming down his face.

When they came, as inevitably they did, Martin took them inside his church and mutely pointed up at the plain glass in the windows. 'That,' he said with total honesty, 'is the only glass you will find here in St Luke's and, as you see, our walls are undecorated.'

The men were reluctant to believe him. They had become addicted to the bullying nature of their work, and the rush of blood that came when they prised out and destroyed a beautiful example of the work of ancient hands before the tearful and distraught eyes of some rural clergyman had become almost as good as sex. They didn't like it when a journey was for nothing. They consoled themselves with kicking the walls and jeering at the tubby little priest and then they left.

Once they had disappeared up the track leading out of the village, Martin went back inside his church and collapsed on the floor in front of the altar. As soon as he could gather his thoughts, he began to pray and he didn't stop. At first unable to mutter any more than *Thank you, thank you, thank you*, soon he managed to put his deep gratitude and relief into words.

He had saved the precious panels. He had asked for help, and help had been given.

It was, he concluded, just one more example of God's love.

The years went by.

Edward didn't last long, for he had been a sickly child and

failed to grow to manhood. After him came his half-sister Mary, and now it was the Protestants who were tied to the stakes and burned alive. Martin watched from afar, distressed and horrified at the violence and the cruelty even while he was wondering if the time was right to unearth his panels and reinstate them in glory in their rightful place. But he seemed to hear a quiet, calm voice inside his head saying, *Not yet.* He thought the voice was probably God's.

He was so very glad he had listened. For Mary only lasted roughly the same length of time on the throne of England as her half-brother and then, upon her death, came the advent of Elizabeth. The country turned Protestant again and, although after a brief resurgence iconoclasm faded away, Martin remembered that quiet voice in his head and decided to leave the panels where they were.

And there they stayed.

Over the next thirty years, Martin continued with his serene, happy life. His parishioners loved him, trusted him, looked upon him as a supporter and helper in times of need and of danger, and a good friend all the rest of the time. He never forgot about the panels, but he never put them back.

He wasn't aware of the growing danger, for he lived his quiet days far from the intrigues of Elizabeth's court. He had no idea, then, of the fear that had grown up among the Queen's spymasters; of the paranoia with which they constantly searched throughout the land for secret Catholics; for old Catholic families sheltering Catholic priests; for clergymen who, while posing as good Anglicans, secretly cleaved to the old Catholic ways.

And so it was that in 1590, when the dark eyes of suspicion fell upon Martin Oude, he had absolutely no idea why they had come for him or what they wanted.

Or, luckily for Martin, what was in store.

Jonathan came out of his long reverie, for he could go no further. What came next was terrible, and he had no heart for it tonight.

He rose to his feet, extinguished the light and, knowing his way in the dark, went to bed.

THIRTEEN

When Theophilus Davey arrived back at Wrenbeare that morning after his brief visit home to change his clothes, eat a bite of breakfast, collect what he needed from his office and summon Jarman Hodge, he had already planned how he would conduct the day. He had instructed Jarman to melt away and seek out the nearest of the neighbouring properties in order to speak to the servants there, and so he approached the Fairlight house alone.

Greeted at the door – if *greet* was the right word for the resentment, loathing and suppressed anger he saw in the servant's face – Theo said immediately, 'Theophilus Davey, coroner.' He was quite sure the servant would recognize him from his earlier visit and knew full well who he was, but it didn't hurt to issue a reminder. 'I require a private room. Find me somewhere, if you please.'

The servant was short and stocky, red-faced, with broken veins in his cheeks and a big bloom of a nose. He smelled of alcohol. He was balding, and what hair he had was dark and worn long to his shoulders with a few strands arranged over the dome of his head.

Why such antipathy? Theo asked himself. He made a mental note to add it to his list of things to consider.

The servant shot him a look that might have made a lesser man back down. But Theo was large and imposing and he carried the authority of his ancient office. Not many people resisted him for long. The manservant made a hawking sound in his throat, then without a word took Theo along a short passage that led off the hall and into a decent-sized room with two windows looking south-east, wood-panelled, furnished with bookshelves, two chests and a large table with an imposing chair standing behind it. Glancing at the shelves, Theo saw thick bundles of papers, yellowing with age, and large leather-bound volumes whose bindings were cracking with neglect.

The room was, he surmised, the study of the late Sir Thomas Fairlight, justice of the peace, and, in all likelihood, nobody had touched his private papers since he died.

Theo nodded. 'This will do well.' He ran a finger across the surface of the big oak table. 'Get someone to dust this, then see that I'm left alone unless I summon one of the household.'

The man grunted something. Theo turned until they were face to face. 'What's your name and what do you do here?' he demanded curtly.

The man seemed to think about refusing to answer. Then, with a shrug, he said, 'Leagh. Once I was the butler. Nobody calls me that now . . .' He shrugged again, dismissively. 'I'm in charge of the indoor servants.'

As he spoke, Theo smelt another blast of alcohol fumes. Leagh muttered something which Theo chose not to hear, then strode away. The very sound of his footfalls on the wooden floor spoke of his anger.

Theo stood quite still for a moment, staring thoughtfully after Leagh's retreating figure. Then he put his leather bag down on the floor beside the chair. He had packed paper, quills and inkhorn, and the little penknife that had been his father's was in its usual pocket in the inside of his robe. There was no point in spreading out the impedimenta of his profession until the table had been dusted, so he followed in Leagh's footsteps and went to find the agents he'd detailed to search the house and grounds.

None of them had anything to report.

Dispirited, Theo wandered around the grounds, familiarizing himself with the layout. The front facade of the house was imposing and it was clear that, in its prime, it would have been even more appealing. Now a tangled creeper grew rampant up one wall, its roots making cracks and crevices in the brickwork, there were broken panes in some of the windows and a big patch of mould covered the wall under the overhanging roof.

Theo walked round to the rear of the house, to the yard, the outbuildings, the stables; the servants' domain. He caught sight of Christopher Hammer in the distance, in a paddock

inspecting the rear offside hoof of a skinny bay mare. Cory
sat on a fence nearby, chewing on a blade of grass.

Crossing the yard, Theo caught the stench of human waste.
The privy was concealed behind an ugly brick wall, and he
remembered the little scullery maid, Tatty, saying she'd seen
a wolf lurking behind the wall when she went out to use the
privy one night. Theo studied the scene, imagining himself
hurrying out of the stinking privy, about to dash back to the
safety of the house and suddenly aware of a big, crouching
shape in the shadows . . . Just for an instant, he had a flash
of empathy with the terrified maid.

'What did you see, little Tatty?' Theo said softly.

He would be asking her for real soon.

Back in Sir Thomas's study, the table now dusted and polished
to a shine, Theo spread out his belongings and, with a clean
sheet of paper before him and a nib charged with ink, he began
to list the people to whom he wished to speak. He had got as
far as *Avery Lond, Agnes Lond* when there was a knock on
the door.

'Come in.'

Leagh opened the door and eased his way inside, tiptoeing
across the room with exaggerated care as if keen to demonstrate that he well remembered Theo's command to be left
alone and was doing his very best to honour it.

Theo sighed.

'What is it?' he asked, deliberately keeping his expression
neutral.

'A message for you, Master Davey sir,' Leagh said,
approaching the desk and bent almost double.

'Let me have it.' Theo held out his hand.

Leagh bowed even deeper and put a piece of paper into the
outstretched hand. Theo waved him away, and he backed out
of the room and very gently closed the door.

Theo was torn between irritation and amusement. In the
end, amusement won, and he suppressed a chuckle. Unfolding
the scrap of paper, the laughter died.

He read the main paragraph of Gabriel Taverner's short
message twice, then swore under his breath. Damn the doctor,

he'd been so sure! *This man died from natural causes*, he'd said, *from starvation or some sickness.* Then there'd been all that anxiety over whether it had been leprosy, only the doctor said no.

And now he had done another examination, this time no doubt taking the trouble to do as Theo had said and carry the body into the sunlight and have a proper look, and found irrefutable evidence that the vagrant had died from suffocation.

Theo swore again, lengthily.

Then, noticing that there was something else written in small letters beneath the main block of writing, he peered at it. Gabriel had added *Sorry.*

Theo smiled. All at once he didn't feel quite so cross.

Throughout the remainder of the long morning, Theo spoke to the members of the household.

First he sent a politely worded request to Avery Lond, asking if he could be spared from tending his wife to have a few words with the coroner. It was some time before there was a response, but eventually he heard the sound of swift, brisk footsteps outside and Avery Lond, after a perfunctory tap on the door, came in.

Theo rose and indicated the second chair that he had set on the opposite side of the table. He said courteously, 'Please, Master Lond, be seated. I am very sorry to have to intrude on the grief of the family and the household but, as I am sure you appreciate, it is my duty.'

He watched very closely as Lond sat down.

Theo had done this so often. He had learned, over the years, that much could be discerned from the reaction of men in Avery Lond's position. Theo had deliberately taken the position of power in the room: he sat in the grander chair; he faced out into the room while Lond's chair was back to the door; it was he who had issued the invitation to sit down. Sometimes a man – or, indeed, a woman – would have the strength of mind to resist. They would do what they could to grasp back the reins, as if thinking, *This may be the king's coroner but it's my house, I refuse to tap at my own doors to beg entry and I'll sit where I like.*

Avery Lond crouched in his seat across from Theo as if he was a naughty schoolboy awaiting punishment.

Theo studied him in silence for a few moments. He no longer smelt of vomit and, indeed, his smooth cheeks indicated that he must have washed and shaved. His attire was entirely black, with barely an inch of white underlinen showing at the neck and cuffs of his tunic. He was a short, lightly built man, and his long neck seemed to flow into his narrow shoulders like the smooth lines of the top of a bottle. He was still very pale – perhaps it was his usual colour, Theo thought, for he had the look of an indoor sort of man – and his face was twisted in a mixture of anxiety and disapproval. His eyes, sunken deep beneath hooded lids, were small, and it was impossible to determine their colour. *Mud*, was the nearest Theo could get.

He decided to begin on a solicitous note.

'How is Mistress Lond?' he asked, making his smile sympathetic and concerned.

'Oh, my wife,' Lond breathed. He shook his head. 'She is abed and her maid has made her a succession of calming draughts, yet still she weeps and will not be comforted.'

'It is a dreadful thing to lose a mother,' Theo observed sententiously. 'And by such means!' he added, dropping his voice confidingly.

Avery Lond nodded. 'I can't get the images out of my head,' he admitted. 'I thank the good, merciful Lord that it was I and not Agnes who heard Denyse screaming and went to investigate.'

'The woman who cares for her . . .' Theo paused and gave Lond a questioning look, although he knew the name full well.

'Mary,' Lond supplied.

'Thank you. Mary did not notice when Denyse got out of bed and went downstairs?'

'Apparently not,' Lond said curtly.

Theo let the silence extend. Avery Lond began to fidget, then to wriggle in his chair, then to shoot a series of glances at Theo from under his lowering eyelids. Finally he said peevishly, 'I don't know what I can tell you! I heard nothing until Denyse's muffled screams awoke me, I saw nothing until

I looked past her and saw – saw the body.' He gulped. 'And regarding that earlier business about the person who was rumoured to have been lurking around the house, all I can do is repeat *yet again* that whoever told you that must be mistaken!' He paused, panting. 'We – Lady Clemence, God rest her soul, Agnes and I – know nothing of any intruder. *Nothing!*'

The final word was hurled at Theo like a weapon.

Theo sat calmly watching him. 'Interesting that you mention the intruder,' he murmured. 'You link the two events, then? The intruder's presence and your mother-in-law's death?'

Avery Lond opened his mouth a few times but no sound came out. His chalk-white face flushed, a pulse beat in his throat and he appeared to be choking. Finally he stood up in a sudden upthrust of energy, leaned towards Theo and spat out, '*There was no intruder!*'

Then he turned and ran out of the room.

Gazing after him, Theo decided it wasn't the moment to ask if his wife was up to a brief conversation.

He spoke to Mary next. She sat perfectly still in the chair opposite to him, hands folded in her lap, her face calm, her voice low-pitched and pleasant. She was a comely woman, with a good figure and a pleasant, if not beautiful, face, and Theo wondered idly if she was married, widowed or single. But it wasn't his business to enquire, so instead he asked her to tell him what she recollected of the previous night. She related with swift economy how she had put Denyse to bed, later retired herself, then slept soundly until roused by the commotion from downstairs.

'The days are long and they are not easy, Master Davey,' she said, 'and when I get to my bed at night, I fall asleep quickly and sleep deeply.' Her eyes held his. 'Lady Clemence, Mistress Lond and her husband appear to believe I am capable of remaining vigilant and on guard for the slightest sound or movement from my charge during all the hours of the day and night, but that is impossible.'

He nodded. 'They are demanding employers.'

She didn't answer save for a slight raising of her eyebrows.

'How is Mistress Denyse? Will she recover from the shock?'

Mary shrugged. 'The screaming has stopped, although that, I imagine, is more likely attributable to Doctor Taverner's potion than any diminution in the girl's fear and horror. At present, we are all so relieved to have the silence that we're not really thinking further ahead than the next few hours.'

He thanked her and dismissed her.

He spoke to the other indoor servants, finally summoning Tatty. The little wall-eyed girl was so terrified at being told to enter the late master's study, however, that Theo took pity on her and suggested instead that they take a walk outside.

He chatted to her about the weather, saying how good it was to see the sun again after the rain, and about how the moisture and the warmth brought out the scent of the roses. He spoke to her as gently as if she was his own small daughter, and soon she lost her fear and began to reply. Theo steered them right round the back of the house so that they ended up in the yard, close to the wall that concealed the privy.

'You saw a wolf out here, didn't you?' he asked, in the same chatty tone in which he'd been making her giggle when he told her how, as a boy, he used to put frogs in his sister's shoes. 'That must have been frightening. *I'd* have been frightened, anyway.'

She nodded, eyes wide, one focused firmly on him and the other turning in towards her nose. 'Oh, yes! It was! I ran inside and told all them in there' – she pointed at the open door into the servants' quarters – 'and they all come out and looked and said it wasn't there and there weren't no wolves no more and was I sure I hadn't made it up and I said no, I *did* see it, I really did, and it was all big and dark and lying crouched along the foot of that wall' – she pointed again – 'but I don't think they believed me, even when I said I'd heard it moaning.'

'Moaning.' He hadn't heard that detail before.

'Yes, *yes*! It weren't a howl, which I know is what wolves are said to do, it was sort of soft, and sad, and I reckoned maybe it had hurt its paw and it was in pain, and maybe it had come here to where there were people because it wanted help.'

Theo didn't think it sounded like typical wolf behaviour.

He wondered if Tatty had been listening in to some bedtime story of Mary's, as she tried to settle her charge; he was sure he recalled some tale of a wild animal having a thorn taken out of its foot and rewarding the man who helped it by refraining from eating him.

'. . . made me a calming drink and said I should go to bed,' Tatty was saying, 'so it was good, in the end, that I said I'd seen the wolf, even if it was very scary, because I got out of washing the kitchen floor and got given a sweet cake and all!' Her childish delight at these small treats was touching.

He smiled down at her. 'Thank you, Tatty, you can go now,' he said. Her face fell, and he added kindly, 'You've been very helpful.'

He watched her trot away.

Back in Sir Thomas's study, Theo gathered up his papers, quills and ink. He knew he should go home, for he could think of nothing else he could usefully do here. Whilst the thought of leaving was heartening – Wrenbeare was a strange household and all the time he was under its roof he felt uneasy, as if there was something chilly and unpleasant crawling over his skin – he felt it held secrets he hadn't even begun to uncover.

'Well, the people here are not going to reveal them to me simply because I ask,' he muttered to himself. He fastened the buckles of his bag and, hoping that Jarman Hodge had had more luck with his enquiries, strode away.

He had not been back in his office long when Jarman Hodge arrived. Theo prompted him with a jerk of the head, and Jarman gave a grunt of acknowledgement. He pulled up a stool and began to speak.

'First off,' he said without preamble, 'nobody in the neighbouring dwellings saw or heard any sign of the vagrant. No break-ins, no thefts, no strangers lurking in the shadows by night or spotted loitering by day. If we're still set on believing that there was someone at Wrenbeare, and that it was the man now lying dead in the cellar of the house up the road, we've only got Christopher Hammer's and Cory's word for it.'

'I believe them,' Theo said.

Jarman nodded. 'Reckon I do too, since I can't for the life
of me fathom out what it would benefit them to lie about it.'

'*First off*,' Theo prompted. 'You said that was the first thing.
What else?'

Jarman paused as if gathering his thoughts. Then he said,
'People were diplomatic, and a few times I had the impression
they were holding back what they really thought out of respect
for the recent tragedy.' He paused again. 'But there's something
very odd there. The family at Wrenbeare – it's as if people
are deeply wary of them. I don't think they're popular. They
clearly keep themselves to themselves, and it took them months
of searching before they managed to engage that woman who
looks after the younger sister.' He met Theo's eyes. 'Nobody
likes to go near. It's like they're scared.'

'But these are all just impressions,' Theo said in frustration.
'Have you no firm facts?'

'Rumours, old gossip, prejudice, maybe, about a family with
the misfortune to have a mad woman in their number.'

'So what does the old gossip say?' Theo pressed.

'Oh, tales of Sir Thomas,' Jarman said dismissively. 'Nothing
we haven't heard before.'

'Really?'

Jarman grinned. 'No, unless you'll credit the tale told to
me by a toothless and batty old gammer who lives on a farm
a mile or so from Wrenbeare. According to her, Sir Thomas
fell in love with an angel and lost his mind as well as his heart
when the angel spread its great white wings and flew away.'

'Unlikely, I agree,' Theo said.

He listened as Jarman briefly gave an account of the
remainder of his findings – they were indeed slim – and then
Jarman got up to go. In the doorway, he paused and turned.
'Still no sign of the weapons?'

'No, not when I left, nor of the heart.'

Even Jarman's habitual expressionless face twitched
slightly at that. 'To break someone open and tear out their
heart,' he muttered. 'What was that for? Hatred? Loathing?'
He shook his head, clearly not expecting an answer. 'What
must Lady Clemence have done, to have earned such a terrible
retribution?'

With a nod of farewell, he took himself off.

Theo, thoughtful suddenly, sat on at his desk, quite still, thinking, for a long time.

And at last the interminable day crawled to its end.

FOURTEEN

I woke early, struggling up out of a dream whose details vanished with sleep, leaving me with nothing more than a confused and slightly frightening sense that I was hunting for something and would endanger myself and others if I didn't find it.

I lay for a short time watching the growing daylight. There were no sounds other than the birds outside and I surmised that my household still slept.

My mind wandered.

Then out of nowhere I remembered an element of my dream – an infant, a soft blanket, a smile of love – and suddenly I thought, *Agnes Lond has no children.*

She was no new, young bride. She was past thirty – someone had told me that but I didn't pause to recall who it had been – and she and her husband lived under the roof of her familial home. It might be threadbare and a little dilapidated, but it was a far better dwelling than that of anyone else for miles around.

So, adequately housed, with food in the larder and her family and servants around, *why* did she and her husband have no children?

I remembered Josiah Thorn speaking about the young Clemence when she had been selected as Thomas Fairlight's bride. *She was ungainly and unattractive, poor girl, and nobody had asked for her hand before.* And, a little later: *Matters might have improved had she turned out to be good breeding stock and given birth to a succession of big, healthy babies but she couldn't even achieve that.*

I thought about that. As I did so, I was forced to recognize the breadth of my ignorance concerning women's reproductive systems. If a woman had difficulties conceiving and carrying babies to term, was that a tendency that her daughters would inherit? Fecundity seemed to pass down from mother to daughter – I could think of several local farming families where the generations seemed to pile up with evident ease, so that grandparents and great-aunts lived with their sons and daughters and a tribe of grandchildren, babies arriving to couples with the regularity of the harvest. So it seemed quite possible that the opposite might also apply.

I knew who I needed to speak to.

Telling myself that I had no choice since I really needed her advice, and trying to ignore the lift of the heart and the spirits that the idea of being with her in the near future was giving me, I got up, washed, shaved, found a clean shirt, brushed the worst of the mud and the stains off my leather jerkin and quietly went downstairs.

I cleared the kitchen without alerting Sallie, although I could hear her singing in her room and knew she'd be emerging quite soon and beginning the bustle that was breakfast in my house. The yard, too, seemed empty, and I was just introducing the bit into Hal's mouth and bucking the bridle when I heard movement behind me and turned to see Tock.

He stepped forward as if to take over the task, shaking his head in consternation and muttering something incoherent. Tock is simple, and he likes his routines. For his master to saddle his own horse is not what usually happens, and Tock's disquiet was evident. Although I knew full well it would take him twice as long, it was easier simply to stand back and let him get on with it.

'Thank you, Tock,' I said gravely when at last he had finished and was leading Hal out into the low sunshine and the long early morning shadows. I mounted and then leaning down to him, said slowly and carefully, 'I am going visiting and shall be some time. Tell Samuel to inform Sallie, please.'

He repeated the instructions under his breath, forehead furrowed in concentration. Reflecting that Samuel would see for himself that I'd gone out since Hal was no longer in his stall, and that it didn't really matter what garbled version of what I'd said reached Samuel's ears, I nodded to Tock, put my heels to Hal's sides and clattered off.

Once I was safely away from Rosewyke and heading towards the river, it occurred to me to wonder if it wasn't far too early to make calls. Then I told myself that she was a busy woman, used to urgent knocks on her door at all hours. I rode on.

It was a beautiful morning. The recent storms seemed to have abated for the moment, and the dome of the sky was clear as far as the eye could see. The sweet, nutty smell of gorse flowers under soft sunshine reached up to me from the hedgerows, and in some way it recalled the scent of some of the tropical islands I'd visited during my years at sea. It reminded me of coconut oil, I realized.

Too soon, for I hadn't managed to convince myself that it was a decent hour for visiting, I was riding along the track that led to Judyth's little house.

The ironic glance she gave me as she opened the door a short time later suggested she shared my misgivings. 'You'll not have breakfasted,' she said as she turned and walked off down the narrow corridor, no doubt assuming I was following, 'so why not come out into the sunshine and have some of mine?'

'Thank you.'

Her courtyard was exquisite. The dew sparkled on the herbs and the flowers, the birds sang, the sun was warm on my back, the mingled scents were as potent as good wine. And I sat on a comfortable chair across a sturdy little oak table from a very beautiful woman who was setting out bread, butter, honey and fresh-picked raspberries on a platter for me as if she did it every day of her life.

'Now,' she said once we had taken the edge off our hunger, 'pleasant as it is to share breakfast with you, Doctor Gabriel, I am quite sure it's not why you're here.' She reached out and topped up my mug from the jug of small beer. 'So, what can I do for you?' She smiled faintly. 'After more mandragora, are you?'

I looked at her, taking in the alert, interested expression in her light eyes. I thought in that moment that it was more than likely she might know the household at Wrenbeare; she was too young, surely, to have attended Lady Clemence unless it had been as a very young child apprentice, but she could easily have been consulted by Agnes Lond as she tried and failed to conceive.

I had two choices. I could present my enquiry as if it were simply a general one, and the result of a stray thought that had occurred to me. Or I could come clean, reveal my interest in the Fairlight family and ask her how much she was prepared to tell me.

I was still looking into her eyes. As well as being beautiful, they were also full of intelligence. She would see through my ruse of a disinterested query even as I spoke it, so I opted for honesty.

'I don't need more mandragora, thank you,' I said. 'It worked just as you said it would, and afterwards the dogs were none the worse for it.'

She nodded. 'Good. Go on.'

And then there was no option but to plunge straight in. 'Do you know the family of Sir Thomas Fairlight, at the house known as Wrenbeare on the edge of the moors?'

Her bright expression turned sombre and I realized she'd heard the news. 'Yes.' Slowly she shook her head. 'I cannot believe what has happened to poor Lady Clemence.' She hesitated. 'And Denyse found her body, I'm told.'

'She did.'

Her eyes narrowed slightly. 'You were there?'

'Yes.' Since I'd come to her for information, it seemed only fair to give some too. 'Not at the time, but soon after. I was summoned by Theophilus Davey, the coroner.'

She nodded. 'Master Davey, yes. He wanted your opinion concerning the body?'

'He did. There was no doubt she was dead, for the heart was missing.'

Judyth's face paled. 'Her *heart* . . . But why? Why should anyone do something so very brutal?'

'I don't know.' Her horror at what I'd just told her was evident in her expression and I decided to capitalize on her compassion. 'Some people are saying Denyse killed her mother.'

'But not you?'

I shook my head. 'No, but it may not be easy to still the gossiping tongues unless the true culprit can be quickly found.' I felt guilty over the way I was misleading her, but I really did need her help. 'I thought you might know the family, as indeed it seems you do, and, in answer to the question you just asked, what you can do for me is tell me everything you can about them.' I saw the quick frown cross her brows and I hurried on. 'This was, as you just said, a brutal crime, and what I've learned so far suggests that the reason for it lies in the past: to be specific, that it is somehow connected with Sir Thomas and what he may or may not have done.'

'Sir Thomas,' she repeated very softly. 'I see.' Then, a smile quickly appearing and as quickly vanishing again, she added, 'Well, I *don't* see, really. Why don't you say what's on your mind?'

I paused briefly to think, then began. 'Clemence Sulyard married Thomas Fairlight when she was a very young woman. He married because he needed a wife to disguise his true nature, and she accepted him because nobody else had asked for her. She was plain and ungainly, and she perhaps felt she had failed in the prime duty of a maiden, which is to be attractive. Then, with marriage, she realized she was also failing in the main duty of a wife, because it was three years before her first daughter arrived and another six until the second one followed.'

'Thomas Fairlight was not attracted to women.'

'Yes, I know, but he must have forced himself to bed his wife from time to time for the two daughters to be born.' I was on shaky ground here but I made myself go on. 'Unless we are to believe that there were but two acts of generation, each of which resulted in the birth of one of Clemence's two children – which could be true but for the fact that I'm told she had miscarriages between the births – then we must surely assume that intercourse was reasonably regular.' I was confusing even myself. Judyth kept resolutely silent, and I had the distinct impression she was enjoying my discomfiture and determined to let me struggle on unaided. 'Someone else I spoke to said that Clemence was not good breeding stock, and then, when I realized that her daughter Agnes is childless, I wondered whether the ease or the difficulty with which a woman conceives, carries and bears healthy children is passed on to her daughters. If she has any,' I added somewhat lamely. I was beginning to feel very foolish under Judyth's silent scrutiny.

For quite some time after I'd finished speaking the silence continued, although thankfully Judyth had looked away and was now staring out over the lavender bushes that encircled the little space where we sat. Then, at last, she sighed and said, 'I will forgive your ignorance, Doctor, since I know full well that what limited professional experience you have so far had of women and their bodies is largely book-learned, although no doubt that is in the process of changing.' She shot me a quick glance. 'It is true that some women are not *good breeding stock*, as you put it.' Her light emphasis on the words made me squirm, and I understood then how harsh and dismissive they must have sounded. 'Sometimes there are very apparent reasons why a woman desperate for a child does not conceive. I can help if, for example, a particularly young and innocent couple are not entirely sure of the correct procedure, or if, as I have known, a thin and undernourished girl does not menstruate regularly and requires a better diet to make her body work as it should.' She paused. 'Sometimes the fault is beyond my help, as when a woman conceives with no difficulty but cannot carry a child beyond a few weeks or months, or when babies are born but are so sickly and frail that they do not survive.' She sighed. 'There is joy in my work, Doctor, but also unbelievable pain.'

I nodded. I didn't feel able to speak, having nothing to say and doubting my voice would sound as steady as I'd like.

Presently she said, 'In asking about Lady Clemence's ability as a breeder, you do no more than follow what almost every other physician does, for you are all men and you view conception, pregnancy and birth as exclusively female matters. Why, can you tell me, do you all fail to realize that there is another side to the process?'

'But the male role is over and done with right at the start!' I protested. 'The rest is up to the woman.'

'Perhaps,' she agreed. 'Yet what makes up the baby? What turns a woman's unfertilized egg into the foetus that nestles inside her womb and emerges as a living child?'

'The sperm of the man,' I replied promptly and impatiently. 'Naturally, I know that!'

'You may know it but you do not understand the implications,' she said sternly. 'You do not have the experience that I have, so sit and listen to what I'm telling you.' She too sounded impatient, and in her case the mood was verging on anger. 'I have known cases of women married to men and unable to bear a child; dismissed, no doubt, as *poor breeders.*' I seemed to hear the dismissive tones of countless men in those two harsh words. 'Then, widowed, those same women remarry and go on to bear healthy child after healthy child. Just why, Doctor Gabriel, do you imagine that happens?' Leaning closer – so close that I could feel the heat emanating from her, see the fury in her eyes – she added in a hissing whisper, 'And what of the old king, eh? Six wives, and but three children from all those hundreds, thousands of couplings, one of them dead before he reached manhood, one of them a sad, twisted woman whose sick mind told her it carried a child in her barren body when in truth it was no more than a growth! All of them, all six queens, poor breeding stock? *Really,* Doctor?'

She leaned back, panting slightly.

And I knew she was right.

It was something that had struck me on occasion before. Judyth was quite right to cite my limited medical experience of women and breeding, however, and I had not studied or indeed thought about the subject very much.

I thought about it now.

After quite a long time I said, 'So you think it might have been Sir Thomas who was the poor breeder?'

'I do.'

'And, if you are right, just what do you think ailed him?'

She gave me a long, pitying look. 'What do *you* think?'

Riding home, I thought about all that she had told me. I should have realized; I knew that. My excuse – and after her critical analysis of me and my shortcomings I felt I needed one – was that, although I knew a great deal about the condition she suspected of causing Sir Thomas's failure, it was in another guise and at a different stage of development. Now, kicking Hal to a canter, I wanted to be in my study, the long record of my years at sea spread out before me so that I could go back over all the cases I treated and documented.

As if to make up for what he saw as his earlier lapse, Tock was waiting, ready to take Hal and tend to him. I hoped he hadn't been standing there all the time I'd been out but suspected he probably had. Samuel, picking up that I was in a hurry, did not detain me as I ran inside the house. There was no sign of Celia, and Sallie, after asking if I wanted dinner soon, shut herself up in her kitchen.

Then I was up the stairs and in my study, precisely where I wanted to be, my books open, a quill in my hand, paper and ink at the ready. And there were my drawings, my paragraphs of description, my detailed accounts of what I'd tried with this man or that, of what had helped, what had had no effect, what had caused pointless pain and made matters worse. I read, I looked, I made notes, I learned.

And what I learned was frightful.

We called it the French disease, the *morbus Gallicus*, and without doubt the French reciprocated and attributed its origins to the English. But in truth nobody could know for sure where it came from, for all that it had been around for decades and probably centuries. Setting aside my own notebooks, I got up and fetched a tome from my shelves. It was the fifth book in the series *Practica in arte chirurgica copiosa*, a work by an Italian surgeon, Giovanni de Vigo, written in 1514, in which he set out the ghastly progress of the disease from the first brownish, ulcerated pimples on the genitals to the headaches, rash, fever and joint pains that followed after a month or six weeks, so severe that the patient would emit cries of anguish. Sometimes the symptoms would abate, but only to reappear a year or more later.

I ran my eyes down de Vigo's words, then fetched a second book, written thirteen years later by a Frenchman, Jacques de

Bethencourt, which, making no bones about it, he entitled *A New Litany of Penitence.* For if he too had little idea where the sickness emanated from, he, like everyone else, knew full well how it was spread. *Morbus venerus,* he called it; venereal disease. It arose, or so he maintained, from illicit love, and so it was the malady of Venus.

Finally I looked at a work written in 1530 by a Veronese physician, Girolamo Fracastoro, in which he repeated the tale of a shepherd named Syphilus, who he claimed was the first man to suffer from the French disease. He ascribed the unfortunate shepherd's name to the disease, and upon reading that, I was reminded that I'd heard other doctors in the Mediterranean refer to it thus, although to the best of my knowledge we did not do so in England.

The innumerable cases that I had observed and treated had been among my sailors. And that was why I had been so slow to comprehend: because I had never had a patient in whose body the disease still surged after a decade, two decades, three. It was an awful thought, to contemplate somebody who, believing themselves to have been sick in their youth but with the malady long past and all but forgotten, suddenly discovered on their body – and in their mind – evidence to the contrary.

The disease was feared and despised. And there was no hiding it, for its symptoms were all too evident. In its last phase there were abscesses, debility and madness and the sufferers were ostracized; despised because the marks they bore were perceived as the stigmata of sin.

There was no cure.

The most I had ever managed was an alleviation of symptoms. I would administer guaiacum, also known as holy wood, and mercury in the form of injections and ointments. Sometimes I'd suggest a sweat bath, as it was believed that profuse salivating and sweating could flush out the poisons. The only thing that did any lasting good was the mercury, and that produced the most terrible side-effects: gaping sores on the lips and inside the mouth, loss of teeth, even kidney failure.

I set aside my books, leaning back in my chair in despair at what I'd read; at the unwelcome reminder that all of us, even learned physicians, are helpless in the face of the virulent power of disease.

After some time, I went back to work.

Judyth had told me something which, although I was reluctant to believe, I suspected was correct: that a woman who has been infected with the disease can, if the sickness is in an active state at the time, pass it on to the child she carries. And a child so infected is sickly, does not thrive, has rashes and sores on the body and inexplicable fevers. There are also quite often deformities, since the bones and the organs do not develop as they should. As I turned the pages, eyes scanning the wise words of others, I accepted that Judyth had been correct.

And I began to understand the truth.

I stood up, stiff from sitting so long hunched over my books. The tray of food that Sallie had brought up unknown hours ago sat untouched. I wasn't hungry.

Now I was on my feet I was restless. I paced up and down the room, impatient for something, although I didn't know what. I felt that I had made a discovery that was somehow very relevant to what was happening, but I couldn't for the life of me think how.

I couldn't contain my sudden energy. I dashed out of the room, down the stairs and outside to the yard. Anticipating my need, Samuel was already tacking up my horse.

FIFTEEN

It was already quite late in the afternoon, judging from the angle of the sun. I knew I should go to see Theo, for he would have been throwing himself into the investigation of Lady Clemence's death all day and could very well have much to tell me.

But all my thoughts were bent on what had occupied *me* all day. I knew myself well enough to understand that I would be no use to Theo or anyone else until I had followed that particular trail all the way to the end.

So for a third time I rode out to Buckland.

I gambled on Josiah having packed up his fishing for the day, if indeed he had been down by the river, and being back at his house, perhaps thinking about his supper. I tethered Hal outside the fence enclosing his small garden and went up the path to the door.

It was open, and from within I heard Josiah humming to himself. I paused only to tap on the door, going on inside and calling out, 'Doctor? It's Gabriel Taverner. Is it all right if I come in?'

I went through the kitchen into the scullery, where he was bent over a bowl washing out a gutted trout. 'Why bother to ask,' he said mildly, 'since you are already here?'

I grinned. 'Sorry. I have to talk to you.'

'Ah.' Carefully he dried his fish and laid it on the marble slab on which the bowl sat, covering it with a piece of cloth. 'Then you'd better come through and sit down.'

I think he knew why I was there, even before I'd said more than those few words.

We took our seats and without preamble I said, 'You told me that Clemence Fairlight was of poor breeding stock, for in nearly twenty years of marriage she bore only two daughters, although she also suffered at least a couple of miscarriages.'

'That is the truth!' he protested hotly, as if I'd accused him of lying.

'The childbearing history is true, I grant you,' I agreed. 'Although I dispute that the absence of more children was any fault of Lady Clemence's.'

'She—' he began. Then, meeting my eyes, he stopped.

'I have spent much of the day studying the opinions of learned men,' I said softly. 'Men who know so much more about their subject than I, and who have taken the trouble to observe and record.' I leaned closer to him. 'I understand that you cannot breach the confidential nature of the doctor's relationship with his patient, so I shall not ask you to.' He relaxed infinitesimally. 'Instead,' I went on, 'I shall tell you what I believe happened to Thomas Fairlight and to the unfortunate

and recently dead woman who had the misfortune to become
his wife.'

Josiah opened his mouth to protest, his eyes wide with
distress. But then, slowly, he subsided. He nodded. 'Go on,'
he said dully.

'Last time I was here,' I began, 'you told me of Sir Thomas's
wild youth. Now what I believe is that in one of those early
sexual encounters he was infected, and he suffered the onset
of the symptoms that I myself treated so many times during
my years as a ship's surgeon.'

I waited to see if Josiah would protest, or make some
comment. He did neither.

'Now the nature of my work at sea meant that I rarely, if
ever, had the chance to follow up a case of *morbus venerus*,'
I continued. 'Sufferers went out of my care, or because of
some injury or incapacity they left the sea, or they were killed.
Thus it is that in my years as a doctor I have never seen what
happens to a man – or, I suppose, a woman – who has carried
the disease in their body for decades.' I had his rapt attention
now; I could tell by how very still he was sitting.

'As I just said, I have today been rectifying this gap in my
experience. I now know how the sickness, pretending to have
left the body, in fact does nothing of the sort. How it lurks,
unseen, unfelt, biding its time, sometimes putting in a brief
appearance and providing the sufferer with a fresh outbreak
of sores, pains, fever, perhaps some abscesses. Then, once
again, the malady goes dormant. But as the years go on the
recurrences grow more severe, and in time the patient's mind
is affected.'

I paused again, for I thought I had heard Josiah give a sigh.
Looking up at me, he nodded and waved an impatient hand.
'Continue,' he said.

'This afternoon I read a description of a man in the throes
of the final stage of *morbus venerus*,' I said. 'I will summarize,
if I may. He went deaf and almost blind. His character altered,
so that where he had been amiable and cheery, he became
violent, highly suspicious, convinced his loved ones were
trying to kill him. He was in constant, agonizing pain, in his
head, in his muscles. His memory went and he could not

concentrate for more than a few moments at a time, after which his mind would soar away into horrible visions that he believed were real events, being enacted in the room where he lay. His face became strangely expressionless. He was unable to control his bladder or bowels. His heart pained him and its beat became inconstant and erratic. He—'

But Josiah put up a shaking hand. 'Enough,' he breathed. I waited.

After what seemed a long time he said, 'It is a terrible disease. A scourge; a fit punishment, some say, for the sin of fornication, although for myself, I do not believe that the loving God inflicts such agonies on his children.'

His remark interested me, and I stored it away for future discussion. Now was not the time.

'You know it well because you have treated a sufferer,' I said. 'No, don't try to protest, for I shan't believe you. And I will further surmise that Sir Thomas infected Lady Clemence and that one, if not both, of his daughters bore the sickness from birth.'

He shot me a look. 'What makes you say that?' he barked.

'Agnes Lond is childless, Denyse Fairlight is gravely deformed in body and diseased in mind.' My words were cruelly blunt, but I was in no mood to dissemble.

'Oho, so you've been reading about that, too, I suppose?' he demanded.

'Yes I have,' I shouted. 'Another source helpfully listed the symptoms of children born to a diseased mother. Sores and rashes, failure to thrive, sickly, jaundiced, with short limbs and twisted bodies. Malformation of the bones of the face, so that the teeth are oddly spaced and the nose a peculiar shape.'

Once again he waved a hand as if in surrender.

'I do not wish to distress you,' I said after a short silence. 'I am certain that I am right, and—'

'If you're certain, why are you here in my house bothering me in my peace?' he flashed back.

I let that go.

'I am working with the coroner as he tries to establish the facts of Lady Clemence's murder,' I said when I was sure I could speak calmly. 'I told you before that we're working on the theory that it was somehow in revenge for the misdeeds of the past; of Sir Thomas's past, specifically. If I am right in my conclusions regarding what ailed him, and indeed what ails his family, then it is possible others lay the blame for their own sickness, or that of those they love, at his door.'

I expected him to shout at me again. To protest that he couldn't possibly confirm or refute my supposition. That I should shut my foul, accusing mouth, stop spreading slander about an innocent man who was no longer alive to defend himself and get out.

But he didn't.

He put his hands up to his face and rubbed it vigorously a few times. Then, lowering his hands, he said softly, 'I did what I could for him, but it was little enough. And, God help me, a part of me thought he had earned his suffering for he was a terrible man, made a thousand times worse by that sickness-induced madness. When his agonized, labouring heart finally gave up, I fell on my knees in gratitude to the Lord for deliverance.'

His hands covered his face again and I saw his shoulders shake as he silently sobbed.

Without thinking, I got up and went over to him. 'Do not punish yourself,' I said quietly, my arm around his back. 'You did what you could, of that I have no doubt. From what I have learned nothing would have saved him, and I'm tempted to think that a man signs his own death warrant the moment the sickness enters his body.' Encouraged by the fact that Josiah was no longer sobbing – and furthermore hadn't thrown off my arm – I went on. Leaning in closer, for what I was about to say was for his ears only, I murmured, 'As to your vast relief when finally he died, do not distress yourself over it. Who amongst us, who spend our lives trying to alleviate the pains of the sick and the suffering, can deny we've felt exactly the same on occasion, if we're to be honest? The honour is in the trying, Doctor. Provided it does not affect the thoroughness and the intensity of our efforts to heal and to save life, what we feel in the privacy of our own hearts is our own affair.'

He was still now, and I felt the tension seep out of him. I returned to my chair.

Presently he dropped his hands again. He was pale, his face drawn. He looked at me, his eyes calm. He said simply, 'Thank you. The death of Sir Thomas Fairlight is a burden I have borne for many years. It is good – more than good' – he smiled faintly – 'to put it down.'

The mood, I felt, needed to be lightened. 'You're welcome,' I said. 'One day I shall no doubt ask you to do the same for me.'

Evening was advancing as I rode away from Buckland and headed for Theo's house. I became aware how tired I was. But my day was not yet finished; I had the strong sense that Theo had been trying to contact me, and, since I hadn't told anybody where I was going when I set out so precipitately to see Josiah, he'd have had no luck.

The door was ajar and there were appetizing smells of supper wafting around in Theo's hall. The sudden, violent gurgling of my stomach reminded me that I hadn't eaten since my bread and honey with Judyth early that morning. I was just wondering if I could beg Elaine for a morsel or two to eat when the door to Theo's office was flung open and he erupted into the hall.

'Where the *hell* have you been?' he demanded. His face was flushed and his hair stood on end as if he'd been repeatedly raking his fingers through it, as no doubt he had. 'I've been hunting all over for you and no less than three of my men have been out to your house looking for you!'

'I was at home from mid-morning to late afternoon,' I said courteously. 'I was up in my study.' Guiltily recalling the deep concentration with which I'd pored over my books, I recognized the distinct possibility that someone had come knocking and I hadn't noticed. If the rest of my household had been absent, then any number of Theo's men could have come and been disappointed. 'I may not have heard,' I admitted.

But Theo had already dived back inside his office, beckoning me to follow. 'What news?' I asked as I followed him.

'Hah! Bugger-all!' he said.

'Nothing found?'

'Nothing.'

'Then why did you want to see me so urgently?'

'Because I thought *you* might have come up with something!' he said, with the air of a man forced to put into words the self-evident.

I suppressed a smile.

'And you have no more idea as to the perpetrator?' I asked.

'No, although I appear to have succeeded in diverting suspicion from that poor little mad daughter.'

That, I supposed, was something.

I almost asked him what he'd been doing all day to have achieved such a paucity of results, but thought better of it.

Theo, I noticed, was deep in thought, a frown on his face. 'I *hate* Wrenbeare,' he said suddenly. 'I hate the mood there. It's . . . not normal. It makes me feel very uncomfortable.'

I understood exactly what he meant. 'Me too.'

He looked up at me. 'Why is that?'

I shrugged. 'The evil nature of the family's past, perhaps.' Before he could ask me to elucidate, I told him.

He was silent for some time when I'd finished. 'So we have some more substance to our theory that Lady Clemence's murder is for revenge,' he muttered eventually. 'Someone acting on behalf of the vagrant, are we thinking? If Sir Thomas infected the man's wife, then—'

'Not his wife,' I put in gently.

'Ah. No, of course,' Theo said. He fell silent again. 'But it's all so uncertain!' he burst out. 'A thin, insubstantial stranger who might or might not have broken in and been chased away, a batty little maid who says she saw a wolf, and *nothing*, not one single thing, to give us any idea of why he was there and what he wanted, or what he saw that he shouldn't have seen, or what he knew of the Fairlight family past that they didn't want made public, and now he's dead, *if* it was the same man, and Lady Clemence is dead too, and I am no further forward than I was the instant I was summoned to view her body!'

I fully understood his frustration and wished that I could offer a glimmer of light on his darkness. 'I'm sorry, Theo, I—'

But with a shout he suddenly plunged into the litter and drift of papers and documents strewn across his desk. He rummaged for several moments, muttering under his breath.

I made out a succession of curses, each stronger than the one before. Then he said, 'I'd put it safely away, for it is precious; sacred, perhaps; but then I got it out again to look at and I was interrupted, and it's here somewhere, it *has* to be!'

Finally he had what he sought.

His eyes on me, he held it out. 'There's this,' he said.

I took it from him. It was the piece of heavy paper, torn across, that we'd found on the body of the dead vagrant.

I unfolded it, smoothed out the creases and, the shock running through me, stared down at the image drawn upon it.

It was beautiful.

The face was androgynous. Perhaps the artist, depicting an angel, hadn't wanted to ascribe either male or female sex to a being purely of the spirit. The hair was light, hanging smoothly either side of the face, and indicated by a series of straight lines. The eyes, deep under straight brows, were full of anguish; of sorrow and pain; of fear. The nose sat well-formed and perfectly straight above the mouth, whose full lips looked as if they had been carved. The high cheekbones stood out clearly, hollows angled beneath them. The rip that bisected the paper ran from high on the subject's right cheek to halfway along the firm chin.

'I can barely tear my eyes off him,' Theo said quietly, looking over my shoulder. 'If indeed it is a he.'

'I know,' I agreed. 'It is utterly compelling.'

'My daughter said he was sad,' he went on. 'She asked if I could make him happy again.' He paused, then said diffidently, 'Do you think it's Christ? The suffering, the deep pain, the compassion?'

'It's not Christ,' I said.

'How can you know?' Theo demanded, stung that I had dismissed his suggestion so summarily.

'This is the preparatory drawing for an angel,' I said softly. 'The angel in the glass.'

'What are you *talking* about?' Theo cried. 'What angel?'

I didn't know if I should tell him. Jonathan had asked for my help, and I'd known without being told that what we did had to be kept secret. It was dangerous for such things to become common knowledge . . .

But Theo was trying to find a murderer. The dead vagrant had to be involved somehow with Wrenbeare and he'd been found with this sketch on his body; the sketch that had been used for the violently erotic panel that had been hidden away with Jonathan's sacred images.

Making up my mind, I handed the sketch back and Theo wrapped it in a piece of plain paper and tucked it away inside his robe, out of sight. I thought he was praying as he did so. Then I said, 'Come with me. We have to go to Tavy St Luke's.'

I was too impatient to see the Angel panel again to be circumspect. I said quietly to Jonathan when he came to the door, clearly surprised to see Theo standing beside me, 'I have to show the Angel to the coroner. I'm sorry, Jonathan, I know you were planning to keep the existence of all six of the panels a secret for a while longer, even if you'll ever be willing to show the final one to anyone else, but I believe this is very important and I have no choice.'

He had been frowning as I started to speak, but now, apparently accepting the inevitable, he stood aside and Theo and I went in. 'Go and sit down,' he said, nodding a greeting to Theo. 'I will fetch the last panel.'

He was not gone long. He unwrapped the sacking and swept aside the straw padding, and the Angel panel lay on its wrappings under our scrutiny.

'It's not medieval, like the others,' Jonathan murmured.

Theo shot me a look and mouthed, '*Others?*'

I'd forgotten he didn't know about the St Luke panels, the flowers, the jolly nuns and the lilies of the field. 'Later,' I hissed.

'I've been thinking, Gabriel, since last we spoke,' Jonathan went on, 'and I believe this can be dated to the later years of Elizabeth's reign, at a time when, with the danger of destruction by the iconoclasts over at last, some of the old families thought it safe to replace their lost glass. I have come across similar examples, and both the technique and the very vivid colours put me in mind of them.'

'Yes,' I said distractedly.

Theo had as yet made no comment. He hadn't taken his

eyes off the beautiful, naked figure, its worshipper kneeling at its feet.

'Unlike the sketch, the figure in the panel is very definitely male,' he observed. 'And he is perfect.' He reached out a hand and very gently touched the snowy wings. He laughed apologetically. 'You almost expect them to feel soft. And the face!' He reached inside his robe for the drawing, unwrapped it and spread it out. 'The beauty is there, but the angel does not look so sad.'

Jonathan gave a gasp, dropping to the floor and leaning down over the sketch. 'It is the same man.'

'The same, yes, but only just a man, wouldn't you say?' I replied. 'Fifteen, sixteen?'

Jonathan was looking from panel to drawing and back again. 'Yes, perhaps. But who is he?'

'The drawing was found in the possession of the vagrant believed to have broken into the Fairlight home, Wrenbeare,' Theo said.

'Then it's not – he can't be Thomas Fairlight, surely?'

I thought quickly, calculating in my head. 'No. I have no idea what Sir Thomas looked like, but if you're right about when this panel was made, then he'd have been too old to have been the model. He was born in the 1530s' – I tried and failed to recall the exact year – 'and he'd have been almost fifty years old by 1580.'

We fell silent. Such was the power of the angel that it seemed to have robbed us of speech.

But presently Theo gave a soft exclamation. 'Jarman Hodge told me something he'd heard, although it sounds like no more than some garbled version of an old legend.'

'Tell us anyway,' I said.

'An old woman said there had been an angel that came to earth, and Thomas Fairlight fell down and worshipped it, but then it spread its wings and flew away and he died of a broken heart.' He shook his head impatiently. 'It was something of the sort, anyway.'

'Broken heart,' I repeated, chilled all at once.

Theo, understanding, said, 'And somebody took out Lady Clemence's heart. *Broke* it, perhaps.'

'Because, years ago, this man, this boy' – I indicted the angel – 'broke Sir Thomas's?'

'But it makes no sense!' Jonathan exclaimed.

Of all the things that we said that night, it was the only inarguably true statement.

SIXTEEN

I slept poorly, my mind far too busy with thoughts and vague ideas that chased each other and never quite caught up sufficiently to make any sense. In the end, as dawn began to pale the eastern sky, I gave up and, drawing on my clothes, went along to my study. With a fresh piece of paper before me and my quill loaded with ink, I began to make a brief account of everything that had happened since I'd been called to see the body of the dead vagrant up on the edge of the moor.

And presently, as so often happens when a logical, step-by-step analysis is made, I was reminded of a little detail that had apparently been forgotten.

The night I went to help Jonathan dig up the panels, Theo had come out to Rosewyke looking for me. When he told me, I'd had the clear impression he was irritated that I hadn't been there when he needed to talk to me. When I'd enquired what it was about, he'd curtly mentioned a big man who looked like a vagrant, creeping timidly into his office and asking about a missing friend.

But I'd been preoccupied, and thought no more about it. I'd presumed, as far as I'd presumed anything, that Theo would have sent someone out to look for his shy visitor if he thought the man had anything useful to tell him, and if not, would have let him quietly disappear back to wherever he'd come from. And I'd had concerns of my own, first the extraordinary discovery of the panels and then the murder of Lady Clemence.

There had been a name that the big vagrant had mentioned; I clearly recalled Theo telling me we now had a name for the dead man. I scratched around in the deep recesses of my mind and finally came up with it: Jannie.

Did the name go with the body, or was it no more than coincidence that had sent the big man hunting for his missing friend just at the time when a body had been found? I had two options: I could tell myself it was pure chance – there were so many vagrants in the land, too many hopeless, homeless, destitute and sick men and women wandering the roads, the tracks and the out-of-the-way places, and nothing, really, to say that the dead body was that of the big man's friend – and forget about it. Or I could postulate that there was a connection, explore that possibility and see where it led.

Well, there was nowhere else to go.

Putting my nib to the page, I began to write.

And soon, as my hand began to move faster to keep up with my thoughts, other half-forgotten facts seemed to spring out at me.

The big, dark wolf seen lurking at the foot of the privy wall at Wrenbeare by little Tatty.

The elderly woman who had discovered someone hiding behind her henhouse; someone who had run off with a capful of eggs.

The limp, withered honeysuckle flower that I'd found on the floor beneath the vagrant's body on its trestle in the crypt of the empty house.

And I thought of that lonely, comfortless ruin of a dwelling up on the fringes of the moor, where the body had been discovered.

Staring blindly out of my window, gradually the realization came that it was now full daylight. For the second day running, I left my house before any of my household was up, and this time I set out for the moors.

I wasn't sure if I would remember the way, but it seemed that my unconscious mind must have been taking note of the route, even as I'd ridden along beside Theo listening to the birdsong. Quite soon the little cluster of buildings loomed up on the track ahead of me, the largest of them standing out, taller than the rest. The door was still off its hinges, still leaning against the left-hand wall that propped it in place.

I tethered Hal carefully. I had a sudden horror of something startling him, so that he ran off and left me stranded there. It was an absurd fancy, for Hal was well-behaved and had never once acted like that. But there was something about that lonely place that seemed to haunt; that made the small hairs on the back of the neck stand up in sudden alarm.

I pushed the door aside and strode into the room.

On my previous visit I'd been too preoccupied with the body to take much notice of the surroundings, and I'd observed little beyond the holes in the roof, the dangerously dilapidated state of the walls and the terrible stench. Now there was no body – the room was empty of any living thing save spiders and a buzz of flies in the smelliest corner – and I slowly turned in a circle, looking all around.

An oval of stones indicated where a fire had been built, although now there was no more to see than some charred ends of sticks which, when I bent down to place my hand over them, were cold and dead. There was no neat stack of firewood; no pail of stream water; no indication that someone intended to return here with a snared hare or a clutch of stolen eggs to cook in a tin pan over a friendly little blaze.

I continued my survey.

In the corner furthest from the swarming flies there was a bundle of some sort. Approaching it, I tentatively poked it with the toe of my boot, so that it unwound itself and I saw it was an old blanket, stained, stiff with dirt, holes along one edge as if it had been singed. I crouched down to look more carefully.

I was quite sure it hadn't been there when the vagrant's body had been discovered and removed, for if it had, surely Theo would have instructed his men to take it away. He'd been searching for a full identity for the body – he probably still was – and he wouldn't have left any clue abandoned there.

And that meant that, despite the dead fire, someone had been here since the vagrant's death.

Fired with sudden certainty, I set about a more thorough

search but, other than a pile of pigeon bones in a shallow grave just outside the door which might have been there for weeks if not longer, I found nothing else.

I untied Hal's reins and mounted. I sat for a while looking around, but there were no other settlements in view.

So where was he?

I reviewed what I did know of his movements and recalled the elderly woman and her henhouse. For want of anything better to do, I turned Hal's head and rode off in the direction of the little settlement where she lived.

'No, no, Doctor, I've not seen him again, nor had none of my eggs not stolen neither!' she said when I approached her in the tidy little yard behind her house. 'I've kept my eyes peeled, see, and I've had my rattlers handy to scare him off.' She reached out for a selection of bent and battered old pan lids, loosely tied together with string, and, holding them up, shook them vigorously. They made an appallingly loud noise. 'Thieves don't like it if you let 'em know you've spotted 'em,' she said authoritatively, 'and anyway my neighbours all come running when I bang my pan lids!' As if to demonstrate the truth of her claim, a woman's head popped out of a window two doors along. 'It's all right, it's just the doctor!' the old woman called out cheerfully. The other woman's expression suggested this was by no means the first false alarm; also that she wasn't best pleased at her elderly neighbour's antics.

It seemed that my visit had been in vain, for the old girl had nothing whatsoever to tell me. As I rode off, however, the neighbour called out to me and came running after me. I drew rein and waited for her to catch up.

'She keeps early hours,' the woman panted, jerking her head back towards the cottages, 'and she doesn't see or hear half what goes on, despite what she's probably been telling you.'

'She didn't tell me anything,' I replied.

The woman grinned. She had a front tooth missing in her upper jaw, but she was shapely, with glossy dark hair, and otherwise handsome. 'Then your elevated status must have made her a mite more respectful of the truth than she normally is,' she said.

'I'm just a doctor,' I protested.

'Exactly,' she replied. Then she said, 'There *have* been other instances of someone lurking around. Her at the end' – she pointed – 'had her dog's old blanket stolen from off the gorse bushes where she'd set it out to air. And there's been eggs taken from the cottages down there.' She indicated a shallow little valley where a stream ran and where a small row of dwellings stood huddled together.

'Has anyone seen the culprit?' I asked.

She hesitated. 'Maybe.'

I waited. She was eyeing me and I wondered if she was after a coin or two in exchange for the information. But then she said in a rush, 'I'm almost embarrassed to tell you because it sounds so silly!' She laughed uneasily.

'Tell me anyway,' I said.

'It's the children, see. They say they've seen him, more than once. Well, not so much seen him as heard him.'

'Heard who?'

'The black giant!' she said with another embarrassed laugh. 'Yes, yes, I know how daft it sounds and we all know there's no such thing as giants, black or otherwise, and the children are making up tales to give themselves a bit of a fright. But they say they've seen him hanging around and more than once they've followed him, only then he sets up that awful noise again and they get scared and run for home.'

'What noise?'

She seemed to be struggling with herself. Finally, as if she knew I wouldn't leave till she'd told me, she blushed prettily and said, 'It *can't* be right, and I know full well they're just making it up, but they say he sobs like his heart's breaking.'

I went straight to Theo and when I reminded him that he'd had a large visitor who said he was looking for a lost friend, he had the grace to look abashed. He muttered something about how could one man be expected to keep every last little detail at the front of his mind when other, far more terrible things kept happening, and the very force of his defensiveness told me that he too recognized that this might be very important.

When he'd finished grumbling he said gruffly, 'I'll set a watch out there. If it's correct that the children of the settlement have seen him several times, then it's likely he's a creature of habit and will probably return.'

'Especially since he's had rich pickings from the neighbourhood, including eggs and a blanket,' I added.

Theo nodded. 'I'll get Jarman Hodge on it,' he said. 'I'll pass on to him what little I know, tell to find our big man, talk to him and bring him in.' Elbowing me out of the way, he strode to the door of his office, opened it and yelled down the passage, '*Jarman!*'

Jarman Hodge knew the little settlement he was being sent to watch over. He knew almost all the settlements in the area within a radius of perhaps five or six miles, and his knowledge of places further afield was only slightly less sound. He made his way there, found a small hazel copse in which to tether his horse where the animal would be out of sight, found a suitable tree behind which to conceal himself and, with the inexhaustible patience born of long practice, settled down to wait.

He had an excellent view of the little row of houses, with their gardens behind and a variety of henhouses and animal pens, and a more distant but adequate view of the dwellings down beside the stream in the little valley. It was late afternoon, the day still warm and sunny, and there was quite a lot of activity. Men and a few women worked in the fields around the settlement, and more women could be observed busy around their cottages and their yards. A skinny girl emerged and took some washing off a row of lavender bushes. An old crone went tottering down her garden path to throw scraps to her hens. Some children appeared, apparently from nowhere, chasing each other, the lads shouting and jeering, the girls shrieking in mock-distress. Presently the workers in the fields began to turn for home, and clouds of smoke from some of the cottages suggested fires were being built up to cook the evening meal.

Dusk came down, and Jarman narrowed his eyes to sharpen his vision.

The sounds from the settlement were tailing off, and the last of the visits to the privy before bed being made, when finally his patience was rewarded. He spotted a movement, on the slope above the little valley, and suddenly he was fully alert. Watching closely, he saw a big shape begin to walk, slowly and hesitantly, towards the cottages. The man's progress – he was so big that surely he had to be a man – would take him quite close to Jarman's hiding place. Still observing intently, Jarman allowed the huge figure to get ahead, then moved out from under the trees and began soft-footedly to follow him.

The big man went right up to the cottages, then paused and stood still turning his head this way and that as if listening. Apparently satisfied that everybody had turned in and he wouldn't be disturbed, he climbed over a fence that was no obstacle to someone of his height and went down the path to the henhouse at the end of the garden. He opened the little low door and, when the hens set up a soft, alarmed clucking, he muttered – *sang* – something that instantly soothed them. Jarman, close now, shook his head in wonder. He'd never come across such a thing before . . .

The big man had reached inside the henhouse and appeared to have found what he wanted, for already he had extracted his arm and was backing away, careful to fasten the door again. With a surprising turn of speed, he ran back up the path, climbed the fence and was away.

Jarman, a fit man and no mean runner himself, was hard put to it to keep up.

The pursuit seemed to go on for miles, but he was sure this was only because he was so anxious not to lose his quarry. After a time, a small huddle of buildings loomed up ahead, the state of them and the total absence of lights, wood smoke or any other sign of human occupation suggesting they were abandoned. Jarman recalled the description of the little hamlet where the vagrant's body had been found and he was all but sure the big man was leading him straight to it; perhaps to the very house.

The big man approached a building whose ruined door leant across the doorway. He pushed it aside and went in.

Jarman, moving so quietly that even someone listening out for him would not have heard, crept up close until he was standing right outside. He had expected to hear the sounds and smells of a fire being set and lit, but none came. Instead he heard a sort of slurping, gulping noise, accompanied by a sort of grunting. The big man, it seemed, was consuming his purloined eggs raw.

He must be very hungry, Jarman thought.

He knew he should have gone straight in and addressed the man. The coroner had sent him to do just that: *Find him, talk to him, bring him to my office*, he had said, and Jarman wasn't in the habit of ignoring his orders.

But all the same he let the man he'd been sent to find finish his meal. Knowing Theophilus Davey as he did, he didn't think he would mind.

Presently the sounds of desperately eager eating ceased. There was a soft belch, then a sigh. Knowing he could not postpone what he must do any longer, Jarman pushed past the door and went inside.

It was dark within, with only a little light coming in from the dusk-darkened sky, finding its way through the holes in the walls and the roof. As Jarman's eyes adjusted, he made out the big man crouched on the floor in the corner. He was bundled into a heavy coat, or cloak, the fabric tight across his vast shoulders. He was bearded, or perhaps it was only that he hadn't shaved for some time. The hair on his face and that on his head were approximately the same length.

Jarman had been not a little worried that his abrupt arrival inside the big man's hideaway might precipitate him into some violent reaction, which was alarming, to say the least, since the man was so much bigger and more powerful and could probably have crushed the life out of Jarman with one large hand. But Jarman knew straight away that he was in no danger, for the big man had cowered into his corner, his hands up to his face, and he was peering at Jarman from frightened brown eyes that seemed to glint with tears.

'I won't hurt you,' Jarman said, keeping his voice low and gentle. The alarm in the big man's eyes did not abate. Moving a little closer – the man flinched away from him – he added,

'You came to see the coroner, didn't you?' No answer except for a whimper. 'It's all right, you're not in trouble' – *at least I hope you're not*, Jarman thought to himself – 'but you said you were looking for your friend, didn't you?' He stepped forward again. 'Jannie, wasn't it?'

Very slowly the man nodded. 'Jannie,' he echoed.

'You travelled together, didn't you?' Very slowly Jarman lowered himself to the ground, hoping he would present a less threatening figure to this sad, frightened man if he didn't loom over him. 'You'd been friends for a long time, yes?'

The man nodded again. 'Since boys, *ja*,' he whispered. 'I cared for him, protected him.' A tentative smile stretched the well-shaped mouth. 'I was big one, I had good fists.' He held one up, and Jarman had to agree with him.

'But you became separated,' he went on. Seeing that the big man hadn't understood, he said, 'You lost each other, and that was why you went to see Master Davey, in case he knew where Jannie was.'

The big man nodded again. Something about Jarman seemed to have won his trust, for now he said, '*Ja, ja*, is right, but I was bad, I said Jannie's name to the man and I was scared, for Jannie said nobody was to know we were there.' He stopped, frowning. 'Nobody was to know *he* was there,' he amended.

'I see,' Jarman said softly. His mind working fast, he went on, 'He had to get into the house without anybody suspecting he was in the area, didn't he?'

He was hoping that by pretending he already knew about the mission, this poor, slow-witted man would think it was all right to confide in him. When the big man's smile came back, wider and more certain now and he began to speak, Jarman felt a stab of guilt at how easy it had been to dupe him.

But then he put the emotion aside and began to listen so intently that there was room in his mind for nothing else.

SEVENTEEN

I knew I'd left the matter of the big man – 'the black giant', as the children had named him – in good hands. Theo clearly understood why I'd suggested he should be rounded up, which was good because I'd only told him half the story.

He needed to be questioned, that was certain, because there seemed little doubt that he had known our dead vagrant and in all likelihood shared the lonely ruin on the edge of the moor with him. As an excuse for taking him in, if indeed Theo needed an excuse, there was the matter of the stolen eggs and the purloined dog blanket.

I knew somewhere deep in the folds of my mind that there was much more to it than two wanderers encountering each other on the road and walking side by side for a few miles, days or weeks.

I knew, although I didn't yet understand, that the heart of this mystery lay at Wrenbeare and so, without telling anyone where I was going, that was where I headed for.

The household was quiet as I approached. As I rode into the courtyard, I expected to see Kit Hammer or Cory, but neither appeared. I dismounted, tethered Hal and walked across to the door. It stood ajar, so I went inside.

I stood in the hall. The light was dim, the flagstones cool beneath my feet. Everything was still. All was quiet.

I went to the foot of the stairs. I called out softly. 'Mary? Are you there?'

There was no reply.

I went along to the room where, in slightly cheerier, happier times – although those were relative terms and the place had never felt joyful – I had encountered Lady Clemence and her daughters. Where, only two days ago, I had stood over the body of a woman whose heart had been torn from her body.

Agnes Lond sat in a high-backed chair by the fire. Her eyes, wide open, stared down at the empty hearth. She must have heard the sound of my boots on the stone floor but she did not look round. Her husband lay on his side, asleep, on a settle on the opposite side of the hearth.

I drew up a low stool and sat down beside her.

'I apologize for coming into your house uninvited,' I said, keeping my voice low. Avery Lond must surely be exhausted, and it seemed unkind to wake him. 'There was nobody in the yard that I could send to ask for admittance, and, when I came up to the door, I found it open.'

She stirred from her apathy, turning to look at me with faint curiosity. 'They have gone,' she said distantly. She sighed.

I studied her. My physician's instinct told me straight away she was far from well, but as yet I had no clue as to what ailed her. I thought she'd lost weight, for empty folds of skin sagged beneath her heavy jaw as if the flesh had recently and quite suddenly melted out of it. There were hollows in her formerly plump cheeks, and her pale eyes were circled in darkness. Her hair, haphazardly tucked under a plain white cap that was slightly grubby, was rough and dry like a sick hound's coat.

I said in a whisper, 'How is your sister?'

She shrugged. 'Peaceful, thank God.'

Recalling all too vividly the piercing, incessant screams, I muttered, 'Amen.'

As the echo of the word faded, the silence seemed to intensify.

The first stirrings of alarm began but I made myself ignore them.

'Mistress Lond, tell me about your father,' I said, keeping my voice calm and quiet.

'Father died,' she said in a faraway tone. 'He was sick, he raved and thrashed about in his pit of foulness, then his heart burst and he died.'

'Yes,' I said. I didn't think now was the moment to discuss Denyse having witnessed the dreadful death. 'But tell me about before that. What was he like? What did it please him to do?'

She turned to me, the protuberant eyes wide open so that

the pale irises were entirely surrounded by white. The rims, I noticed, were red and scaly. 'You already know, I think.' Her voice was cold.

'I know a little,' I admitted. 'I surmise more.' Deciding I had nothing to lose, I went on, 'I believe his appetites were for boys.'

I stopped, very much hoping she would pick up where I had left off. After some time, she did.

'Boys. Yes.' She sighed again, deeply, as if drawing it up from the very depths of her. 'There had been others, or so it was believed, but then he saw the angel, and he was never the same again.' She shook her head, her face drooping in sadness. 'He had us – Mother, me, Denyse – and he had *position.*' I sensed she wanted to shout the word, but she restrained herself to a sort of suppressed hiss. 'I tried, I tried so hard, to make myself be enough for him, for although I wasn't the son and heir that he wanted, I was his child, his daughter, and he should have loved me.' A tear ran down her face. 'But he didn't want me. He wanted his angel. Always, always, it was boys.'

It seemed cruel to push her when she was clearly in distress, but I did.

'Boys, yes, I understand,' I said. 'I believe there was evidence of these unnatural desires, here in your house, and that you – your mother, your husband, you yourself – wanted above all else to ensure that nobody ever unearthed it. I believe that when a sick, hungry, desperate vagrant came to your house and somehow managed to get inside, he saw, or found, or tried to take away, something that, if it were to be seen by outside eyes, would have blasted apart for ever the image of your father that you try so hard to keep alive. The honourable, upright, God-fearing justice of the peace that you want so much to keep in the world's memory would be shown for what he was. For what he did.' I paused, watching her closely. Her face hadn't moved by a fraction.

I went on. 'I believe that someone from this house ran after this vagrant and, finding him alone in his ruin of a hiding place, put a cloth or a small pillow over his face and held it there until he was dead.'

She went on staring at me.

'It was your husband, wasn't it?' I nodded towards Avery Lond, curled up on his settle, his back to us. 'But I believe it was your mother who made him go and commit the deed, for it was she who had the most to lose.'

Agnes Lond gave a faint tut of annoyance, as if some minor event in the daily life of the household had gone amiss, causing mild annoyance. She looked away, muttering, 'He always does as Mother commands him, but afterwards he complains lengthily and bitterly to me. He's so *weak*.' She spat out the word. 'I tell him, if you don't like it, find a house for us so that we need not always be here under Mother's roof. Shut in with the past,' she added in an almost inaudible whisper.

It was so utterly quiet in the house that I heard the tiny sound of her words quite clearly.

Silence. Profound silence. But it was still the afternoon of a pleasantly warm and sunny day, so why was there no evidence of people going about their daily work?

Just now she said *they have gone*. I thought she was referring to Christopher Hammer and Cory, the groom and the stable lad. So where were the rest of them? I tried to recall the indoor servants. There was a housekeeper I'd heard someone refer to as Joice, a fat man with straggly strands of shoulder-length hair and a bald dome who smelled of alcohol, and various maids including the wall-eyed girl who said she'd seen the wolf.

And the woman who looked after Denyse.

'Where's Mary?' I said sharply. 'Is she with Denyse, keeping her calm?' *Sweet Christ*, I thought, *I hope somebody is.* 'It's very important that Denyse is made to feel safe!' I added, my voice rising, when Agnes still didn't answer.

Very slowly Agnes turned her head so that she was looking at me. 'Mary has left.'

'And the housekeeper? And the man with the greasy hair and the big nose?'

'He is called Leagh,' she said. Then, with a sudden grin, 'He *has* got a big nose, hasn't he?' She giggled, quickly suppressing it. 'And the housekeeper's name is Joice. But they have gone. I *told* you,' she added with irritation. 'You're meant to be a physician, so why don't you *listen* to people when they speak to you?' She shot me a haughty look, in which was distilled all the arrogance, confidence and pride of her long line of illustrious forebears.

Who had come, I thought, to this. A dirty, neglected house, desertion by the staff, brutal murder and madness running rife.

Agnes Lond had turned back to her steady contemplation of the hearth. She had begun humming.

Dread flooded through me. Leaping to my feet, I ran for the stairs and up to where I remembered Denyse's room to be, at the far end of the corridor. The door to Mary's room was open, the bed stripped, no sign of anybody in residence.

But there was someone in Denyse's room.

She lay in her bed, the bedclothes tucked around her shoulders, the once-white linen sheet with its embroidered border neatly turned down.

And, like her nightgown, soaked in blood.

Denyse's throat had been cut.

I searched the rest of the bedchambers. All were empty. I ran back downstairs and raced through the kitchen, the scullery, the pantry, the rest of the servants' quarters.

Not a soul.

Slowly I walked back to Agnes.

I stared down at the still figure of Avery Lond and, as I had expected, I saw that it was not moving at all. There was no soft rise and fall of the chest. No expansion and contraction of the ribs as the lungs took in and expelled air. There was no visible wound, but a cushion lay on the floor in front of the settle.

Like his sister-in-law upstairs, Avery Lond was dead.

With the greatest reluctance I'd ever felt in my life, I sat down once again on the stool and gently took hold of Agnes's hand.

'Did you kill them?'

She nodded.

'And what about the vagrant?'

She nodded again. 'Oh, yes. He had to be killed too.'

'Your mother commanded your husband to do it because you had to stop him speaking about what he'd seen?'

She sighed but this time she didn't nod. Nor did she speak.
'How did your husband know where to find him?'
She gave me a cold look, her eyes full of contempt. 'We
saw him run off and watched to see where he went. When he
took the track up onto the moors, we knew there were only a
handful of places where he would find shelter.'
I thought of Jannie, curled up on the filthy floor. Then I
saw in my mind's eye the huge figure of his friend crouching
over him, whispering his love and his concern, trying to tempt
him with some morsel of food, some tiny sip of hot drink,
weeping as Jannie turned his head away. 'But he was not alone
there,' I said. 'He had a companion, who—'
'You refer of course to the big simpleton,' she interrupted
dismissively. 'But he was not there all the time. He had to
forage for food, and it was simply a matter of waiting until
he went off again.' She sniffed, and her over-long nostrils
seemed to flare briefly. 'The man was too stupid to think to
look behind him.'
Because all his thoughts would have been bent on the
desperate state of the man he loved, I reflected sadly. Even as
he'd lumbered away from the hovel, he'd have been trying to
work out where he could steal some food.
I said softly, 'But it was for nothing, for what the vagrant
took from this house was still on him when his body was
found.' She looked up at me then, vague surprise in her eyes.
'The sketch,' I said. 'The page of heavy paper, that must have
torn when one of you tried to snatch it from his hand as he
ran away.'
But slowly she shook her head. 'No.' I thought she wasn't
going to go on, but then she said in a rush, 'It was Father's,
and all that he had left. He gave up everything else but at the
last he couldn't bear to part with that drawing. He kept it
hidden and nobody knew he still had it, until one day Mother
found him with it in his hands, staring down at it, such love
and adoration in his face, the tears streaming from his eyes.'
Her expression hardened into hatred, cold, cruel, chilling.
'Mother screamed at him and she tried to take it away, but he
held on tight and it tore in two, and she only had the lower
left corner. She threw it on the fire, cursing his name, cursing

what he had done and what he had unleashed upon her. 'Upon us all.' Her head dropped. 'He hid the half that he held on to,' she whispered. 'And then that man came' – I thought I saw her shoot me a swift, crafty look – 'twice, he came *twice*, the first time nosing around and peering in the windows, and then the second time he broke in, he came right inside, and I don't know *how* he knew where to look for it but when he was *here*, in this house where he had *no right to be*' – her voice rose to a shriek – 'he went straight to the very place where Father always kept it and by the time we realized that he was here and what he was doing, he already had it in his grasp and he *wouldn't let go*.' The last words were screamed at such volume that I heard her voice crack.

She was panting hard as if she had just been running. I waited a few moments, then I said, 'So why did your husband not remove it from the body?' She didn't answer. 'He knew the vagrant had taken it!' I cried. 'Once he was dead, it would have been a simple matter to search him and reclaim it.'

She looked at me with disdain. 'It wasn't important,' she said. 'It wasn't because of any *drawing* that he had to die.'

I didn't understand.

I glanced at Avery Lond's body. I wondered how she had killed him. Then suddenly I thought: *He didn't suffocate the vagrant. Agnes did.*

I felt ice run up my spine. The woman sitting before me had killed the vagrant, her sister, her husband. Her mother? I didn't know, hadn't even tried to find out. And *why* had she killed them? Had Denyse had to die because she wouldn't stop screaming? Had she suffocated her husband because he had discovered what she'd done to her sister and come flying down the stairs, horror all over his face, to confront her? But no, that couldn't be right, because surely the only way she could have put that cushion over his mouth and nose was if he was relaxed in deep sleep.

Avery Lond, I thought, had died because he was weak and wouldn't stand up to his formidable mother-in-law.

But I thought perhaps I could supply an answer, for I was beginning to suspect what was the matter with Agnes Lond.

She too was a child of Sir Thomas Fairlight, who had borne a terrible scourge of a sickness that passed from man to woman, from woman to child. And Agnes had been shut out from her father's affections because he preferred to expend his love on boys. Agnes Lond was probably as mad as her dead sister.

And I realized, as I sat there trying not to alarm her in any way at all, that there was a fair chance she might kill me too.

I sat there beside her, wondering what to do. It felt as if I was in a dream. Time had stopped, there wasn't a sound to be heard, and Agnes Lond and I might have been alone in some strange little bubble cut off from the rest of the world.

But then she made a small movement. Turning to look at her, I saw she had a large knife in her hand. There was blood on the blade.

She said in a tone of utter reasonableness, 'I am sorry but I don't think I want to talk to you any more.'

Then she lunged at me.

I had time to fling up an arm to protect my throat, and the knife struck the underside of my forearm and was deflected off into my shoulder. It felt as if she'd punched me. I felt the blood begin to flow – a lot of it – and my head swam. I saw her stand up, the knife still in her hand, and give a little nod, as if some small domestic task had been completed to her satisfaction.

Then she wasn't there any more.

She has disappeared, I thought. *Vanished.* In my shocked state, blood pouring out of me, it seemed quite a logical assumption.

I think I was going in and out of consciousness. I remember pain, acute pain that throbbed in time to my heartbeat, and being mildly concerned because I knew that each heartbeat was pulsing more blood out of me. Then it all seemed to go black.

I came back to myself to find that I was lying with my head in someone's lap, and that someone's firm hand was pressing a soft cloth to the wound in my shoulder. I risked a swift opening of my eyes and saw that there was a big white bandage wrapped tightly round my forearm, and it was hurting a great deal. Shutting my eyes again I said feebly, 'Ouch. That's too tight.'

'It is not,' said a calm voice. 'It needs to be just so, to stem the bleeding.'

I knew that voice.

I opened my eyes once more and looked up at the woman bending over me. It was Mary, and I realized that she had probably just saved my life.

'I thought you'd gone,' I said, quite taken aback to discover my voice was no more than a feeble whimper.

'I came back,' she replied shortly.

Had she been upstairs? Did she know? 'Denyse is—' I began.

'Sssh,' she hushed me. 'I know.'

I struggled to rise. 'I have to—'

But moving was not at all a good idea, for instantly the room began to whirl around and I thought I was going to be sick.

'Stay still,' Mary said, gently but firmly pushing on my uninjured shoulder. 'You are far too weak to move yet.'

I obeyed. Her lap felt soft, and there was a blanket over me. I was shivering.

I saw images of the very recent past. Agnes, sitting humming to herself. Agnes, with a knife in her hand.

Agnes.

Once more I tried to sit up. 'Agnes has a knife!' I tried to cry out. 'It's not safe, we have to—'

But Mary said quietly, 'Agnes is dead.'

'Dead.' A pointless repetition of the one word was the best I could manage.

'She was on the stairs when I arrived,' Mary went on. She sounded very sad. 'There was no knife, or at least I didn't see one. Oh, I'm not denying she had one, and used it,' she added swiftly at my faint protest, 'for the evidence is right here lying in my lap.' She smiled briefly. 'I asked her if she was all right, and she shook her head and said, "I will never be all right, Mary. I know that now." Then she started walking up the stairs, and when I followed her, she broke into a run, and she went on, past the first landing, up the little stairs to the servants' quarters in the attic, and then she was out on the ledge and over the parapet. I tried to grasp hold of her, but she pushed me away.' There was a huge bruise, I noticed, on her right wrist. 'She jumped. She threw herself off the roof.'

And calm, imperturbable Mary gave one harsh sob.

'You cannot move yet,' she said very firmly a little while later. 'I just told you. I shall leave you here only for as long as it takes me to prepare some food and something to drink, and I shall make up a fire because you don't seem to be able to stop shivering. Then,' she went on, raising her voice as I tried to interrupt, 'both of us will pray very hard that someone comes to call – your friend the coroner said he would be back late today, so I have every confidence that our prayers will be answered – and we will tell him what had happened and ask him to send for Doctor Thorn, who will sew up your wounds.' She glanced at me. 'If nobody has come by sunset, I will ride for the doctor myself.'

'Is there really nobody else here?' Nobody else living, I might have said.

'No. Agnes told her husband to dismiss the outdoor staff. When he demurred, protesting that it wasn't right to send them away with no warning and nothing to tide them over, she shouted at him to shut his mouth and go and tell the staff there was no more money to pay them, they must pack their bags and be gone. She herself did the same for the few remaining indoor servants, most of whom were only too pleased to go.' She paused, her face distressed. 'Some – the more perceptive ones, perhaps – had quietly slipped away already. Now,' she said briskly, 'I shall make your drink, and I'll bathe your wounds so they are ready for the doctor.'

It was good, I reflected with weary irony as she set off for the kitchen, to have something to look forward to. It was many years since anyone had stitched me up, but I was sure it was going to hurt as much as it had always done.

* * *

Some time later, we sat before a bright blaze and I had managed a cup of a comforting hot drink and a piece of bread spread liberally with butter and raspberry preserve. I was no longer feeling faint, although still in a lot of pain. To take my mind off it, I said to her, 'You have lived in this house for – for how long?'

'Two years, nearly.'

'You will, I am sure, have some understanding of the house-hold, and have come to some conclusions.' She made no comment. 'Will you share them with me?' When still she did not reply, I said, 'They are all dead, Mary. Can it harm them now? Besides, I am a doctor, and used to honouring confidences.'

'You are also close to Master Davey,' she said shrewdly, 'and will probably share with him everything you know.'

'Yes,' I admitted, 'I probably will.'

Then, after a brief pause, she said, 'I believe I do understand, as much as anybody could, for I have asked discreet questions here and there and I have kept my eyes open. Some of the servants have been here for many years – Leagh and Joice, for example – and they have long memories.' She paused. 'It is a very sad tale, and it has its roots in the past. He could never control his urges, that was the trouble.'

'Sir Thomas?'

'Yes,' she said with slight impatience, as if implying, *who else?* 'Everything that has happened here was because Sir Thomas Fairlight did not love his wife, nor his daughters, because he had given all the love that was in him to somebody else.'

'The boys, yes I know,' I said. 'Agnes told me.'

'One boy in particular, I believe,' Mary went on. 'He came into Thomas Fairlight's life soon after Denyse was born, when Agnes was six years old. Denyse was far too young to be jealous but Agnes felt the pain of rejection very deeply, although at that tender age she could not perceive that her father's deep love for the boy was sexual and not paternal. She was desperate for her father to love her, but he barely noticed her at all. Then the boy went away – I do not know why or how that happened, although I believe Thomas's priest remonstrated with him and may have been influential in persuading him he must give up his life of vice and be the man whom the community believed him to be; the man his family so badly needed. And I believe that he managed to do so, and that for a time, at least, matters were resolved. But then it became clear that Sir Thomas – he had received his knighthood by then – was very unwell, and he sank into madness.'

'I know about his sickness,' I said softly.

She glanced at me. 'Do you?'

'I have spoken to Josiah Thorn.' She was revealing secrets to me, and it seemed only fair to reciprocate.

'But he was Sir Thomas's doctor, and tended the whole family,' she protested.

'Yes, I understand that, and he was not indiscreet,' I assured her. 'I already knew enough to guess, and his silence confirmed that I was right.' It wasn't exactly how it had happened but I wanted to protect my friend. Especially as he was soon to sew up my wounds; it really wasn't a time to risk anything that might antagonize him . . .

'So, Sir Thomas died, with his secrets safely buried and only a half of one sketch of a beautiful young man to remind him of what he had lost,' I said when Mary didn't speak.

I felt her slight start of surprise. 'Agnes told you?'

'Yes.'

She shook her head sadly. 'And then that tramp turned up,' she whispered. 'I don't know what happened, but I can only assume he was rifling through Sir Thomas's private papers searching for money or valuables, and it was only by chance that he had the old sketch in his hand when he was apprehended.'

'Either that,' I agreed, 'or the sketch was what he had come for.'

She said heavily, 'Yes. That is what I feared.'

'It is the more likely explanation, surely,' I went on, 'for why else did he have to be killed? Why else would Lady Clemence, Agnes and Avery claim so persistently that there had never been an intruder here?'

She nodded. 'He must have known, that poor, starving man,'

she said softly. 'He came here looking for that sketch, and, for Agnes, for Lady Clemence, seeing him with it brought the past back with dreadful clarity.'

'It was Agnes who killed him,' I said. 'She followed him to the hovel where he was sleeping and she suffocated him. He was thin and weak, and she was a solidly built, strong woman.'

'Did she confess?' Mary asked in a small voice.

'Yes.'

'And the others . . .?'

'Her sister and her husband, yes. As to her mother, I don't know. She did not say that she had killed her.'

'She would have been covered in her mother's blood,' Mary observed, 'and she was not.'

'You saw her soon afterwards?'

'I did. It was I who went to wake her and tell her what had happened.'

'And there was no time for her to have changed her clothes and washed off the blood? To have hidden the weapons and—' I didn't go on.

Mary shook her head. 'There was not. Moreover, I would swear to the fact that she was deeply and peacefully asleep when I went into her room. Is that likely, do you think, in someone who has just murdered their own mother?'

'I would say it was not,' I said slowly. 'Except that . . .'

'Except that Agnes Lond had lost her mind,' Mary finished for me.

There came the sound of footsteps; two sets. I heard Theo's deep voice and another lighter one answering him. Mary and I looked at each other. I struggled to sit up straighter.

She rose to her feet as Theo came into the room, the vague figure of one of his agents behind him. 'Before you speak, Master Davey,' she said, 'will you please ask your man there to ride for Doctor Thorn at Buckland, as he is required to attend Doctor Taverner.'

Theo did as she asked, and Gidley – I could see who it was now – hurried away. Then Theo came hurrying towards me, kneeling down in front of me.

'Are you badly hurt?' he asked. I couldn't read his expression.

'No. Cuts to my arm and shoulder that will need a few stitches, that's all.'

Now his emotion was clear to see; it was relief.

While we waited for Gidley and Josiah Thorn, Mary and I told Theo what had happened. He went upstairs to look at poor Denyse in her bed and he stood over the body of Avery Lond for some moments. He went outside, presumably to look at Agnes, splayed on the ground behind the house. Then he came back to where Mary and I sat beside the fire and very vigorously poked it up, adding quite a lot more fuel. All of us, I think, were glad of the bright flames.

I took advantage of Mary's absence as she went to fetch us all a measure of brandy to ask him, 'What of the big man? Did Jarman Hodge find him? Did he bring him in?'

'His name is Paulus Fiske and he is now tucked up in a cell that leads off my cellar,' Theo replied. 'He's not a prisoner – well, to be fair I suppose he is, since I've locked him in, but that's only to stop him running off again. He's been fed – not that he ate much, the state he was in – given hot water to wash in, and he has a couple of blankets to keep out the chill.'

'And what does he say?' My impatience was boiling up. 'Did he come here hunting for the other one? For Jannie?'

'There is a story to be uncovered, that's for sure,' Theo said, 'but as yet I know very little of it. He – this Paulus Fiske – is in deep distress, he's afraid, he's lost and quite alone, all of which, added to the fact that he was starving and filthy, is why he's now asleep in my cell, warm and fed. And,' he added, eyeing me with a faint smile, 'why I'm very much hoping this Josiah Thorn will be able to patch you up, since it's you who is going to watch while I speak to Paulus Fiske tomorrow morning, and tell me how to penetrate his secrets.'

EIGHTEEN

J osiah Thorn's hands might have been old but they had lost none of their skill or their delicate touch. I couldn't say that it didn't hurt when he stitched my shoulder and the soft flesh on the underside of my forearm, but it was bearable and he was quick. As he remarked, it did a doctor a power of good to experience the treatment he meted out to others.

He told me very firmly that I was on no account to ride away that night. In case I decided to do so anyway, he told Mary to hide my clothes, which she had taken away to cleanse of the blood that seemed to have permeated and splattered over everything I wore. Unless I was proposing to ride home to Rosewyke in my skin, it looked as if I'd be staying at Wrenbeare.

I didn't relish the prospect, since I'd be sharing the house with three dead bodies and not a living soul. But Mary took pity on me and so, to my surprised pleasure, did Theo, and both of them offered to stay with me.

Gidley was dispatched with more messages, this time to Theo's and my respective households to explain that we would not be home that night. 'Don't you give too much in the way of explanations, lad,' Theo warned him. 'No need to alarm that pretty sister of yours, Gabe, that you've taken a wound. Especially,' he added rather crushingly, 'since it's not a very serious one.'

Mary made up beds and then, after making sure Theo and I had all we needed in the way of food and drink, she bade us a quiet good night and retired to her room. It was late now and, given the events of the day, I didn't blame her. Theo and I finished off the small amount that remained in the late Avery Lond's bottle of particularly fine brandy, then we too sought our beds.

*   *   *

In the morning, I dressed in my freshly laundered clothes and after both of us had put away a reasonably decent breakfast prepared by Mary, Theo and I set off for his house, and the confrontation with Paulus Fiske. Mary left with us, although I noticed that, before he let her go, Theo made sure he knew where to find her if he needed her. She said little in answer to our questions about whether she had a place to go, and if she would be all right, save to say briefly that she was going to stay with the friends she'd fled to when Agnes Lond dismissed her from Wrenbeare.

Earlier we had watched two of Theo's men load the three bodies onto a cart and depart off up the road. They would be taken directly to the empty house where Theo rented the crypt, since, as he said, it would be grim for Paulus Fiske to share the cellar beneath Theo's house with them. 'Poor bugger's near enough demented as it is without making it worse,' Theo remarked glumly, 'and I need to get some sense out of him.'

Theo asked if I would go down to the cell and examine the big man. 'He's been fed, watered and washed again this morning,' he added, 'and is altogether in a better state than when he was brought in.'

I agreed. 'What am I looking for?' I asked.

Theo gave me a slightly uneasy glance. 'Not sure. The man's . . . well, I'm not certain he's right in the head. He moans a lot. Weeps.'

'I see.'

I went down into the crypt and the guard on duty let me into the cell.

With a couple of Theo's agents stationed unobtrusively out in the hall and a third, a particularly broad and strong man, just outside the front door, the interview with Paulus Fiske was carried out in Theo's office, Fiske sitting facing Theo across the large desk and myself standing just behind Fiske. As Fiske squirmed and wriggled in his chair, Jarman Hodge slipped quietly into the room and came to stand beside me.

The big man couldn't see Jarman or me unless he turned his head, and as his frightened eyes were fixed on Theo, I was able to study him without his realizing it. He was huge, or it was fairer to say he had been huge, for now, although he still had the massive bone structure, the height, the breadth in the shoulder and the chest, the flesh had fallen off him and he looked as if he was close to starvation. He wasn't hungry just now, though, for Theo's wife Elaine had sent down to the cell a very generous breakfast, and Paulus Fiske was still slightly troubled by the wind that had been the inevitable result of wolfing down food on an empty stomach.

Theo, apparently thinking that delay would only increase Fiske's nervousness, began as soon as we were all settled. 'Now, Paulus, you came here a few days ago looking for a friend, but before I could begin to help you, you fled.' Paulus gave a soft moan. 'Now, yesterday evening one of my agents saw you steal some eggs, and—'

'I was hungry!' Paulus protested. 'I am very sorry, I know it is wrong to steal, and I will work to pay back the money if I—'

'Never mind about the eggs,' Theo said shortly, cutting across the flow of distressed words. Paulus, I noticed, had a marked accent, and I thought I detected the particular sounds of English spoken by a man from the Low Countries. 'My agent followed you to a house on the edge of the moors, where earlier we had found the body of a vagrant, and you told him that the dead man was called Jannie—'

'*Ja, ja*, Jannie, Jannie Neep,' Paulus said eagerly. 'My friend.'

'Jannie Neep, yes,' Theo went on, 'and you said that this Jannie had come here for a particular purpose, which was to break into a big house called Wrenbeare that is the home of the Fairlight family.'

Watching Paulus from behind, I saw him stiffen. I thought at first it was from a sudden increase in his fear, but, edging forward so that I could see his face, I realized I was wrong, for his expression was one of furious anger. He said 'Thomas Fairlight,' in a tone of cold fury, and then he spat on the floor.

Theo, glancing briefly at the gobbet of spittle, said softly, 'I see.' Then, his blue eyes suddenly intent, he leaned across his desk towards Paulus and said coldly, 'I will forgive that, since I sense you are very distressed, but in return for my leniency you will now tell me your tale, right from the start.'

And, meekly and obediently, surprising us all, Paulus Fiske did exactly that.

They had been boys, Paulus Fiske and Jannie Neep, fugitives, lost, desperate, very hungry, when they first fell in with the Frenchman Artus Bennart. Would it have been better if they had stayed huddled in their ditch that night and allowed Artus Bennart to walk on by? It was hard to say. He saved them from destitution, perhaps from death, but was the price worth paying?

Artus Bennart was an artist: a master in the art of stained glass. His work was very beautiful and much sought after, but in his native France, where he was returning when he encountered and picked up the two boys, there were many men whose work was on a par with his. And so, after a brief visit to his tiny house in Chartres to collect one or two essential papers, he was going to England. For the English wanted to replace the beautiful glass they'd been forced to give up and see smashed under the iconoclasts and nobody in England could make it any more.

Artus Bennart was a hard man driven by the urge for self-advancement, and in the course of a tough life he had learned that the most important factor was to look after yourself, because nobody else did. Accordingly, other, weaker people were there to serve him in that aim, and the two boys, enfeebled by all that they had been through and neither very sound in the first place, were like very small flies in the web of a particularly ruthless spider.

Paulus Fiske at almost fourteen was already a large lad, tall, big and strong, eager to please because he had learned already that if you pleased those with power over you, they were less likely to beat you, starve you or otherwise abuse you. He became Artus Bennart's workhorse and, from the day he and Jannie fell in with the master in stained glass, he rarely went to bed without some part of him hurting.

In contrast, Jannie Neep, who was perhaps six months or a year older than Paulus – neither of them knew exactly how old they were, or where and when they had been born – was slim and graceful, he moved like a dancer, he had a body like that of the most perfect young Greek god and the beautiful, distant, serene face of an angel. As soon as Artus saw him, staring up anxiously from that ditch in the last of the daylight, filthy, bones all but poking through his smooth skin, he thought he might have found his model and his muse. Once he'd taken both boys to an inn and hosed them down, he knew he had been right.

'We sail for England on the evening tide, my lads,' Artus told them a week or so later when they had walked for several days north-westwards up to the coast, and the English Channel, grey and unsettled under rain and lowering skies, stretched out before them. 'I hate England and I hate the fucking English,' he added bitterly, 'and I'm going there purely to make as much money as I can as swiftly as possible, then I'll be off back home.' He looked at the boys out of narrow, calculating eyes. 'Now I'm not going to be too fussy about how I go about acquiring it, but when I go home, I intend to be laden down with gold.'

He stared at the boys for a moment, and something in his face sent a shock of alarm through Paulus. Then he said in quite a different tone, jockeying, joking now, 'Ever been on a boat before?' Both boys shook their heads. 'Well, you'll heave and retch as if you're trying to bring up your guts all the way through to your arseholes, but you'll get over it.'

His prediction was accurate. Neither Paulus nor Jannie ever forgot that interminable voyage, and even when they were on dry land once more in Plymouth, Jannie – always the more frail – went on being sick for another miserable three days.

The boys didn't know it, for Artus told them nothing unless there was no choice, but he had been contacted back in Chartres by a Devon family; old Catholics, who wanted to replace a triptych of stained-glass panels of the Holy Family that had been wrenched from the walls of their private chapel forty years ago by Thomas Cromwell's thugs and which, before their own horrified eyes, had been crushed under the boots of the looters and the hooves of their horses. Now, newly arrived in Plymouth, Artus chivvied his workhorse and his model on the last leg of their journey, and so they came to the small inland town on the fringes of a great moor – neither boy ever learned its name – outside which lived the family who had engaged Artus Bennart.

Artus did not allow his workhorse and his muse any free time. When they weren't hard at work in their various ways, Artus made them stay in the dirty little room attached to the barn in which he worked. But one day Artus got drunk. He had just completed the first of his commissions, and the family were delighted with the Virgin and Child panel he had made for them. Jannie Neep had been his model for the Madonna; the beautiful boy could easily pose as a woman, for his androgynous looks were very adaptable. Artus had been extremely well paid and his purse was heavy with coin. Such was the family's happiness at having found so fine a master in the craft that in addition they presented him with a bottle of excellent French brandy, the very smell of which reminded him poignantly of his distant home. He drank too much of it and fell into a drunken stupor.

Paulus and Jannie – who had not been paid and who didn't get so much as a sniff of the cork of the brandy bottle – took their chance and went out exploring.

And so it was that Thomas Fairlight, reluctant family man, married to an unappealing, discontented woman, father of two daughters, man of wealth and position in the area and recently made a justice of the peace, first set eyes on Jannie Neep. Thomas had been out riding and, hearing the sounds of splashing and merriment from the little stream that flowed close to his route home, went to investigate.

Lust was instant, for Jannie and Paulus had taken off their clothes and were splashing in the stream. Jannie's body was perfect. As was his face, which Thomas saw when he managed to tear his eyes away from the boy's loins and look at it. Smooth, straight fair hair; high, well-marked cheekbones; firm jaw above which the cheeks were still a little full with the residue of childhood. Bright, light blue eyes under straight brows. Perfect nose. Lips, wide, well-marked, utterly sensual.

Or so the besotted Thomas Fairlight said to himself.

He followed the lads back to the dirty room beside the barn. Unable to leave the object of his sudden and furious desire yet afraid to approach – Paulus was an alarming figure – Thomas waited.

And, very late that night, Artus Bennart woke from his drunken sleep with a crushing headache, a very queasy stomach and a desert-dry mouth, all of which symptoms miraculously melted away when the well-dressed man lurking outside told him why he was there and what he wanted.

'The boy looks like an angel,' Thomas had said to Artus Bennart, 'and therefore he shall be an angel; an angel in glass, naked, beautiful, everlasting, and you shall depict me kneeling at his feet in worship.'

Privately Artus thought the concept was crude and somewhat vulgar, but Thomas Fairlight, as if aware that what he so fervently desired was not entirely something to be proud of, was prepared to pay well over Artus's usual fee. Artus set to work straight away, doing as Thomas asked and providing a preliminary sketch to ensure the face was exactly right.

Artus completed the panel, and Jannie, who had been forced to spend far too many long hours posing naked in a cold barn, was very relieved. The image was beautiful; as beautiful as the very best of Artus Bennart's work. And, to begin with, it was enough for Thomas Fairlight.

But very soon the gratification of his eyes was no longer enough. He approached Artus, and Artus allowed him to pay for Jannie's body. On a terrible night of pain, shame, more pain and, ultimately, horror, Thomas Fairlight, forty-seven years old, respectable and admired man of wealth, husband and father, justice of the peace, seduced beautiful, vulnerable, pitiful, fourteen-year-old Jannie Neep.

Soon, as is the way of addiction, once or even twice was not enough, and snatched nights merely led to a vastly increased appetite. And then Thomas demanded to buy Jannie from Artus, and, given the size of the purse and thinking about that little house he had in mind back in Rosigny-sur-Seine, Artus agreed. Paulus, horrified at what had happened and what was about to happen, tried to protest, tried to save Jannie.

Artus beat him to unconsciousness with a heavy stick and sold
Jannie anyway. By the time Paulus recovered Artus was gone,
and so was Jannie. Thomas, Paulus later found out, hadn't
dared indulge his passion for the boy right there in his own
neighbourhood, and had taken him far away.

But Thomas's seduction infected the object of his love, and
quite soon Jannie's beauty turned to ugliness. Thomas, horrified at what he'd done, took him covertly to Plymouth and
paid for his passage back to France. Jannie, sick, in great pain,
fevered, barely knew what was happening, and violent sea
sickness made it all worse. As soon as he had packed him off,
Thomas, terrified now, sought out his tubby, kindly, well-loved
parish priest, whose name was Martin Oude, to confess his
sins and beg for forgiveness. So desperate was he – and also
so afraid that his sins would somehow come home to haunt
and accuse him – that he gave up the Angel panel into the
priest's keeping, and Martin buried it safely away between the
two parcels containing the panels from St Luke's Little Chapel.

Jannie disappeared into the filthy slums of the ports along
the northern coast of France. And back in Devon, Paulus, in
whose world Jannie was the sun, began searching for him.
When he couldn't find him in England, either around the places
where they had been together or in Plymouth, he followed
him back across the Channel. In slow stages, for periodically
he had to work in order to eat, he retraced the route he and
Jannie had taken together, back to the small town in the Low
Countries where their friendship had begun. The hope that had
sustained him all that long way – that he would find Jannie
well and happy, having returned to the place where he and
Paulus first met – was to be dashed, and it took Paulus many
weeks of distress and misery to recover. When he did, and
when he had laboured for a further few months to rebuild his
strength, he set out once again. He never stopped looking for
him, concentrating his search on the ports along the north
coast of France, asking questions, hunting in the taverns, the
inns and the foul dives that clustered in every port.

And in the end, long, lonely years later, he learned by sheer
chance in St Malo that a destitute vagrant had been begging,

pleading with people to give him money because he had to go to Plymouth. A priest had taken pity on him, Paulus discovered, or perhaps he merely wanted to get the dirty, smelly man off his church steps. Jannie had sailed for England.

Paulus, who had always managed to earn money by virtue of his strong body and his willingness, purchased his passage and went after Jannie. He knew where his friend was going, and he managed to catch him up as he struggled up the track that went up onto the moors.

Paulus had been talking with barely a break for some time, and all of us could hear that his voice, probably unused to speech, was suffering. Theo said curtly, 'Wait,' and went outside. I glanced at Jarman, and we heard the door to Theo's family quarters open. Soon he returned, bearing a tray on which there were four glasses and a jug of beer. We all drank deeply, for although it had been Paulus doing the talking, listening to his tale was almost as hard.

'So, Jannie came back,' Theo prompted. Like Jarman and me, I guessed, he was impatient to hear what happened next. 'And he was planning to visit the Fairlight family at Wrenbeare.'

Paulus gulped down the last of his beer and nodded. '*Ja*, that is right.' He drew a deep, shuddering breath. 'Jannie, poor Jannie, he knows he is dying, and I too, I can see that he is very sick, with the sores on his face and his body, and although I try, I try very hard to make him eat good food and drink good drink, he is not interested and he says, over and over, "Leave me be, Paulus, for I want to be dead."'

'But he went to Wrenbeare,' Theo said again. 'Why? Did he hope to see Sir Thomas and demand some sort of payment from him?'

Then Paulus raised his head and looked straight at him. From that mild face and those gentle eyes, the sudden hard, critical stare was alarming. 'Of course not,' Paulus said. 'Jannie loathed and feared Thomas Fairlight, and when he found out that he was dead, he rejoiced.'

'Then *what did he want*?' Theo thundered.

Paulus shook his head. He was smiling gently, a very faint

expression as if it was only for himself; or, perhaps, for the shade of Jannie Neep. 'It is maybe hard to understand for you who never saw him as he was in youth, but Jannie was truly beautiful. But now it was no longer so.' A sob burst from him. 'To have destroyed that beauty, for this alone I hope Thomas Fairlight burns in hell,' he said with sudden vehemence. Then, his voice breaking with passionate grief, he cried, 'There was one thing only that Jannie wanted before he gave himself up to death, and that was to see again how beautiful he had been before Thomas Fairlight ruined him, infected him and broke him. He remembered the Angel panel, and went to Wrenbeare just to ask if he might have a look at it. He knew they wouldn't recognize him. He went once and they chased him away. He was so desperate that he risked going back again, and that time he managed to get inside. He knew where Thomas Fairlight's own private room was, for once he had been taken there. He could not find the panel but in the secret place that Thomas had shown him he came across the preliminary drawing that Artus Bennart had done.'

The sketch, that torn half of a sketch of the beautiful, sorrowful face that Theo had believed to be Christ's. Not the Saviour grieving for the sins of mankind and for his own impending fate, but poor Jannie Neep, terrified of the sins of one man who he knew would not stop until he had sated his lust on the object that had aroused it.

'And Lady Clemence found him with it in his hands,' Theo said heavily.

'*Ja, ja,*' Paulus agreed, 'and she thought at first he was just a thief and, although alarmed, for she believed the sketch had been lost long ago, she felt no more than that. Then Jannie began to plead, and told her who he was. "I want to see myself beautiful one last time," he said.'

He paused, his face working with the emotion. 'Jannie, my Jannie, told me that she *shrank* from him, that fat, ugly old woman with her pale and bulgy eyes and her face like a horse, she pulled away in disgust and horror. She told him with vicious, cruel words that he was hideous, vile, repellent. Then he too became angry and he said that all that had happened to him was because of what Thomas did to him, and that it was Thomas's fault, not his, that he had been ruined and his golden image destroyed.'

Yes, I reflected. I could readily see Lady Clemence spitting out so cruelly in her horrified terror as she stared at the ruined wreck that used to be Jannie Neep, her husband's adored angel, inside her own house . . .

'He came back to me that night and I knew he had failed,' Paulus said. Tears were running down his face. 'I told him he was beautiful to me, that I still saw him as I always had done. It did no good.' He wiped his sleeve across his face. 'I tried to help him, I had been trying all the time I had been there with him, going out and searching, but I couldn't find it. I went out again that night,' he added, his voice breaking as his grief overcame him, 'for I think to myself, if I can find it, then perhaps it will be enough, and my Jannie will no longer wish only to die.' His hands went up to cover his face and for a few moments he sobbed bitterly. Then, with a visible effort, he wiped his face and sat up straight. He looked at Theo and nodded, as if to say, *I'm ready.*

'What were you looking for?' Theo demanded. I'd been watching his impatience build up while he waited for Paulus to recover himself and I was quite surprised he'd managed not to bellow out the question.

Paulus stared at him. 'I did not believe the Angel panel was still at that house,' he said. 'As soon as we learn Thomas is dead, and dead for fourteen, fifteen years, I think, but of course they will have hidden it! And so, while I am out finding good food with which to tempt my Jannie, also I hunt, I hunt everywhere, but I go too near the village and I am chased away by a man who shouts and threatens me and calls his dogs.'

Was that how those pieces of brilliant glass had been uncovered? I had been wondering all this time who had first exposed them to the light of day, assuming it was some burrowing animal . . .

'I could not help my Jannie,' Paulus was saying. 'There was nothing to be done but for me to take him in my arms and hold him while he wept.' He was staring down at his huge hands lying in his lap, relaxed now as if, with Jannie's death, their purpose was gone.

Then, looking up at Theo, he said simply, as if it was obvious, 'She had broken his heart, that cruel, vicious woman, and then he died. And so I broke hers. I opened up her ribs and I cut it out, and I buried it out on the moors.'

There was utter silence in the room.

Then Theo cleared his throat and said, 'Are you confessing to the murder of Lady Clemence Fairlight?'

And Paulus Fiske said, '*Ja.*'

'You didn't think to tell him that his beloved Jannie didn't die from a broken heart but was suffocated?' I asked Theo.

It was some time later. Paulus Fiske was back in the cell and Jarman Hodge had melted away. Theo and I were alone.

'And what purpose would that serve?' Theo said, and I sensed anger beneath the words that I knew wasn't directed at me or my question.

'None, perhaps, save that it is the truth,' I said quietly.

'Truth! Huh!' Theo muttered.

I understood. I too was feeling slightly . . . shabby, I think best described it. Paulus Fiske had done a terrible deed, and Lady Clemence's murdered body was a violent and horrific image in my head that I knew would take some time to fade, assuming it ever did. But, dear Lord, you could understand why Paulus had done it! Loving Jannie Neep as he had done throughout his long, lonely, sad life, it must have been all but unbearable to have found him again, just at the time he was dying and wanted to satisfy one last, pitiful wish. Only to have his ruination at Thomas Fairlight's hands thrown back in his face so viciously by a fat, ugly, frightened old woman.

I said, 'If you're worrying about what will happen to him – the arrest, I suppose, the trial, the execution – I don't think you need to.'

'Why? You planning to spring him from my cell down there and see him on his way back across the sea?' Theo demanded.

I shook my head. 'He's dying, Theo.'

Theo turned to stare at me. 'You're sure?'

'Yes. I'm not sure what's the matter with him but, from what I saw and was told by him when I examined him earlier, I'd guess it's some grave and chronic malady of the stomach or the guts, probably caused by a lifetime of too little food with too little goodness in it.'

'I fed him,' Theo muttered. 'Elaine's made sure he's had good food since he's been here.'

'Yes, I'm sure she has, and also that Paulus will have greatly appreciated the kindness,' I said gently. 'But it's far too late.'

Theo was rummaging among the papers on his desk and presently he held up the piece of paper we had found on Jannie's body. 'If you're right, then I dare say he'd like to have this,' he said gruffly.

'Yes. I'm sure he would.'

He coughed once or twice, then said, 'How long has he got?'

'Not long.' I couldn't be more specific, and in any case I was reluctant to say what I was thinking: with the death of Jannie Neep, Paulus had lost the one person whose presence somewhere in the world made a hard life worth going on with. But it was such a sad thought. 'We're speaking in terms of weeks, perhaps even days, rather than months.'

Theo nodded. He didn't say anything for quite some time, but then muttered, 'Under the circumstances, I'd better take my time writing my report.'

My prediction was right. Paulus Fiske didn't have weeks, only a handful of days. He was found by the guard who took down his breakfast four days later, lying on the blankets Theo had provided, his face very peaceful.

In his enormous hands he held the torn page on which Artus Bennart's skilful hand had drawn Jannie Neep's beautiful face.

NINETEEN

I left Theo at last and rode wearily home. I wanted to sit by my own fireside with good, plain food – although I had no appetite I knew I should eat, for the loss of blood had made my head spin – and a very large mug of beer.

Celia came into the hall to meet me. She seemed to know without my telling her that I was worn out and had little wish to explain why and, bless her, she simply told me to go into the parlour while she went to ask Sallie to bring food and drink. 'Then I'll tell her she can retire for the night,' she added softly.

I was slumped over the table, my head resting on my arms, when Sallie brought the loaded tray. She set out bread, cold meats, sweet tarts and a tankard of ale, then, giving Celia a look, swept out again. The sound of the door from the kitchen into Sallie's room reverberated through the house as she very forcefully closed it. I looked up and met my sister's eyes and she gave a rueful smile.

'Oh, dear,' she said. 'I believe I have offended her, but I rather thought you'd like us to be alone.'

'You thought right,' I said through bread and cheese. Celia, tactful, wise, left me to my food and my ale and only when I sat back, replete, did she come to the table and sit down beside me. I poured out a mug of ale for her, and she raised it in a silent toast before taking a sip. 'I am sure you have been into danger,' she said with a glance at the bandage on my forearm and the dressing on my shoulder, 'and I am very, very glad to have you safely home.'

'Thank you.' I drank again and refilled both our mugs. 'The wounds are not serious,' I said.

'But, to judge by how pale you were when you came in, they bled a lot,' she remarked calmly.

I glanced at her – I'd forgotten how observant she is – but thought it better not to answer.

Then, trying to play down the drama and the danger, I told her briefly all that had happened since I'd left home the previous day. And, when I'd finished, she said in a horrified whisper, 'Gabe, she could have killed you!'

'But she didn't.' I reached out, took her hand and clasped it, giving it a firm squeeze as if to demonstrate that my injuries had not taken away my strength.

'All right, I believe you!' she said, removing her hand and wincing.

She must have had questions she was longing to ask but

she kept quiet. We sat there side by side in the gathering darkness. Presently she got up and lit a couple of lamps. 'I think it's time for bed,' she said, putting one down on the table in front of me. 'I'm tired, and you must be too, even more so.'

'Yes,' I admitted, 'I—'

There was a soft knock on the big oak door. Celia glanced at me. 'I'll send whoever it is away,' she whispered, although nobody standing outside the heavy door could possibly have overheard her even if she had shouted. 'You're not fit to tend any patient tonight. You need to sleep, Gabe.'

I went and put my arm round her. 'I know. It's all right, I'll see who it is and what they want, and do my utmost to get rid of them as soon as I can.'

I went to the door and opened it.

Jonathan Carew stood on the step.

'I'm so sorry to disturb you so late, Gabriel,' he began, just as I was saying, 'Jonathan! Come in, there's half a jug of very fine ale in the parlour just asking to be finished off!'

Celia, who must have seen and taken in Jonathan's ashen face just as I had since she'd been standing just behind me when I opened the door, said in an admirably ordinary tone, 'I'll leave you to have a swift talk to Gabe alone, Jonathan, for I am rather tired and was just on my way to bed.' She gave me a look that clearly said, *As should you be!*

Jonathan apologized again for arriving so late, and she said politely it didn't matter and not to worry. Then she gave us both a sweet smile and headed for the stairs.

She disguised her curiosity very well, I had to say that for her. But I would have bet a gold coin that closing her bedroom door and settling down to sleep were the last things on her mind just then.

'I am so sorry to keep you from your bed when I know full well you are injured and need to rest,' he said as I led him through into the parlour and indicated Celia's empty chair. I wiped the mug she had used with a clean cloth and poured out ale for Jonathan and me.

I shrugged, which made the cut in my shoulder give out a sharp stab of pain. 'I'm all right.'

He smiled. 'You're not, but I must talk to you. I'll try to be brief.'

I waited.

'I have heard what's happened,' he said presently. 'I know about the deaths at Wrenbeare, and quite a lot about how it all came about. Theo Davey's been to see me.' He paused. 'There are, however, one or two gaps in the tale, and I believe I can fill them in.'

I was very surprised. How could Jonathan know anything about past events in the Fairlight household? He had only been in the area for a few years, and had arrived long after Sir Thomas's death. But I could tell from his pallor, the hollowness of his face and his general demeanour that whatever matter had been so deeply troubling him was still very far from being resolved. If anything, his suffering seemed to have intensified.

Trying not to show my anxiety, I drank some ale and said, 'Shouldn't you be filling in these gaps for Theo?'

He shook his head. 'No. Well, I should, but I'm not going to.' Again he hesitated, and I sensed the struggle in him. 'What I'm about to say is in the nature of a confession, Gabriel, and before you say anything, no, it's not something I will ever share with another priest.' He looked down at his hands. I noticed again how well-shaped they were.

'There is an incident in my past and known, I believe, only to me, and it weighs heavy. Because of what I learned from it, I am convinced that the deaths at Wrenbeare are very closely linked with the St Luke panels, although I do not think anyone else could possibly have perceived the connection.'

'Ah.' As I heard his words I was momentarily surprised. But within an instant it was as if a quiet voice inside my head said, *You were aware of this; you knew that somehow the one matter was bound up in the other.* I waited. Then I said, 'How did you know the panels were hidden in a woody dell in Tavy St Luke's?'

I watched Jonathan's face. Several expressions seemed to cross it in swift succession. Then he sighed, put his hands over his eyes and said, more to himself than to me, 'Why not tell? Would it not be a relief, after all this time?'

I didn't speak.

After a time, Jonathan lowered his hands, sat up straight and began.

'I told you a while ago that I was haunted by the ghost of a man I'd once briefly met.'

'I remember.'

'He was once the parish priest of Tavy St Luke's. Not my immediate predecessor, but the incumbent before that.'

'You told me your predecessor was a tall, thin, aesthetic-looking man stooped with arthritis. The one before,' I added softly, 'was he a tubby little man?'

And Jonathan, with a groan of despair, said, 'Yes.'

His name, I could have added, thinking back to Paulus Fiske's story, was Martin Oude, and a long time ago he was Thomas Fairlight's parish priest.

But I kept quiet, and let Jonathan tell me what was tormenting him so relentlessly in his own time and in his own way.

For some moments he didn't speak. Then, with a glance at the jug of beer, he said apologetically, 'Is there any more of that in your kitchen? It's a long tale that I'm going to tell you, and it'll be thirsty work both talking and listening.'

Without a word I went out to the pantry and refilled the jug. I topped up our mugs, then sat down again and waited.

'I trust you will indulge me,' Jonathan began, 'if I go back rather a long way, but I want you to understand why I—' But it seemed he couldn't finish whatever he'd been about to say. 'I want you to understand.' He shot me a pain-filled look, his green eyes boring into mine. Then, visibly bracing himself, he said, 'I'm Cornwall-born, and I was the third son of a family with considerable prestige in their local area. As is the case with many third sons, the career options for me were slim, but I showed early intelligence and at first it was decided I should train for the law. The concept appealed to me very well but circumstances which I do not need to go into led me instead into the priesthood, and that too was more than accept-able, especially when, once I had gone up to Trinity Hall in Cambridge to read canon law, I began to understand that there were many roads open to me in addition to that which led to becoming a vicar. I perceived very early the overwhelming power of the Church.' He stopped, shot me a brief, intense look and added quietly, 'They say that power seduces, and in my experience that is true. I was, however, a very willing partner in my own seduction.'

I studied him, willing him to go on. My shoulder was throbbing in time to my heartbeat and I longed to go to bed, but already Jonathan Carew's tale had begun to draw me in.

'Throughout the 1580s,' he went on, 'there was a constant threat of Catholic invasion, and men were fearful of some sort of attack from Spain, and of plots to assassinate the Queen. Then the last decade of the century began, and Francis Walsingham's spy network stepped up to full efficiency. Catholic plots had been discovered, far too frequently for the spymasters' peace of mind, and the plots were by no means all as simple and doomed to disaster as the most infamous ones.'

I knew something of the matters to which he referred. Although I had been at sea until late in the decade, you would have had to be blind, deaf and stupid not to perceive the dangers faced by the Queen and the country.

'And the spy network,' Jonathan said heavily, 'was ever on the lookout for new recruits.'

With a sense that all of a sudden I had an idea of what might be coming, I forced myself to ignore the pain in my shoulder and my arm and gave him my full attention, allowing the smooth flow of his words to take me back into the past.

And this is the story he told me.

Jonathan Carew has been spotted.

The Cambridge college where he studies with such intensity is a place of high-browed, thin-faced men who mutter to themselves, who maintain silence even at mealtimes as they frown deeply and, in the privacy of their own heads, continue to work on the abstruse problems of church law that obsess them. Some of them are lost deep inside their own thoughts and they fail to notice those who watch them so closely. But watchers there are, and they have a variety of motives for their careful attention. Some hope to learn secrets. Some hope to uncover conspiracies, and by so doing, gain advancement, wealth and prestige, even though it probably means betrayal and a terrible end for someone else.

The rumour of what happens in the dark, secret cellars where the interrogators do their work is enough to strike fear in the most courageous heart. The rack. The Scavenger's Daughter. The Iron Maiden. The Iron Boot. And every sinister device is designed to inflict agony, the very fear of which can drive a man to spill the words he believes his tormentors want to hear, whether they are true or not.

Among those who observe from the shadowed recesses are agents of the spymaster. They are constantly on the lookout for the right sort of men, for the need is unceasing; in fact, it is increasing. So says the spymaster. So *said* the spymaster, for now in April 1590 Francis Walsingham lies on his deathbed in the London house on Seething Lane and is past all speech.

The network of spies that he set up, however, is as strong and as solid as ever, and new young blood is constantly recruited to replace those who for whatever reason – quite often death, for it is a hazardous profession – can no longer perform their duty. Walsingham had two main fears: that Catholicism would return to tear England apart, and that someone would sneak in under his constant vigil and take the life of the Queen he had served so loyally, so devotedly and so well. Those who have inherited the spymaster's crown feel as fervently as he did, and the fight goes on unabated. Catholic priests do indeed arrive in England, far too regularly, and, until the execution of Mary Stuart after the failure of the Babington Plot three years previously, there was the constant fear that the Catholic faction would rally behind her, kill Queen Elizabeth and put Mary on the throne.

Thanks to Walsingham and those who saw with the same vision, this did not happen. Elizabeth lives and reigns still, and the men of Walsingham's network intend to keep it that way.

They are never short of work. In such anxious times, Catholic conspiracies can be suspected all too easily, and it is quite often all but impossible to separate genuine, accurate intelligence from malicious rumour. A man has long held a loathing of a neighbour who cheated him of a few acres of pasture, for example. So what better revenge can there be than to drop a word in the right ear suggesting that the neighbour has been seen to open his door by night to mysterious black-garbed strangers arriving from the coast? Strangers who mutter Latin prayers and carry the rosary . . .

A particular sort of mind is required to sort the time-wasters from those who bear genuinely useful information. And, on this spring day in Cambridge, the spymaster's agent believes he has found a young man who possesses such a mind. So, as Jonathan Carew finishes his sparse midday meal and gets up to return to his studies, the agent falls into step beside him and mutters an invitation in his ear. Not very long afterwards – men don't refuse this particular invitation, and the path has been cleared by the authorities for Jonathan's unobtrusive disappearance from the college – he is on his way to London.

The old priest is brought in six weeks later.

Jonathan has been kept busy, and he has fulfilled the promise that the agent saw in him. He is horrified by what he sees. Had he known, had he had an inkling, he would have run away from the spymaster's agent as if the fires of hell were opening at his feet. He is not often summoned right into the dark chambers where the torture is done, but *not often* has already been far too frequent.

He does not know what to do.

The old priest is called Martin Oude and he is in his seventies. He was born in King Henry's reign and, until the King did away with the monasteries, he was a monk. He became a priest; he had been a devout and sincere Catholic and then, when the world changed, he was an obedient Protestant. He endured the destruction of so much that was precious and beautiful, first under Henry and then under the boy king who followed, and he meekly bowed his head before the storm. Then came Mary, eyes burning with such a fervour that it leapt out and ignited the terrible bonfires, and so many died, hands clasped in a desperate, final prayer as they howled their agony. The world changed yet again with the ascent of Elizabeth, and Martin Oude, like many others, began to think that tolerance had come at last.

But it hadn't.

They have told Jonathan that Martin Oude is suspected of sheltering a Catholic priest newly arrived from France. Martin is the vicar of a tiny Devon parish not many miles inland from Plymouth, and it has been reported that he takes in strangers in need, helps them, feeds and sometimes houses them, and doesn't ask nearly enough questions as to where they have come from and what they propose to do now that they are here.

And in this nervous England, where the paranoid men who claim to *know* look constantly and fearfully over their shoulders for the next foreign spy and the next Catholic plot, being kind to needy strangers and feeding them when they are hungry, clothing them when they are naked, tending them when they are sick and taking them in when they need shelter – doing, in fact, exactly what Christ exhorted all his children to do – is sufficient cause, apparently, to throw suspicion on a man.

And the suspicion is enough to have him arrested and brought in to answer the paranoid men's questions.

Martin Oude, a tubby, cheerful sort of a fellow when he first arrived and apparently with little idea of what awaited him (for if he had even suspected, he would have ceased being cheerful and the happy smile would have turned into a rictus of terror), has been altered to his very core by nearly a week in the deep dungeons.

A week of *answering questions.*

And, naturally, all that goes with it.

Jonathan Carew has not been required to ask the questions, to wield the terrible instruments, to throw pails of water over the tubby priest when the pain makes him pass out before he has finished answering.

All that Jonathan has done is to listen from a corner of the dungeon and try to determine if the words that come out of Martin Oude's crushed and bloody lips are the truth, or whether he is merely gabbling out anything and everything he can think of purely to stop the pain.

That is the trouble with torture, as Jonathan can so plainly see and as he thinks his lords and masters, if not the cold-eyed men wielding the terrible devices, ought also to realize.

It's so very hard to *tell.*

*   *   *

On the evening of the sixth day Jonathan goes to visit the prisoner. He has not been ordered to do so: he goes of his own volition, for something in him has broken free from the obedience and the wish to conform, and not question his superiors, that have hitherto bound him.

He can no longer stand by and do nothing.

It is his country that has asked this service of him; his Church that sanctions the methods, for they are deemed to be worth the damage they do, to the souls of the perpetrators almost as much as to the bodies of the victims. Jonathan is in Holy Orders, and he knows he owes obedience to his Church, his masters, his Queen.

But he is sick to the depths of his being, and he knows that he must act because otherwise he will wither away and die.

Martin Oude lies in the damp and stinking straw on the cold stone floor. He cannot get comfortable, for he has nothing to support his head and the racking has done something serious to the muscles and the joints between his shoulder and his neck.

Jonathan has brought two soft, plump feather pillows. Gently he eases up the old man's head and puts the first pillow under it. The old man lets out a sigh.

Jonathan has realized from the brief touch that Martin Oude is feverish. His skin is burning and he twists and turns in pain. He is delirious.

'So beautiful,' he murmurs. 'The physician with his patient, and amid the flowers preparing his herbs. The nuns, so blissful in their simple goodness. The wonderful colours of the borders, and, joy of them all, Our Lord and the lilies of the field. They labour not, neither do they spin, yet I say unto you that Solomon himself in all his royalty was not clothed like one of these. Oh, how beautiful, how exquisite!' He takes a sharp and clearly painful breath. 'How innocent,' he whispers.

He remembers favourite verses from the Bible, thinks Jonathan.

'Beautiful, yes,' he agrees softly.

The old priest tries to reach for his hand but there is a broken bone in his wrist and he cries out sharply. Jonathan stretches out and very gently puts his cold fingers against the hot flesh.

'I saw no harm in them, d'you see?' the old man pleads. 'They were so lovely! It was as if they were washed with the warmth of the sun and empowered by the enchanting power of the moon and stars! Why should they be evil when they held such beauty? Things of beauty come from God, when all is said and done. And the face of Our Lord, his profound eyes full of love, his smile so kind! Why was that suddenly an object of repugnance? Tell me that, please! And tell me, too, what the loving Christ says when he looks down on the deeds of his children, who he loved so much that he gave his life for us! Did he not tell us that his greatest commandment to us was to love one another?'

There is more; a lot more.

Martin Oude is lost in the past, defending himself not against the accusations that are currently being hurled at him – and of which Jonathan knows without doubt that he is entirely innocent – but against something from long ago; a crime which the spymasters don't even suspect him of having committed, and which surely nobody cares about any more . . .

The old priest rambles on, quite often forgetting he's meant to be a Protestant vicar now and going back to the faith of his youth. He talks of vaguely Catholic images of saints and wonders, of relics, of miracles at shrines, of well-dressing and ancient folk traditions.

He is old, he is forgetful, he confuses events of his own past with the legends and tales told to him by others, Jonathan thinks. His heart aches with pity for he can see, despite the dim light in the cell, what has been done to Martin Oude.

But presently he realizes the old man is repeating himself; saying the same thing, over and over, with increasing insistence: as if he is desperate for Jonathan to hear and to understand. And Jonathan begins to suspect that the old man really is hiding a secret.

He is.

What is on his mind, so powerfully that it gives him no rest, is the thought of those panels he took from the wall of

222 Alys Clare

his church forty-three years ago and hid safely away until such time as the danger was past. For he can still see them, those five panels, and their beauty, their magic and their mystical power all remain as strong in his ageing mind as the day he hid them.

He is not guilty of anything else, for he is a true innocent. But Jonathan begins to understand that this matter that so preys on Martin Oude's mind is there for his interrogators to pick up.

And that in all probability they have already done so.

He's guilty of something, they'll mutter to each other. And they'll be quite right, although the something can present no danger to Queen or state, or even, surely, to the Church. Having detected this pathetic little secret, they will not rest until they get it out of their victim, and when they do, even they will appreciate that it's trivial and unimportant.

And, even knowing this, then they will kill him.

All of this runs wildly and painfully through Jonathan's mind. But the old man is still muttering – his voice is all but inaudible now – and Jonathan goes on listening.

And what he hears he will never forget.

At last, after what seems a very long time, the old priest has exhausted himself. The delirium has passed and he seems to have forgotten all about the matter that obsessed him such a short time before. Now he lies back on the cold, wet floor, his head on the soft pillow, and he looks up at Jonathan in full awareness.

'They will come for me again tomorrow, won't they?' he asks pathetically. Tears of pain, fear and despair run from his bloodshot eyes.

'Yes,' Jonathan agrees. 'I'm afraid they will.'

There is quite a long silence.

Then, his voice clear and strong, Martin Oude speaks two words.

Two little words, but they change Jonathan Carew's life.

What Martin Oude says is, 'Kill me.'

*   *   *

And, gravely and calmly, Jonathan Carew says the words and performs the actions that his faith requires of him when death approaches. Then he picks up the second soft feather pillow – he was very careful to bring two – and, having first spread a fold of the old priest's soiled robe over his face, he puts the pillow in place and holds it very, very firmly.

There is barely a struggle.

After a surprisingly short time, it is done.

Jonathan keeps the pillow where it is while he checks. But the pulse has ceased, the heart has stopped. He holds the pillow in place for a while longer, then removes it.

He draws the fold of cloth away. He has arranged it thus in case a thread of cloth or a tiny, stray feather should be shed from the pillow to betray this deed that he has just done.

He kneels beside the dead body and he prays. When he is done, he goes on kneeling there, keeping vigil with Martin Oude while his soul departs.

Jonathan knows that he has done the right thing. The old man asked him to do it, and the alternative – the horrors and the agony that tomorrow would undoubtedly have brought – was not to be contemplated. To obey the command 'Kill me' was the compassionate response, the only response.

So Jonathan Carew tells himself.

Yet the commandment says quite plainly, *Thou shalt not kill.*

And he has just taken a life.

As yet, kneeling there beside the cooling body, he has absolutely no idea how he is going to live with it.

Jonathan has understood that Martin Oude was talking about the stained glass that was removed from his church – his little Devon church – during the iconoclasm of 1547, when Edward VI ascended the throne. Before the men came to obey the royal injunction to 'destroy all shrines, pictures, paintings, and all other monuments of feigned miracles so that there remain no memory of the same in walls, glass windows or elsewhere within their churches or houses', the little priest made quite sure that his church's glass would be safe.

And Jonathan thinks, as finally he gets up from the cold,

damp floor and the cooling body of an innocent, loving old
man and stumbles back to his own room, why? What did it
matter? Was it worth all this agony, all this dying?

He discovers, over the ensuing days, that working for the
spymasters has lost its appeal.

Jonathan becomes rebellious, outspoken. He speaks up for
the oppressed, he is strident in his criticism of the use of brutal
torture. 'Don't you see that it does no good?' he shouts coura-
geously but unwisely to his superiors. 'A man in agony will
tell you anything you want to hear if he believes you when
you say you'll stop if he breaks his silence!'

His superiors hear him without comment. They watch, and
they wait.

Increasingly Jonathan is haunted by Martin Oude's words
on Christ's love. How horrified the Lord must surely be at
what was being done in his holy name.

And the clever, narrow-eyed men in the spy network know
that it's time Jonathan Carew was ejected from their number.
They've had enough of him; they don't trust him any more.
He's sent off somewhere where the work is largely of a clerical
nature, lengthy, monotonous and largely unimportant – a sort
of penance posting – and then the living of Tavy St Luke
becomes vacant when Philip Snell dies and they decide it
would be quite ironic and amusing to send him there. They
believe that by booting him off to such an out of the way,
forgotten, unimportant, tediously dull and excruciatingly
boring place where nothing ever happens and that they believe
he will hate, they will be giving him the constant, painful
reminder that he has brought his exile – and the end of his
glittering career – entirely upon himself.

'You asked some time ago how I knew the panels were here,'
Jonathan said.

He had been talking for a long time. He was clearly very
tired, but he was a lot less pale and he looked – lighter, was
the best way I could describe it to myself.

'Martin Oude told me he'd buried them in "the dell", and
I surmised that he meant some location close to where he had
his incumbency. I tried to search when I first came here, but

I discovered very soon what an impossible task it was. I didn't forget – I don't think there's been a day when I haven't thought of Martin Oude and the promise I made to him – but I let the matter slip to the back of my mind.

'Until one day those two lads came running into the village shouting that they'd found jewels in Foxy Dell. I should have realized, for I had heard people speak of Foxy Dell, only I suppose I thought that a local landmark sufficiently well known to have been given a nickname wouldn't have been chosen as a hiding place. But perhaps it had not yet acquired its name in Martin Oude's day.' He paused, slowly shaking his head. 'But I knew, then. Even as the realization dawned, I seemed to hear Martin's agonized whispering, and it didn't stop. Then I began to see him as well.' Briefly he covered his eyes with his hand.

'You saw him when you were in the pulpit that Sunday after the lads' father had fought with Farmer Haydon,' I said. 'You went quite pale, and you clutched at the sides of the lectern as if it was the only thing keeping you on your feet.'

'It was,' he said quietly. 'That was the first time that Martin appeared to me. I saw him – believed I saw him – standing at the far end of the aisle, and he was smiling at me with such kindness, such love.' He broke off.

After a few moments I said, 'I don't imagine he'll be back. You've done what he wanted, Jonathan. The panels are back where they should be and soon, when the time is right and it's safe, you will unveil them. Martin Oude will be able to rest in peace.'

He nodded.

I stared suddenly, for I'd just thought of something. 'But what about the Angel panel?'

Jonathan looked at me without speaking for a few moments. Then he said, 'It must have been Martin Oude who added it to the two parcels of panels from the church, for it's too much of a coincidence to think that—'

'He did!' I interrupted. Once more I heard Josiah Thorn's words: *Ah, I remember how that tubby little priest remonstrated with him . . .*

Thomas Fairlight, afraid, guilty, ashamed, had confessed his

love and his lustful hunger for Jannie Neep to his priest, and
the priest had told him he must give up the Angel panel even
as he gave up the boy he adored. And Martin already had a
hiding place for stained glass panels and so did not need to
hunt out another one . . .

'He – your Martin Oude – slid Thomas Fairlight's pride
and joy – his Angel panel – among the five from his church!'
I cried.

And Jonathan, a very tentative smile on his face, said, 'Yes.
And that was what I came to tell you.'

I asked after a while, 'What should we do with it?'

'I think,' Jonathan said slowly, 'that we should hide it again.
Oh, not where we found it!' He managed a laugh. 'I don't
think I have the courage to risk Farmer Haydon's mastiffs
again, even with the benefit of your little bottle of potion.' He
looked at me, his face serious again. 'I believe it has evil in
it,' he said quietly.

So did I.

'Then we'll find a suitable place and consign it to the
forgiving earth,' I said.

And while we did so, I thought, I would find a way to ask
Jonathan Carew to pray for the souls of Jannie Neep and
Paulus Fiske.

Except that there would be no need to ask him, for without
a doubt he would think of it for himself. They would be there
in the forefront of his mind, beside Martin Oude.

Presently he got up to leave, and I saw him to the door. We
said our goodnights, and I watched him walk briskly away.
His steps were swift and sure now; he was, I thought, on the
way to recovery.

I locked and bolted the door, then made my way wearily
up the stairs.

Celia must have heard me, for she appeared at her end of
the gallery.

'What a tale,' she said, the horror still showing in her face.
'That poor, poor man.'

I wasn't sure if she meant Martin Oude or Jonathan. Possibly she referred to both of them. But I was exhausted, and sad with the residual emotions from hearing Jonathan's story, so I just said lightly, 'I knew you'd be listening. You always did have flappy ears.'

She came swiftly to stand beside me, giving me a very warm, intense hug. It hurt, but I didn't say so. Then she let me go.

'Good night, Gabe. I hope you'll sleep all right, and the pain won't keep you awake.'

'It won't.'

I went along to my room, undressed and got into bed. It felt wonderful.

I knew there had been no need to warn my sister to keep Jonathan's secret. Celia, after all, carried in her memory deeds even darker than his.

TWENTY

Although Celia and I had been to London in March, where among other entertainments we witnessed the King's official entry into the City, we decided that another visit to the capital was exactly what we needed after the drama of recent events. My fellow Symposium members and I had a vague arrangement to meet at some point in the latter half of the year, and when I wrote to them suggesting the second week in July, they agreed.

Celia said we ought to take Jonathan with us. I said he wouldn't come, she said of course he would, basing her certainty solely on the fact that he'd once said he'd lived in London before coming to Tavy St Luke's. In the end, since it began to look as if my sister and I were going to fall out over it just as we used to do as children when both of us were convinced we were right, I asked him.

He gave me his singularly illuminating smile and said, 'There's nothing I'd have liked better, Gabriel, but I'm afraid I cannot be away from the parish for more than a few days at a time.'

I almost said, 'Could you not ask another priest to take the services for you during your absence?' but, just in time, I swallowed the words. I didn't know if it was possible to arrange a locum, although I thought it must be. What would happen if a vicar was taken ill? If he died suddenly?

Jonathan, I thought, had used the fact that he could not leave his parish for the length of time required to go to stay in London for a couple of weeks as an excuse to turn down Celia's and my invitation. I was sure he'd been truthful when he said there was nothing he'd like better; there had briefly been a hungry look in his strange green eyes when I'd said London, as if he was imagining all the delights of the city, seeing them arrayed before him like jewels on a velvet cushion. And I thought I knew why he had refused: it was because he did not feel he deserved such a treat.

Somewhere in his soul, in his heart, Jonathan was still doing penance for the death of Martin Oude.

Since I continued to be stiff and in some pain from my wounds, Celia decided it was up to her to be the leader of our two-person party. She carried out her role with nonchalant efficiency, arranging the hire of the same rooms we'd occupied on our previous visit, in the house where I had lodged while studying at the King's College of Physicians and, on the long journey to London, being very firm about what time we stopped each evening and selecting the finest available inn for our overnight stay.

London was busy muttering about the new King, and about the progress, or lack of it, of his plan to unite his two king-doms of England and Scotland under one crown. About his Catholic wife, about his favourites. There was more frivolous gossip too, of course, and his new subjects had already noticed how keen he was to get away to the countryside and go hunting whenever he could but was a terrible shot and had to have animals finished off by better men; how his manners left quite a lot to be desired, with his tongue too large for his mouth so that he slurped and dribbled when he ate; how his after-dinner conversation was crude and even scatological, with bawdy jokes about farts and turds; how the Queen preferred the cosmopolitan delights of London and had a particular fondness for patronizing poets, playwrights and artists; how the ten-year-old son and heir, Prince Henry, had already impressed his peers with his quick and ready wit and his dignified demeanour. There was talk, too, of the new English translation of the Bible, and King James himself was said to have worked out what must surely be the incredibly complicated arrange-ments for its accomplishment.

He had been busy, this new King, for in addition he was rumoured to be the author of an anonymously published pamphlet entitled *A Counterblast to Tobacco*, in which, as well as roundly denouncing the *vile custom* and its *filthy smoke* and *black stinking fume*, the author also rejected the supposed medicinal benefits of smoking and claimed that the hot, dry nature of burning tobacco was quite alien to the cold, wet nature of men's brains. He had quite a lot to say on the subject of the humours, and, since this ancient doctrine was the subject of my presentation to the Symposium, I anticipated a heated discussion when my fellow physicians and I met.

Celia was quite determined, however, that my prime requirement was for a succession of cheerful leisure activities, and we went on the river, browsed the shops and the markets and joined the audience in the Globe Theatre to watch the King's Men – the new name for Will Shakespeare's Chamberlain's Men – perform a couple of plays. The first, *Titus Andronicus*, was in hindsight perhaps a poor choice, since its subject was revenge of the most bloodthirsty kind, and we had recently experienced something of the sort in our own lives. As we sat through human sacrifice, beheadings, the lopping-off of hands and the cutting-out of a tongue, the serving to a woman of her own sons in a pie and a final mad slaughter of almost everyone else left alive, Celia reached out and took my hand, whispering, 'It's only a play, Gabe.'

For contrast, the second play we saw was *Much Ado About Nothing*, a light, frivolous piece about a group of people meeting in Messina for the celebration of a wedding, and the various tricks and mix-ups that threatened to prevent the right couples ending up together. I lost track of the plot quite early on, but it didn't seem to matter much as the actors were attractive and appealing, throwing themselves into the action with enthusiasm, and the pompous, self-important Dogberry and his inept crew of amateur watchmen made the groundlings laugh extravagantly when they weren't busy lobbing sundry objects at them.

The glittering diversions of London could not, however, dispel the gloom of my mood. I went to the Symposium meeting and allowed myself to become far too heated as I defended my increasingly solid belief that the doctrine of the humours was outdated, to say the least, and ripe for investigation by the wider medical world. My colleagues fought back, reminding me that a part of our oath as physicians was to ensure that the methods and the treatments of our predecessors were faithfully perpetuated. 'We walk in their footsteps and we must respect them!' one of them cried, watching me anxiously as if I'd just demonstrated evidence of incipient madness.

'But what if they were wrong and what we do does no good?' I shouted back.

Both my friends paled. It was as if I'd torn up their ancient, precious medical books before their eyes. I shouted a bit more, stomped up and down the room a few times, then abruptly all my fury went out of me and I shook their hands and apologized.

They seemed to know without being told that I'd been through some distressing experience recently, and they were aware I'd been wounded. Good friends that they were, they suggested we wind up our session early and go and have a few ales.

My thoughts reverted repeatedly to Wrenbeare; to that house of dark memory, where a man's inability to control his base nature had led to the deaths of six people, not counting himself. Celia had been quite right when she tried to encourage me to disassociate fact from fiction, and I didn't tell her about the nightmare I had after *Titus Andronicus* because I sensed she was feeling enough remorse already, it having been her suggestion to see the wretched play.

I could have wept for Jannie Neep and the loyal, loving Paulus Fiske. Yes, Paulus had committed violent, brutal murder, and none of what had happened had really been Lady Clemence's fault, but his simple logic – *she had broken Jannie's heart and so I broke hers* – was understandable. Poor Paulus had experienced so little love in his life. It was small wonder that he should have acted in such a way to avenge his friend's death.

But Clemence too was to be pitied, I thought as I lay awake long into the night a few days after our second visit to the Globe. Ugly, unwanted, unable through no fault of her own to produce the nursery full of lusty sons and beautiful daughters that were required of her, bitterness had eaten into her until all she had left was the echo of her late husband's status. For that too to have been taken away by the visit from that little wraith from the past must have been something she simply could not contemplate.

And Thomas Fairlight's disease-induced madness had come down to his daughters, keeping one trapped in the distorted body of a mad child and turning the other into a murderer.

I thought of Theo, with six corpses to dispose of and on whose deaths he would first have to write lengthy explanatory reports to send to whomever he was required to answer to; I realized I didn't know who this was, unless it could be Lord Cosmo Underhay, our local justice of the peace. That little puzzle also kept me awake for some time. I realized, as Theo filled my thoughts, how much I valued him, both as a coroner and as a friend. The fact that I derived enjoyment from his company even when we were bending side by side over the most noisome corpses and the bloodiest murder victims said a great deal for the man.

But the person I thought about most often during those sleepless London nights was Jonathan Carew. As far as I was concerned, I approved utterly of his action in giving Martin Oude a swift death, for the alternative was not to be contemplated. I would have done exactly the same thing myself, but then I wasn't a priest. Although I was a physician, and our most binding oath is to do no harm, I believe I could quite easily have convinced myself that putting a pillow over Martin

Oude's face, and thus saving him from a far more agonizing and prolonged death, was the right thing to do.

But Jonathan, I realized, was a different sort of man.

Because I both respected and liked him, I found myself wanting to find some way of convincing him that his action had been necessary and humane. I came to understand, shortly before I finally fell asleep as dawn began to lighten the sky, that there was absolutely no way I could do so. Until our treasured vicar accepted in his heart and his very capable mind that he'd acted as the loving Lord to whom he had dedicated his life would undoubtedly have commanded, Jonathan would just have to suffer.

Celia noticed over breakfast the next day that I was not looking my best.

'Did you not sleep?' she asked quietly.

'Not very well.' I tried to smile. 'I always forget how noisy London is.'

She studied me. 'Would you like to go home?'

Home.

The river, the sloping hills and the secret valleys, the sea not far away, the soft, sweet air. My beautiful house, and Sallie, Samuel and Tock. I smiled suddenly, thinking of Sallie's face when Celia had given her a gorgeous russet silk petticoat as a small thank you, as my sister said, for all her kindness; poor Sallie, quite overcome, hadn't known whether to laugh or cry and had done a bit of both. Then she had fled into her room off the kitchen, returning some ten minutes later red in the face and beaming, twirling her skirts so that the yards and yards of frilly edged silk whistled and hissed. She had, I think, been Celia's devoted servant even before that. Now, perhaps, she was her friend as well.

The village and the villagers. Josiah Thorn. Theo and his family.

Jonathan Carew.

Judyth.

I thought of her clean, sweet-smelling, tidy little cottage and the sun on her herb beds. I thought of her curvaceous body, her shiny dark hair and her light, clear eyes. I hadn't realized I was smiling until I heard Celia suppress a soft chuckle and murmur, 'Gabe, she's only one aspect of home.'

It's uncanny, and at times decidedly uncomfortable, how often my sister seems to read my mind.

Home.

The yearning in my heart told me how much I wanted to be there.

'But we've only been in London for just over a week,' I demurred. 'You surely have more visiting that you wish to do, for I'm certain there are a couple of shops and a market stall that you haven't yet patronized, and you were talking about a second trip on the river and seeing another play. Besides, we've booked the rooms for a fortnight, and I'm not at all sure we'll be offered a refund. And it's such a long—'

'Yes, Gabe,' she interrupted, 'I know, it's such a long way, and we'll be wasting some of what we paid for the rooms, and we ought to make our stay here worthy of the journey.' She sighed, giving me an exasperated frown. 'My question remains: would you like to go home?'

So I just said, 'Yes.'